The Missing Father

A Jayne Sinclair Genealogical Mystery

M. J. Lee

About M. J. Lee

Martin Lee is the author of contemporary and historical crime novels. *The Christmas Carol* is the eighth book featuring genealogical investigator, Jayne Sinclair.

The Jayne Sinclair Series

The Irish Inheritance

The Somme Legacy

The American Candidate

The Vanished Child

The Lost Christmas

The Sinclair Betrayal

The Merchant's Daughter

The Christmas Carol

The Missing Father

The Inspector Danilov Series

Death in Shanghai

City of Shadows

The Murder Game

The Killing Time

The Inspector Thomas Ridpath Series

Where the Truth Lies

Where the Dead Fall

Where the Silence Calls

Where the Innocent Die

When the Past Kills

When the Evil Waits

When the Guilty Cry

When the Night Ends

This book is a work of fiction. Names, characters, organisations, places and events are either a product of the author's imagination or used fictitiously.
Any resemblance to actual persons, living or dead, events or locales is entirely coincidental.

Copyright © M J Lee 2022

Look for more great books at writermjlee.com

This book is dedicated to all those
who died in the Fall of Singapore or suffered in the
prisoner of war camps.
You have not been forgotten.

CHAPTER ONE

March, 1943
Chungkai Camp, Thailand

It was a day just like any other.

Captain David Stephens held the hand of a man as he died, talking constantly to him in a low voice so as not to disturb the others. The doctor had seen him that morning but nothing could be done. The man had already drifted into that semi-conscious state where reality and dreams collide.

Before the war, he had known Harry Jarvis. He had been fit and healthy then, a boxer for the regiment. Of course, Harry didn't recognise him any more, trapped as he was in the depths of delirium, talking incessantly about his mother and the ocean, reliving some long-forgotten trip to the seaside during Wakes week.

Harry was smiling when he died. One moment he was chattering away and the next he was gone.

The captain wrote his name, rank and number in the school exercise book, taking care to ensure he made no mistakes. It was the one thing he could do, a last respect to the man.

There were four other names already for that day.

A slow day for deaths.

A good day.

He stood up and wiped his forehead, the sweat and grime staining the rag he wore around his neck.

Across in Bed Three, a man cried out for water. He went to the bamboo barrel they kept in the corner and, using the coconut shell, filled it half full, carrying it carefully to the man.

He would die soon, the captain was sure. He'd seen it before. The tiredness in the eyes, the faraway look as if the threshold between life and death had already been crossed, the future already here in the present.

A future where there was no hunger, no pain, no mosquitoes and no unrelenting prattle about the damp heat of the jungle.

He raised the man's head and let the water trickle across the dry lips.

What was this man's name?

He couldn't remember.

There was a time when he knew all of them, but most had gone now. The new ones were coming in every day.

He took the tiny picture wrapped in its greaseproof paper out of his pocket and stared at it as he often did. His wife and child, gone now, gone forever, but in some strange way, still here with him, his memory of them keeping him alive.

The doctor approached him slowly, a rusty belt holding up his ragged trousers, a sweat-stained shirt all that remained of his once pristine uniform. 'Can you get the detail to bury Bed Twelve as soon as they can? There's three more coming in from upcountry later today and we need the cot.'

'Will do. I'll ask the bugler to play the last post as they bury him.'

The captain had lost the polite formalities of the army long ago. For him, they no longer seemed to matter. But the formalities for the dead still remained.

It was a matter of respect for their life. And for the manner of their death.

'I think Bed Three will be free later,' he added glancing at the man to whom he had just given water.

The doctor looked across at the patient, a sad helplessness in his eyes. 'Make him as comfortable as you can,' he said quietly.

'No more quinine?'

'We'll save it for the new arrivals. Perhaps one of them is strong enough to survive.'

The captain nodded.

It was a day just like any other.

CHAPTER TWO

Saturday, December 07, 2019
Didsbury, Manchester

Jayne Sinclair was sitting in front of her computer waiting for the call. On her left, she had a large glass of Sauvignon Blanc. On her right, Mr Smith was intent on cleaning every inch of his fur, stretching his legs and body into awkward positions to reach the most difficult places.

The notification pinged at exactly 8.00 p.m., just as she had agreed with the client. She'd been working on this project since the morning. Hopefully, it would be her last before she finally took a break; a trip to Australia with her stepfather Robert and his wife, Vera.

She needed this break, she wanted this break and she was definitely going to treat herself.

She clicked the app and the client's well-known face appeared instantly. 'Hi Jayne, great to see you. What's the weather like in Manchester?'

Cecile Barton's accent was peculiarly transatlantic, a voice that had served her well as the irascible policewoman with a gruff exterior and a heart of gold in the long-running detective series, Driver. Her father had emigrated to America in the 1960s when she was just six years old, making his fortune from a car dealership in Southern California. Now she wanted to find out her roots.

Jayne looked out the patio window into her garden. It was black as ink outside with a harsh wind tumbling through the trees. She had the central heating on full but she was still wearing a cardigan over her jumper and had long woolly socks on her feet.

'Same as ever for Manchester in December, cold as a penguin's nose.'

Cecile Barton laughed. 'You'll be pleased to know it's a balmy seventy degrees here at the moment.'

Jayne did a quick calculation in her head: about 21°C. 'That sounds perfect, a lovely day.'

'That's why I live in LA. Blue skies, warm days and luscious men. But that's another story. What do you have for me, Jayne?'

Cecile Barton had contacted her two weeks ago with an interesting brief – to find out as much as she could about Cecile's English heritage. 'Both my mum and dad have already passed and I never asked them where we came from or anything about our family history. I'd like to find out if I was related to kings or royalty. I certainly feel that's where I come from,' she had said.

Jayne had taken the basic details and quickly discovered that Cecile Barton's origins were far more prosaic than she imagined; most of her family had been mill workers in Bolton, having moved there from Manchester just after the 1881 census. In their first meeting the client had been disappointed by Jayne's discoveries. 'Are you sure there's nothing royal, or at least a hint of the aristocracy in my background?'

'Not that I can see from your family tree at the moment. I'll delve back further for the next session and there may be something earlier.'

This was now the next session, but Jayne wasn't looking forward to giving the news to her client. She decided to start with something positive. 'I've found the First World War record and the medals of your great-grandfather, John Barton.'

'Oh, that sounds interesting. He was a war hero?'

'I think anybody who fought in that war was a hero, Cecile.' Jayne pressed the 'invite to share my screen' button on the app. 'As you can see, he was already a reservist in the Loyal North Lancashire Regiment when he was called to the colours in 1914.'

'Reservist?'

'A part-time soldier, held in the Reserves until needed.'

'Right, so he was already part of the army?'

'Not a regular soldier though, somebody who trained perhaps twice a year.'

'Okay.'

Jayne could almost hear the shrug in the voice. 'He was called up and finally went to the Western Front in 1915.' She clicked on the page showing his war record.

'Western Front?'

'It's the name for the trenches in France. I've checked the regimental history and he probably fought in the second Battle of Ypres and the first Battle of Loos.'

'They fought over the toilets?'

Jayne coughed to cover her smile. Cecile Barton may have been an excellent actress but she wasn't the sharpest knife in the drawer. 'No, it's a place in France. Not a good time for his battalion. They attacked in the face of uncut German wire, machine guns and gas. When, after a second attempt, the survivors rallied in the trenches, only three officers and 159 other ranks remained on their feet, with sixteen officers and 489 men having fallen.'

'That's terrible.'

'It was war, casualties at this time were immense. I've included a history of his regiment in the file I'll send after this meeting.'

'But he wasn't hurt?'

'I don't think so. There's no record of any wounds until 1917 when he was invalided out of the army with trench fever.'

'What's trench fever?'

'A nasty disease transmitted by body lice. It was endemic in the armies on the Western Front. He must have had a severe case because he spent six months in hospital and received a disability pension after the war. Here are the records.' Jayne shared the screen but the client seemed to have lost interest at the mention of body lice, saying, 'What about the other ancestors?'

Jayne clicked back to the family tree she had compiled. 'It was John's father, also called John, who took the family to Bolton in the 1880s, probably to find work in a textile mill as a spinner.'

'Anything else?'

The client was definitely losing interest. 'We have your great-great-great-grandfather, Silas Barton, who is listed as a copper worker in Manchester in the 1841 census.' Jayne shared the image. 'He was married to an Anne and had one child living in Deansgate. I've checked the address on Google. It's where the Science Museum is now, but the street itself and the house have been demolished.'

'That's sad. I would have liked to have gone back and seen the house.'

'In the rapidly expanding cities of the Industrial Revolution, not much survives, I'm afraid. I've taken Silas a little bit further back to his marriage to Anne in 1822 in Manchester Cathedral. Her maiden name was Hyndman.'

'Manchester Cathedral, that sounds very upmarket.'

'Maybe he was a regular parishioner and that's why he was married there. I'll need to check more in the Manchester church registers of the period to find out. If you remember, this was just three years after the Peterloo Massacre, and Manchester was still a hotbed of radicalism.'

She stopped for a moment, taking a sip of her wine. In the corner, Mr Smith had just arched his back and stretched his front legs forward, before checking his bowl to see if there were any titbits left. On discovering he had eaten everything, he snorted twice and then settled himself down in the corner. Despite the weather, he was probably looking forward to a long night out on the prowl.

Jayne returned to her client. 'That's where I am at the moment. I've reached a brick wall on your grandmother. We know her maiden name was Reid but I still haven't found her birth details yet. Plus, I want to go further back with Silas. Who were his parents? I'll get back to you by the end of the week, I need to go to Manchester Central Library to check the parish records.'

'Thank you, Jayne, you've done a thorough job, but I don't know if we'll continue. I was expecting my ancestors to have been more…'

'Noble and aristocratic?'

'Precisely.'

'But I think they were, Cecile. They worked hard, they fought for their country and they raised families. And look at what happened, one of their number is now a famous and successful actress in Hollywood. We can't change our past, Cecile, just celebrate it.'

'I don't know, Jayne, I'd like time to think about it.'

'No worries, I'll send you the document and the family tree I've compiled so far.'

'Right, can you bill me for the work?'

'I'll do that, Cecile. I hope you continue. I think all our ancestors' lives are interesting no matter where they came from or who they were.'

'I'll think about it and let you know. Thank you for your work.'

The screen went blank. One part of Jayne was happy that Cecile Barton wanted a break. It meant that Jayne could concentrate on preparing for her trip. There was just so much to do and so little time to do it all. At least she had already arranged for Mr Smith to stay with a neighbour while she was away. Finding somebody to look after him had been number one on her list of priorities.

She took a large sip of Sauvignon Blanc, found the Barton file and sent it to the client. She stood up and stretched before taking her glass of wine and walking to the patio doors.

Outside the wind had increased, rattling the window frame and the outside fence. 'Are you sure you want to go out tonight?' she asked Mr Smith.

He ignored her and continued licking his fur.

Their moment was disturbed by a loud ring from the front door. Jayne glanced at the large clock on the wall. Nearly 9.00 p.m. 'I wonder who that can be at this time of night?' she said out loud.

Mr Smith ignored her, as he usually did.

CHAPTER THREE

October 28, 1938
Keppel Harbour, Singapore

The country sort of crept up on them like a cat stalking a bird.

One minute it was a long grey smear hovering above the horizon. Next, it was a thicker, blacker line like a stroke from a blunt pencil in a schoolbook.

Arthur Horton leant on the rail, stretching over as far as he could to stare down at the white wave of water being churned up by the bow of the ship. They had come so far in such a short time, each mile hotter than the last.

He looked up again. The shore had a definite green tinge now, with an irregular fringed top.

As they were getting closer to this foreign shore, everyone around him was quiet. Ronnie Arkwright, Ted

Rogers, Tommy Harrison, Ray Teale and even Serjeant Murray all just stared at the approaching coastline.

'Do you want one, Arthur?' Ronnie offered him one of his Capstans.

Ronnie Arkwright was his best mate in the platoon. For some reason, they'd hit it off straight away even though they were completely different personalities. Ronnie was quiet, but when he spoke everybody listened, including Serjeant Murray.

Arthur shook his head; he'd smoked more than the ship's funnel recently. He looked across at the members of the platoon, gazing toward the land, their faces marked by the sun after the sea voyage. Their newly issued tropical khaki; sleeves rolled up above the elbows, long shorts drooping down below their knees, shirts open at the collar, all still bore the sharp creases of storage in Aden.

He leant out over the gang rail once again and saw the whole scene repeated on the other decks. Long lines of young men, all pressed to the side, staring out at the distant shore.

Even the officers seemed to have been infected by the men's mood. Their jovial, public schoolboy jests replaced by a quietness that was unusual for them.

A thick, clogging waft of cigarette smoke filled his nostrils and mouth. He heard Ronnie cough twice and watched as the dead Capstan made a perfect swallow dive into the dark waters of the sea.

He squinted to see the shore better.

Its green was more pronounced now and he could clearly see stands of thick forest on the edge of a palm-fringed beach. It wasn't like the pictures he'd seen at all. Not the colours, anyway. The water wasn't a vivid aquamarine blue. The beach wasn't a golden yellow. The trees weren't a rich tropical green.

All he could see was a slash of dark, muddy brown sea, a stroke of grey beach and a mist-laden green jungle rising to no great height.

'Is this it?' he said, louder than he meant. 'Is this really Malaya?'

The rest stayed silent.

'Give us a fag will you, Ronnie,' Arthur asked his mate.

'You just said you didn't want one.'

'Well, now I do.' He took the Capstan, lit it and inhaled deeply, feeling the tobacco reach into the depths of his lungs. He blew the smoke out and watched as it drifted and danced in the rays of the sun.

The sharp acrid taste took him back to the time when they were training in York. A horrible place that camp was. But the town was lovely; old-fashioned narrow streets, friendly people who didn't mind squaddies, great beer, and the Minster. How he loved the Minster. On his days off, he would go and sit there, listening to the songs of the choir as the sound soared to the rafters, echoed off the stone pillars, and escaped out of the pale red of the Rose Window.

He wasn't religious at all, but on those days, when the singing was so beautiful, God would have had to have been an old curmudgeon not to listen.

The sound of cheering brought him back to the present. They were much closer to the shore now. He could see houses regularly spaced along the coast, facing the sea.

The lads were cheering at an ancient tramp steamer, which was sailing between them and the shore. An old man was hanging out his washing on a line across the stern. A young child with a round, shaven head was waving and smiling at them.

'Hey mate, fancy doing my washing while you're at it?' shouted a broad Manchester voice from above.

The man ignored them, going about his work as if they didn't exist.

The harbour was full of activity; all the ships of the world jockeying for position in the port. Of course, their vessel took precedence. Everyone else seemed to be trying to get out of their way.

He could see the city now in the distance. Its grey blur shrouded in an even greyer blanket of haze.

Then he smelt it.

A cloying, clinging smell, full of rotting vegetables, fruit, charcoal, car exhaust, fish, more fish, and above it all, a top note of the putrid aroma of people; a blend of sweat, hard work, sorrow, despair, and sacrifice, mixed with just a smidgeon of joy.

The docks were in sight now. Ships gushed black smoke out of charred funnels. Derricks and cranes like mothers, carefully feeding their cargo into the voracious mouth that was the hold. Endless rows of warehouses with piles of goods, crates and bales from all over the world. The rattle of chains, the constant chug of compressors, the steady whirr of winding gear.

He wished Maggie was with him to witness it. Something they could have shared together. Instead he was here with eight hundred other men, lining the decks, staring at the shore.

He wiped the sweat dripping from his face onto his uniform. It was as if someone had turned a tap on in his body and decided it would constantly ooze liquid from every pore.

With all the other lads, he cheered and cheered and cheered as they finally docked in the centre of the city, a brass band playing a welcome to the conquering heroes of Manchester.

In Singapore, Arthur would melt away to become nothing.

But he wasn't to know that.

Not yet, anyway.

CHAPTER FOUR

Saturday, December 7, 2019
Didsbury, Manchester

Jayne opened the door and was surprised to see her neighbour, Alice Taylor, standing in the rain, a coat held over her head.

'Sorry, Jayne, for calling round this late.'

'Come in quickly before you drown out there.'

The woman stepped through the door, drops of rain falling from her coat as she shook it. Her grey hair was slightly damp and she was dressed as she always was, whether it was summer or winter – a light green twin-piece with matching pearl necklace. Alice's husband had died over ten years ago, and since then she had busied herself with the local Women's Institute, helping at a community centre and being a stalwart member of the local Church of England congregation. She was a well-known figure in the area, pedalling all over town on her ancient bike, forever going somewhere and doing something.

Her energy and zest for life always amazed Jayne. In fact, she didn't know anybody, including herself, who was always as busy as Alice Taylor.

'Is it about Mr Smith? I hope you can still take him when I go to Australia?'

Right on cue, the cat wandered out from the kitchen and wove in and out of Alice's legs, his tail held high. She reached down and stroked his head and along his back. For once, instead of moving away, he just stood there lapping up all the attention.

'That's fine, I'm looking forward to looking after my little hero.'

Mr Smith was purring loudly now. The cat who definitely had the cream.

'I'll give you a little snack when you come round later,' she whispered in his ear.

'Snack?' asked Jayne.

'He often comes round to my house for his supper. He likes his liver and vegetables, does Mr Smith.'

'He's been going round to your house to eat? But I feed him every night.'

'I'm sure he's just a little peckish. It's a busy life, isn't it?' She nuzzled her face into his.

Jayne stared at Mr Smith. He obviously had a life she knew nothing about. 'How can I help you, Alice?'

As if suddenly remembering why she came round, Alice stood up. 'Oh yes, sorry. Remember we talked about my adoption…?'

'Of course, I was happy to help.'

'Well, the documents arrived in the post today.' She held up a buff envelope.

Six weeks ago, Jayne had gone round to Alice's house to see if she could look after Mr Smith when Jayne went to Australia. Alice had invited her in for tea and biscuits, sitting her down in the lounge. After a few minutes of small talk, the elderly woman had asked: 'You look into family history, don't you, Jayne?'

'I am a genealogical investigator, if that's what you mean.'

'Well, I wonder if you could help me with something.'

'Of course, not a problem.'

Alice seemed to be turning something over in her mind. 'I haven't told this to many people before, but I was adopted when I was just over three years old.'

'Really?'

'They were a lovely family, the Simpsons. No children of their own and I had a wonderful time being brought up by them. We weren't rich, but we were happy. We lived in Hulme, I knew all the neighbours. The house has since been knocked down, of course. They built those awful flats where it used to be.'

'What would you like to find out?'

'I know it's a bit late in life but I'd like to discover who my birth parents were. I know my mum's name, it was

Margaret, and I think my dad died in the war, but I never knew his name. My mum, she wasn't the most stable person apparently. Liked to drink, according to the Simpsons. She passed away in 1941 – well, that's what the Simpsons told me. I was just two then. They said I was adopted by them a year later in 1942.'

The old lady remained silent for a while, then she stood up and went to an old cupboard, opening a drawer. 'I only have one picture of my birth mum and dad.'

She handed over an old black and white print, obviously taken in a studio. A woman was standing next to a man in an army uniform. She was tall and sharply featured. The man looked younger than her and had a broad smile on his face. She was wearing a wedding dress, carrying a bouquet of flowers and a silver horseshoe. He was in his army khaki, a soft cap on his head and the shiniest boots Jayne had ever seen.

'They both look so happy,' Jayne said. 'This must have been taken on their wedding day. Do you know when that was?'

The woman shook her head. 'I don't even know his name.'

'I can help you, if you want.'

'It's strange, I've never wanted to know until now. I always thought of the Simpsons as my parents. But I had my eightieth birthday this year and I've decided I can't avoid it any more. I need to find out before I die.'

'It's quite a big decision to make at eighty.'

'I celebrated down at the community centre – we had cake, and games and everything. It was a lovely day. I think I decided after that it was time to find out.'

'It could be painful discovering the truth.'

'I know, and that's why I've put it off for so long. John, my husband, God bless his soul, always wanted me to do the research, but I wasn't ready… until now.'

'Do you know anything?'

Again the woman shook her head.

'Not even your mother's surname?'

'Not even that. I can't remember anything about that time.' The woman paused for a long time, staring into mid-air, until she eventually spoke. 'I've tried so hard to remember her, but I can't. Perhaps I was too young.'

'Or sometimes the mind has a way of forgetting the hard times we don't want to remember.'

'True, our memories are never so exact. It's funny but the only thing I can recall is the smell of her perfume. It was sweet and floral. I've spent my whole life looking for the perfume but I've never found it. Strange, isn't it?'

'Did your adoptive family not tell you anything else?'

She sighed. 'The Simpsons wanted me to be their daughter, so I took their name. They didn't even tell me I had been adopted until I was forty. They told me they had visited me in a children's home, but I don't remember the place at all. That's when they gave me the picture. They didn't know anything themselves, other than that both my mum and dad were dead.'

Again a long silence, which Jayne was reluctant to interrupt.

'I've tried so hard to remember being in the children's home too, but I just can't. Perhaps it's a sort of protection, not remembering I mean. One reads so many bad things about those places.' A long sigh, followed by the return of the smile that Alice normally wore every day. 'Now it's time to find out what happened.'

'You never applied for a passport?'

Alice shook her head. 'John didn't like flying. We always took two weeks in Bournemouth every year. He was a creature of habit was John.'

'Right, the first thing we need to do is contact the adoption service in Southport to find your birth certificate. They'll also have the names of your parents, and once we have the names, we can discover a lot more.'

'How do I do that?'

'No worries, I'll help you. Come round to the house tomorrow and we'll fill in the forms together.'

The woman seemed to think for a moment. 'I'm afraid I can't pay you, Jayne.'

'No worries, let's call my work payment for looking after Mr Smith.'

'But I want to do that, Jayne, he's such a character.'

'And I want to help you find your relatives, so let's call it evens.'

The next day, Alice Taylor had gone to Jayne's house and they had completed the forms for the adoption agency.

'Is that it?'

'I'm afraid there's one more procedure. Because you were born before 1975, you also have to visit a counsellor.'

'Why?'

'It's the law, I'm afraid. There is the possibility of suffering emotional trauma as people discover the truth about their past. The counsellors are social workers who help guide people through the process of opening their adoption records. Don't worry though, we can go to see them together. Where were you in care?'

'A children's home in Salford, I think. At least that's what the Simpsons told me.'

'I'll contact the council and arrange to meet a social worker. We may be able to find your care-home records, if they still have them.'

'That's it?'

'That's all there is. We just wait for the reply from Southport.'

The woman frowned. 'Should I also take a DNA test?'

Jayne smiled. 'How do you know about those?'

'I was watching TV the other night and they showed a man having a DNA test. They found his relatives afterwards, they hadn't seen each other for sixty years.'

'We could do a DNA test with any of the usual providers. But there are no guarantees you'll find relatives. It depends if they have also taken a test and their DNA uploaded to a site like GEDmatch.'

'It sounds so complicated.'

'Don't worry, let me do it for you.'

'Is it painful?' she asked dubiously. 'Taking the test, I mean.'

'Not at all, just a swab on the inside of the cheek to collect saliva. We'll send off for a kit from one of the testers, probably Ancestry, and Bob's your uncle.'

'Actually, Bob might be my uncle. I don't know at the moment.'

They both laughed.

Two weeks later, Jayne took Alice to meet the counsellor and sent back the DNA sample to Ancestry. Now Alice was standing in front of her with the first results from the adoption records office in Southport.

'Have you opened it yet?'

'No, I was too worried. Can we do it together?'

'No problem, come on through to the kitchen. Can I get you some tea?'

'No thanks, I don't think I can handle any more tea. I've been on edge ever since this came.'

Jayne held up the envelope. 'Shall we open it?'

Alice took a deep breath and nodded.

CHAPTER FIVE

November 28, 1938
Tanglin Barracks, Singapore

They had a busy morning for a change. Roll call taken by Serjeant Murray was speedily done, followed by a breakfast of sausage, bacon, egg and beans in the NAAFI. The sausages weren't a patch on those from Jones, the butchers from the Ashton Road; the bacon wasn't crispy and the eggs had a strange, earthy taste, like they'd been rolled in mud; but Arthur loved a fry-up in the morning and the army always gave you a good one, even here in Singapore.

'Who was it who said an army marches on its stomach?' he asked his mate Ronnie Arkwright.

'Dunno, but whoever he was, he was dead right.'

Both of them were already dripping with sweat even though it was only eight in the morning.

'Looks like it's gonna be hot again,' said Arthur, dipping his bread into his egg yolk.

'When isn't it hot?'

Ted Rogers leant across the table to grab the salt. 'Apparently this is the cool season. In May it gets hotter than a Turkish sauna.'

'I'm gonna waste away, me. Won't be anything left. If I collapse from heat stroke, it'll be the army's fault. Why don't they make it cooler?' The last sentence was moaned by Tommy Harrison.

'Listen, Tommy, if moaning were in the Olympics, you'd win a gold medal,' answered Ronnie. 'You'd beat that Jesse Owens fella every day of the week'

'I just tell it like it is,' sulked Tommy.

'Right, let's be havin' you.' Serjeant Murray towered over them, his immaculately pressed uniform as crisp as ever.

'But I haven't finished yet, Sarge.'

'That's Serjeant to you, Harrison, and you'll have to eat quicker next time. Parade ground in three minutes.'

Serjeant Murray marched off, not hearing a muttered 'Bloody army' from Harrison.

Once they lined themselves up, Serjeant Murray inspected them, finding fault with everybody.

'Those boots look like they've been dancing in mud. Shine 'em so I can see my sparkling eyes in 'em, Horton.'

'Yes, Serjeant.'

'Your solar topee has a scuff mark on it, Arkwright. Has one of the local dogs been wipin' his backside on it?'

'No, Serjeant.'

'Then it must have been you. Get it cleaned, lad.'

'Yes, Serjeant.'

'Dearie dearie me, you've got egg on your shirt, Harrison. The army doesn't like squaddies with egg on their shirts, makes them look untidy, unsoldierly.'

'It was breakfast, Sarge…'

Murray placed his finger across his lips. 'Shhhh, you only talk when I ask you a question, Harrison. And then you only say, "Yes, Serjeant", "No, Serjeant" or "Three bags full, Serjeant". Is that understood?' he whispered.

'But…'

'Is that understood?'

'Yes, Serjeant.'

'You will report to the Provost's office,' he whispered again before leaning in close to Harrison's ear and bellowing, 'YOU… ARE… ON… A… CHARGE.'

He then smiled, stepped back and twirled the ends of his moustache with his fingers. 'While I deal with Private Harrison, the rest of you have an important job. The colonel has decided in his infinite wisdom that Tanglin Camp is looking slovenly. Your job is to take that whitewash,' he pointed to a row of buckets, 'and paint every stone on the ground white. Is that clear? But take care, my lovelies, do not get any paint on your uniforms or you will be joining Private Harrison at the Provost Marshal's office.'

He checked his watch. 'Paint away, lovelies. You have until noon to get it finished.'

So they had spent the morning painting rocks white. Ronnie had even taken a few potatoes from the cookhouse and painted those too, laying them out in a pattern to form the letters S.O.S.

Now they were back in the barracks after lunch. The army had decided that soldiers could take a long siesta in the afternoon. Arthur was sure it was because the officers fancied a break in their mess rather than for any military reason.

'I mean, if we were at war the enemy wouldn't shout, "I say, chaps, time to stop fighting, we need forty winks", would they?' Tommy Harrison imitated the upper-class voice of an officer.

A boot went sailing past his head, thrown by Ronnie. 'Pipe down. I'm tryin' to get some kip.'

For some reason, Arthur Horton didn't feel tired. As the others lay on their bunks sleeping, reading or just staring into space as the fan above their heads stirred the hot, humid air, he decided to write to his wife.

Block 13
Tanglin Barracks
Singapore
28th November, 1938

My dearest Maggie,

Well, we're here. We spent nearly four weeks on that boat. I'll be glad if I never see one of those things again. There was no room to sleep or eat. Me and the other lads of the platoon had to make do as best we could. You can imagine the pong as we were all crammed beneath the decks. Tommy Harrison didn't wash himself or his socks for the whole time!

Anyway, we arrived in Singapore on Tuesday. You should have seen the docks. Full of coolies, those are the local labourers, carrying sacks on their backs without a care in the world.

It's hot here too. Every day the sun beats down. The lads and me just sweat and sweat and sweat. We don't have to do anything at all, sitting here and writing to you is bringing me out in a flood.

The barracks are pretty nice. There's me and fifteen others from our section in one block. I've got a locker for my stuff and the bed is pretty comfortable. We've even got electric fans. But they don't seem to help much, they just move the warm air around a bit more. We don't need a blanket to sleep at night, it's far too hot!

Anyway, enough of me. How are you, dear? Not letting your mother get you down too much, I hope. And when you have time, can you send me the wedding photos and any photos I took with the Box Brownie on our honeymoon in Llandudno? You looked so beautiful on the day we were married. I know our honeymoon wasn't very long but who could have guessed I was going to be shipped out so quickly and, even worse, sent all the way to Singapore. I guess it's one of the dangers of marrying a soldier.

I spoke to Captain Moriarty on the boat. They do have married quarters here and even some for privates. I put the application in last week to him. You should have seen the number of forms I had to fill in. They asked for your maiden name, your mum's maiden name and lots of other questions. I made most of it up. For the life of me, I couldn't remember. Well, you don't, do you? I then had to write a letter saying why I thought I deserved married quarters. I wanted to write 'because I'm stuck out here defending the Empire far away from my wife'. But Serjeant Murray, he's our platoon leader, said that's not what they want to hear. So he helped me write it. Captain Moriarty said it was well written and the best letter he'd ever seen. It was all about improving regimental efficiency and the family giving a solid foundation for a soldier to avoid the inequities of the Orient. A load of rubbish, but I'd write anything if it meant you could join me here.

Anyway, Captain Moriarty has passed it on to Major Tudor, the company commander. If he likes it, it will go to the Battalion Adjutant and the CO for approval.

As I'm writing this, I'm crossing my fingers, dearest heart, and praying every night and day we can be together again.

I miss you so much but I'm sure we'll be together soon. I hope you can bear living in Singapore, it's so hot. Anyway, I must go now. I keep your picture beside my bed and I'm always thinking of you.

Your husband,
Arthur

CHAPTER SIX

Saturday, December 7, 2019
Didsbury, Manchester

With Alice sitting next to her at the kitchen table, Jayne sliced through the top of the envelope with her fingernail and took out three sheets of paper and a leaflet.

'Here goes,' she said. Alice leant forward, reading over her shoulder.

'The first is a letter from the Southport adoption office. They've found the details of your birth parents and your adoption papers and are suggesting the next steps on your journey.'

'Jayne, please tell me my parents' names.'

She picked up the next sheet of paper and showed it to Alice. 'You were born on May twenty-third, 1939. Your mother's name was Margaret Horton, maiden name Elliot. Your father's name was Arthur Horton.'

'Arthur and Margaret – they're both good, gentle names.'

'And there's more. Your parents named you Mary.'

'What?'

'I think your adopted parents, the Simpsons, probably changed your Christian name as well as your last name.'

'Mary Horton. It sounds so strange. Mary Taylor would have been my married name. I don't know if I feel like a Mary.'

'Would you like to see the details of your adoption?'

Alice nodded slowly.

'You understand that full adoption was introduced into England and Wales by the Adoption of Children Act 1926. This Act contained a number of important provisions. First, only in exceptional circumstances could a child be relinquished for adoption without the consent of their birth parents. Second, adult individuals as well as married couples could adopt legally. And third, adoption replaced the former parental ties with a new relationship with their adoptive family.'

'So the Simpsons became my legal family?'

'Correct. Another act, in 1939, encouraged the supervision of adoption by local authorities employing professional social workers and regulating the adoption agencies. But this wasn't fully implemented until 1943.'

'Please just show me the letter, Jayne.'

The letter was a photocopy of a standard form with typewritten names and addresses added in. It was titled 'The Salford Orphans' Home' at the top and dated November 7, 1942.

In the matter of MARY HORTON, an infant.

Whereas an Application has been made by JAMES SIMPSON of 43, HALLEY ROAD, HULME, MANCHESTER and LOUISA ANNE SIMPSON (his wife) for an adoption order in respect of MARY HORTON, an infant.

AND whereas the parents of the said infant, ARTHUR HORTON and MARGARET HORTON (NEE ELLIOT) are no longer living, it is confirmed that the applicant(s) be authorised to adopt the infant from THE SALFORD ORPHANS' HOME.

This application having been confirmed by the sole surviving relative of the said infant, ANGELINE ELLIOT (AUNT) of 102, RUMBLE STREET, GLOSSOP, DERBYSHIRE.

SIGNED: RALPH TRAFFORD - CHAIRMAN

SIGNED: HELENA ARBUTHNOT - BOARD OF TRUSTEES

There was a long silence as Alice digested the information. 'I was just three and half years old when I was adopted and both my parents had already died…' she said quietly.

'It seems you had one surviving relative, an aunt. Given her surname, I bet she was your grandmother's sister.'

'I wonder why she didn't take me?'

'Perhaps she already had too many children of her own or wasn't physically capable of looking after a three-year-old infant. But the Home obviously did their job because you were placed with a good and loving family.'

'I was very lucky in that respect. Is there anything else we can do?'

'With this information, we can find out a lot more.' Jayne booted up her laptop and logged into the General Record Office. 'First let's order your birth certificate. The birth indexes on the GRO site only go up to 1934 but we can find the information we need on another site.' She called up FreeBMD. 'Let's just type in your name and we'll use Salford as the registry office.'

The search result came back with no hits.

'Not to worry. We'll expand the search to every registration district.' She pressed the key again and this time three results came back, with only one being for the period April to June 1939.

Horton, Margaret   Elliot   Manchester 6d 278

'There you are, I think that is you. Your mother's name was Elliot and you were registered in Manchester, not Salford. We'll now enter the index reference into the GRO form, getting your certificate delivered as quickly as we can. You should have it in the next three or so days.'

'Really?'

Jayne nodded. 'Before we leave the GRO site, there's a couple of other things we can do. From the picture, your parents were married, so let's order their marriage certificate.'

Jayne went back to FreeBMD and entered Alice's parents' details into the marriage search. Just one entry came back this time.

APRIL – JUNE 1938

Horton, Arthur Elliot   Manchester 9c 1838

'So we know they were married between those months.' Jayne repeated the steps on GRO to order the marriage certificate. 'Now, the final thing we can check is the death certificates for both your parents. Let's look at your father first.'

She entered the details in the deaths section of FreeBMD.

'I've expanded the date range so it's now from 1939 to late 1942, when you were adopted.' She checked the screen when the results appeared. 'It looks like there are thirty-three deaths with the name Arthur Horton for this period. If we eliminate all those over the age of fifty – your father was a serving soldier, after all – that still leaves twelve people. It'll cost us a fortune to order death certificates for that number.'

'So what do we do, Jayne?'

'We wait, Alice. When the marriage certificate comes it will give us his age and we can narrow the search parameters. So, now let's check your mother. We'll presume she was using her married name of Horton; we can always check her maiden name later.'

Jayne entered the details in FreeBMD once more. 'There she is.'

APRIL – JUNE 1941

Horton, Margaret   25   Manchester 1c 56

'She was twenty-five years old when she died, which means she won't be on the 1911 census, unfortunately, but with a bit of luck, she may be on other documents like electoral registers. First, let's order her death certificate.'

A hand clasped Jayne's as she moved her mouse.

'Let's not order the death certificate yet. We've found out so much so quickly, I'm having a hard time taking it all in.'

Jayne looked across at the old woman. 'I'm sorry, sometimes I get a bit carried away in the momentum of these searches. Of course, we can wait until you're ready.'

Alice Taylor scratched her head. 'I want to find out more, it's just… The Simpsons told me she died as an alcoholic. I don't know if I'm ready to read the details yet. And we have come so far so quickly. I now know the names of my birth mum and dad. You don't know how happy that makes me. Perhaps, a couple of days from now, we can do a bit more… if it's not too much trouble. When the birth certificates or the DNA results arrive.'

Jayne patted the back of the liver-spotted hand. 'Of course, Alice, whenever you're ready. And it's not too much trouble, I'd love to help you find out more about your family.'

A few minutes later, Alice decided to return home.

'Let me walk you back. It's a horrible night and we don't want you falling on the path.'

Jayne escorted Alice back to her house, stopping at the front door.

'Thank you, Jayne. It's strange but I feel like a huge weight has been lifted from my shoulders. It's like things from my past that I didn't understand are beginning to click into place. And now I finally know my father's name. Arthur Horton. A good name, a solid name.'

'Discovering family history often does that: completing us, helping us understand events that happened in the past. The good and the bad.'

A faint smile crossed Alice Taylor's lips. 'It's who we are, isn't it?'

CHAPTER SEVEN

Block 15
Tanglin Barracks
Singapore
12th January 1939

My dearest Maggie,

Happy New Year. I hope you didn't get too tipsy with the next-door neighbours. You know what you're like when you've had a few, hah, hah.

We're all settled in pretty well here, the lads and me. They're a happy bunch. Ronnie Arkwright's my best mate. He can be a bit off sometimes but mostly he's as straight as anybody. The sort of man you don't want to get on the wrong side of, know what I mean? Then there's Tommy Harrison. He's from Accrington. A young lad still wet behind the ears and a bit strange, like Henry from no. 12. He's all there but a bit of a moaner.

Ted Rogers and Ray Teale have the bunks next to mine. Those two know how to drink like fish. Beer seems to go down their throats faster than you can say Manchester United.

Harry Jarvis, Colin Tracy, Ray Lloyd and Fred Mytholmroyd all hang around together. We never see them apart. The four stooges we call them, after those American comedians nobody likes.

There was another lad, Ben Travis, but he got malaria real bad. He's in the camp hospital now and there's talk about him being sent back to Blighty.

He was as sick as a dog but I'd try to get malaria as well if it meant we could be together again. They give us these pills, quinine they are. We're supposed to take them because it stops malaria. But they taste like a wrestler's used jockstrap. Ben could never stomach them. He was forever throwing up. That's why he ended up in hospital. Lucky man though, if he can get back to England.

I realise I haven't told you much about the camp. It's big. There's a cinema, canteen, shops and laundry, even a hospital. It's like a small town. If we didn't want to go into the city, we would never have to. Everything's here. There's even a golf course reserved for officers. Silly game anyway, not like football.

I read in the Straits Times that United lost 2–1 to Everton. They're near the bottom of the table again. I hope they don't go down to the second division. I'd never be able to show my face in the street if they did.

Anyway, you can see I'm keeping up with the news. We get it pretty quickly out here. The Straits Times even prints the football scores on Monday. And there's always the radio. Ronnie got one from somewhere (no questions asked, no lies told) for our barracks. So now we can listen to George Robey and the latest tunes from the BBC on the World Service.

Sometimes I think you're listening to the same programme as I am. Except it's breakfast in England and teatime here. When I think like that, I miss you so much and want to hold you tight, like we did at Belle Vue when we were courting. Do you remember that evening we went out?

Anyway, mustn't be too sad. We'll be together soon. I had to rewrite the letter about married quarters. Major Tudor said it wasn't quite right to hand to the Adjutant. So I did it. Couldn't see the difference myself but he said it was all a matter of tone. It wasn't pleading enough, I think, for him. It's done now. I hope you can come here soon. I miss you so much.

I went out with the lads last week. We saw Gracie Fields and Victor McLaglen at the Alhambra in We're Going to Be Rich. *That Gracie Fields can sing like a nightingale. And to think she started out as an ordinary mill girl from Rochdale. You see, there's hope for all of us yet. Maybe you and me can be rich soon, hah, hah.*

The others went to the café for a drink but I went back to the barracks. They can meet girls there but you don't have to worry about me. There's only room in my heart for one girl and that's my own darling Maggie. Well, lights out has been called, love, so I've got to go. Keep yourself well and never mind what Mrs Dempsey says. She's just another know-all who knows nowt.

Your husband,
Arthur

Block 15
Tanglin Barracks
Singapore
10th March 1939

My dearest Maggie,

Sorry, I haven't written for so long but we've been extremely busy recently. I haven't had time to think, let alone write.

Last week we celebrated Ladysmith Day. It meant we had to troop the colours in front of General Bond, the G.O.C.

For about a month before that they had us tramping up and down, and marching here, marching there, marching blooming everywhere. My feet hurt, my shoulders are sore and my back aches. I hope I never see another parade ground for the rest of my life.

It all went very well, though. And you would have been proud of us. We all looked so smart and the colours were so beautiful. It made me proud to be a Tad. Even the general said we were as good a body of men as he'd ever seen. So there. Stick that up your pipe and smoke it, as George Formby says.

I'm glad it's all over, though. And so are the lads. Remember the one I told you about who got malaria? His name was Ben Travis. Well, he got it real bad and passed away last week. So, he will be going back to England but not in the way he wanted. All the lads take their quinine now even if it does make them sick.

Life goes on as usual. We get up about six; have breakfast at seven. It's just getting light then. It's the best part of the day. When it's cool and there's the lovely smell of washing in the air. I always love it. Like Stockport on a summer's morning, if you know what

I mean. I know you've asked me to describe what I do and my life in the letters, but you know I've no way with words, dearest heart. I always know what I want to say but it never really goes down on the paper. I hope you understand.

Anyway, after breakfast we do our work like drill or training or looking after the camp.

In the afternoon, we have a nap for a couple of hours. All the Europeans in Singapore have a rest then. It avoids being in the heat of the day. The Asiatics don't, though. Different sort of blood, I suppose. Later I might look after my uniform but mostly that's done by the Dhobi men. Then it's time to head down to the canteen for my tea and maybe listen to the radio for a while. I'm afraid it's all very boring, dear.

We don't see the officers much. They always seem to be playing golf or in the officers' mess. The NCOs really look after us. Serjeant Murray is my platoon leader. We get on well. I hope he'll put me up for promotion soon. Because if I get the promotion, it will be easier to get married quarters. My application is with the CO now and as soon as he signs it, then we'll be alright. But Serjeant Murray says we may be changing CO soon and so it's difficult for the old CO to promise something he won't be able to deliver.

I think I understand, but then it means we'll have to wait a bit longer before we're together. I don't know if I can last much longer, I miss you so much.

Thank God all that stuff with Hitler and the Germans has been sorted out. I knew it would. No one wants to go to war any more, do they? Not after the last little lot anyway.

The lads are all well and we've been going down to the town together. It helps beat the boredom. One day we went past one of the temples and watched the local Chinese praying with their joss sticks and banging their head on the floor in front of these statues. It was very strange. And the colours, the brightest reds you've ever seen, all over the place. It was packed as well. Full of people praying or sitting having a chat. It wasn't quiet like our local church and I didn't see a priest anywhere. Seems like they don't need them to speak to their Gods.

Ronnie took a bunch of incense sticks, and knelt in front of the statues, praying like the old women. It was really funny. This tall man from Manchester dressed in khakis and these old Chinese women. Just like something from George Formby. We were laughing our heads off. Then I saw Ronnie's face as he turned round and he were deadly serious.

Sometimes I wonder about Ronnie. Far too much devil in him, I think.

It seems Harry and Rita have really hit it off then! Well, I told you our Harry was a good sort. Far too good for her. When are they announcing the happy day? August would be best. I always think August weddings are beautiful. Shame we got married in June. But we couldn't wait, could we?

Well, Maggie, I have to go now as it's time to eat. Lord, I do miss you. You help me understand things. Without you, I always feel lost, like a little boy. To be honest, I don't know why I joined the army any more. Some days I feel like running away, getting on a boat and going straight back to England. But I know they'd catch me and then we'd never be together again. I've got to be patient and trust the regiment to bring us together. I know they will soon.

Please look after yourself. I haven't received any more letters from you since I got the first one, so please write soon.

Give my love to everybody in Salford. I'm glad they liked the Christmas presents even if they did arrive too late.

Remember to save your kimono until I get home. I want to be the first to see you in it.

Your husband,

Arthur

CHAPTER EIGHT

March 16, 1939
Tanglin Barracks, Singapore

Life soon settled into the comfortable routine of all colonial forces in the heat of Singapore.

The mornings were for getting things done. Not much, mind you, just the basics of army life; keeping the camp tidy, the occasional exercise session, visits to the doctor and the like. The men rarely saw their officers, their lives being ordered and ordained by their serjeants and corporals.

The afternoons were siesta time; sleeping in the barracks with the other men, listening to them fart and burp and moan. The early evenings, before it went dark at seven, were for sport or education. Some boxed, others ran or played football, still more attended courses. Arthur found himself on the battalion cricket team. He had always been fond of cricket, spending far too much time at Old Trafford watching the Lancashire stalwarts like Cyril Washbrook and Eddie Paynter.

He modelled his swashbuckling batting style on the latter, being particularly strong off the back foot and through the covers. He was the only private on the team, the rest being officers or serjeants. He found it slightly awkward at first, but soon became used to it, being able to mimic the mannerisms and language of the officers with ease.

Besides, they couldn't leave him off the team as he was the opening batsman and leading scorer. In the matches against the other battalions in the colony – the Gordons, the Royal Artillery and the Loyals – he had proved himself capable of taking apart most bowling.

'You could have played for Lancashire, Private Horton,' said Captain Tolliver one day.

'Not me, sir, I wasn't good enough and, besides, I had to work. On Sundays, I had a few innings in the Lancashire League but that was all I could do.'

'I played for Hampshire Second Eleven after leaving Winchester.'

'Jolly good, sir.'

He'd heard the officers using these words and he copied them. Not in the barracks, though, the other men would have made fun of him.

Evenings were for relaxing in the NAAFI or listening to the radio in their barracks. Ronnie, Ted, Tommy,

Arthur and the others had pooled their money and bought one from an Indian trader on Arab Street.

'Ninety Straits dollar.'

'Nah, too much for this, it's just worth thirty dollars. See, the cover has been scratched, it's not brand new.' The others weren't used to haggling for anything so Ronnie did the bargaining and seemed to be enjoying himself.

'It brand new. Eighty Straits dollar.'

'Nah, mate, look at it. Not worth that, but seeing as how you seem to be a fair chap, we'll go up to forty dollars.'

The Indian smiled and his head wobbled. 'Special price, sixty dollar.' He held his hand out.

'Split the difference. Fifty dollars and no questions asked where it comes from.'

The man nodded his head and they shook hands.

Ronnie reckoned it was probably stolen but none of them really cared. They weren't allowed to listen to it during the day, Serjeant Murray made sure of that. But in the evenings, after the sun went down, they could switch it on, breaking up the boredom of the long, hot nights.

The funny thing was most of the programmes came from England. It was strange listening to the BBC Dance Orchestra, cabaret shows, talks on farming, and even readings from the Bible whilst outside their barracks, crickets scratched, bats squeaked and geckos croaked.

The news from the radio was never good. Before they left England, the problems with Herr Hitler seemed to have been resolved. But then more issues constantly kept appearing; the war in Spain, Mussolini in Ethiopia, the Danzig corridor and Czechoslovakia.

'Oh, turn it off, Arthur, and put on the dance music.'

'Just a couple of minutes more, Tommy, they say there's going to be war.'

'They always say there's going to be war. And besides, what's it to do with us? We're out here in the middle of nowhere, remember?'

'Oh, have it your way.'

Arthur turned the dial to pick up another channel, hearing the music of Mantovani coming through loud and clear.

'That's better, I can dance to this.'

Tommy stood and waltzed around with an imaginary partner in his arms.

'Sit down, Harrison, you're making the floor shake, you are..'

They hardly ever saw the local colonial population, except sometimes when they had a day off and could walk in the streets of the city.

Even then, the squaddies noticed that they were looked down upon, not worthy of attention like a stain on a dress or mud on the bottom of a shoe. The women especially seemed to shrink away from them as they approached, as if they were untamed wild beasts.

Days and months passed very quickly, the absence of seasons making the passage of time particularly difficult to follow.

Every day was the same. The sun rose roughly around 7.00 a.m. and set around 7.00 p.m., varying only by less than ten minutes through the year.

'It's because we're close to the equator, see,' Ronnie explained it to Arthur as he was writing to Maggie one afternoon. 'The days are always the same, the temperature is always between 28 and 32 degrees and the humidity is always ninety per cent.'

Harrison overheard him and spoke up in his squeaky voice. 'What I wouldn't give for a proper cold Manchester day. You know the type. In February, when the rain and sleet comes racing over the Pennines and drills deep into your bones. Never thought I'd miss those days.'

A drop of sweat slowly fell from Arthur's forehead onto the latest letter he was writing to home, smudging the ink.

Lord, he missed Maggie.

The corporal in charge of the post came into the barracks. 'Listen up, you lot. Teale?'

The man put his hand up and a letter was thrown at him. 'Arkwright. Tracy. Morris. McLoughlin. Hughes. And the last one—' the corporal held up the pink envelope and smelt it, '—lovely,' he said, smiling. 'And the lucky Tad is… Horton.'

The letter flew across the barracks to Arthur. He smelt it first before ripping it open. Maggie's perfume, he'd know it anywhere. Sweet and floral, just like her.

He stared at the words on the letter.

Manchester
February 5, 1939

Dear Arty,

Just a short letter to give you some BIG news. I'm expecting. I don't know if it's a boy or a girl but my mum held an egg over my tummy and she says for certain it's a girl.

Are you as excited as me?

I wanted to make sure before I gave you the news. According to the doctor, I'm about eighteen weeks pregnant.

Arthur glanced at the date at the top of the letter. February 5th. It had taken nearly six weeks to get to him. What the hell had happened? He carried on reading.

It must have happened near to when you left. Remember the night when Mum went out, leaving us two alone?

I hope you are as happy as I am. Please write and tell me. I've kept it from all the neighbours but you know what a nosey lot they are. Mrs Wilde asked me yesterday why I was putting on weight. Ugly cow!

Anyway, never mind her, but I am already beginning to show and you will be a father sometime in late June, I think.

I'm so happy, Arty, and I hope you are too. I miss you so much, your arms around me holding me close at night. It's so cold here at night and the weather is awful.

Missing you, my big fella.

Please write soon.

Your affectionate wife,
    Maggie

Arthur looked up from the letter and whispered, 'I'm going to be a dad.'

'What's that, Arthur?' asked Ronnie, from the next bunk.

'I'M GONNA BE A DAD,' he shouted.

'Pipe down, Arthur, you're not the first, you know. Old Jarvis has got three kids, haven't you?'

'Three as I know about anyway. Only have to look at the wife and she gets pregnant.'

Arthur ignored them and ran to his locker to get his pen and paper. Sitting on the bed, he tried to tell her how excited he was.

Block 15
Tanglin Barracks
Singapore
16th March, 1939

My dearest Maggie,

What wonderful news. I'm so happy for both of us.
Are you having morning sickness? Not craving anything? Apparently my mum used to crave tripe and vinegar when she was pregnant with me.

I hope you're looking after yourself, eating well and not smoking so much. You're a proper little chimney once you have a drink.

But it is wonderful news. Your mum must be so happy, her first grandchild. I wish my mum were alive to see this day, she would have been over the moon.

I wish I could be there with you and not stuck out here in Singapore. It means I won't be at home for my first child's birth. I'll try to get home but I'm sure they'll say no.

In my next letter, I might have some good news. I can't say anything yet because you know how superstitious I am. But I'm touching my lucky penny at the moment and holding on to the table. I hope it'll happen because it will be great for both of us.

So, dearest heart, you're going to have our baby. I'm so happy. I want to create the family that I never had. I'm going to work extra hard to get you out here soon. I suppose it will have to wait for the birth now, but at least it gives me time to ask the army, but you know how slow they are.

I have to go now, dearest Maggie.
Love you, and our new baby, with all my heart.

Your husband,
  Arthur

'You finished that letter yet, Arthur?' shouted Ronnie from his prone position on the bunk.

'Nearly.'

Ronnie suddenly sat up. 'I've had an idea, lads,' he said to the whole barracks room. 'I think we should go out to celebrate tonight. Arthur's going to be a dad.'

'I don't know about that, Ronnie, I mean…'

'Sometimes you're such an old woman, Arthur. Get your cleanest uniform, we're going out. And that's an order.'

CHAPTER NINE

Sunday, December 8, 2019
Didsbury, Manchester

The following morning Jayne woke up early and decided to drive out to Buxton to visit her stepfather and his wife.

She had been thinking about Alice's case ever since her neighbour had left. Jayne knew exactly the steps she would follow. But it all depended on the elderly woman. Suddenly deciding to discover your own family at the age of 80 was a big decision.

Jayne understood the emotional trauma that Alice was going through and how she could only take in a little bit at a time. Simply discovering her father and mother's name was enough at this moment.

She fixed herself a coffee and fed Mr Smith, who was once more preening himself in front of the radiator.

'I wonder how many times you are being fed a day. Is Mrs Taylor the only person who feeds you?'

As usual, the cat ignored her.

She made sure he had water in his bowl, picked up her car keys and was just about to leave when the phone rang.

'Hello, Jayne Sinclair speaking?'

'Hi Jayne, how's it hanging?'

It was Ronald Welsh. Since the Dickens case she had been using him occasionally to help with research, particularly in the cases involving trawling through the archives at libraries. He was resourceful, a stickler for detail and never gave up – exactly the qualities Jayne needed in a researcher. The fact that he lived on a diet that consisted solely of baked beans, toast and tea didn't bother her… much.

'Hi Ronald, good to hear from you. I was about to ring.' She crossed her fingers, hoping he wouldn't call her out on her tiny white lie. She had planned to phone him that morning but she had totally forgotten. 'I'm afraid I have some bad news. The job for Cecile Barton in the States might not be going ahead.'

'Really? That's a shame, I was looking forward to ploughing through the Manchester rate books and the parish registers for Manchester Cathedral. The baptisms, marriages and burials are possibly the largest for a single parish in the country. There are over 450 leather- and vellum-bound volumes, covering the period from 1573 to the present day.'

Jayne could hear the excitement in his voice. 'I'm sorry, I think the client wasn't too chuffed to find out her ancestors were only copper and textile workers.'

'But that's just recently, Jayne. Lots of families go through ups and downs. Look at that Danny Dyer fella on the telly, he discovered he was related to King Edward III and Thomas Cromwell even though he grew up in a council flat in Canning Town. The civil war did for his family.'

'I know, I know, Ronald – however, she's thinking it over. My experience tells me when clients do that it usually means they don't want to proceed. It may still happen, but I thought I'd better warn you. Where are you off to today?'

'Chetham's. The library is letting me look at the books collected by John Byron and donated by his ancestor Eleanora Atherton in 1870. Tomorrow I'm off to Liverpool. There's a sale on at Adam Partridge Auctioneers with some interesting books in the catalogue. They're too expensive for me but I know there's a few job lots and I'm hoping to discover something interesting buried in the junk.'

Ronald had a passion for old books. It was his discovery of a first edition of Charles Dickens' A Christmas Carol that had led to them meeting and becoming friends.

'Good luck on the hunt, Ronald. I'll call you if I hear back from the client. We need to meet up in the next couple of days. I want to brief you on a some of the outstanding cases that may need research whilst I'm away in Australia.'

'When are you leaving?'

'A week today, I can't wait.'

'I've never been on a plane, you know. The whole idea of being in a small metal tube with four hundred other people and 20,000 feet in the air scares the hell out of me.'

'Yet being three floors underground surrounded by old books doesn't?'

'No, why would it?'

Jayne could hear that he couldn't really understand the question. Ronald was one of those people who was far more comfortable surrounded by books than people. He lived alone in a small house left to him by his late mother and seemed to have few friends. Jayne had once asked him if he ever got lonely and received the curt answer: 'Only when I'm with other people.'

He was definitely not a people person, but given a research problem which involved digging through the most obscure archives or library resources, he was the best Jayne knew at finding the correct documents.

Given any research problem, Ronald was like a dog with bone, never giving up until he had dug out the marrow of truth.

Jayne opened her diary. 'Today is the eighth, so let's meet up on Thursday for lunch. I'll treat you to some beans on toast.'

'I've expanded my diet now,' he said proudly. 'I make sure there's cheese on the toast as well. Has to be Lancashire, though, I can't stand cheddar.'

Jayne wondered what the taste difference was. 'Okay, let's say Essy's at noon?'

'It's a date. I mean a meeting… lunch,' he blustered.

Jayne smiled. 'It is, Ronald, see you then. Bye.'

She put down the phone.

The cat was still licking his fur and outside it was a perfect winter's day. The wind and rain from yesterday had vanished, to be replaced by one of those eggshell blue skies when a hint of warmth was in the air. Perfect for a drive out to the Peak District.

Jayne picked up her car keys once more, took one last look round the kitchen and headed out to Buxton.

CHAPTER TEN

April 13, 1939
Great World, Singapore

'Come on, Harrison, you're pretty enough.'

Harrison was still grooming himself in the only mirror, one of the prize possessions of Block 15. He combed his hair once again and ran a touch of Brylcreem through the ends. But he could do nothing about the red acne that stained both of his cheeks.

'Let's be having you.' This was Ronnie, smart as usual. 'Time to celebrate. Arthur is going to be a dad and we've spent the last month marching up and down that bloody parade ground. Now it's time to wet our whistles.'

They piled out of the barracks, all as smart as tailors' dummies in their best uniforms. But before they had walked ten yards down the hill, they were already sweating.

Then out past the duty serjeant at the guard house. 'Gate closed at two a.m., lads. Make sure you're back before then.'

'Yes, Serjeant,' they chorused back to him.

A waiting taxi. Sod the expense, they grabbed it.

'Take us to Great World.'

'Where, ah?'

'G-reat W-orld,' mouthed Harrison slowly, as if talking to a child.

'Oh, Tua Seh Kai.'

'That's right. Two Say Key.'

'Sure, three dollar.' The taxi driver held up four fingers.

'Sod off. It's only two dollars,' argued Colin Tracy.

'Thursday night. Three dollar.' Again, the taxi driver held up four fingers.

'Let's not hang around. The girls will be waiting,' said Ronnie.

'Okay. Okay. Three dollar. But only if you drive quick, okay?'

The taxi driver smiled. 'Sure thing.'

They all piled into the Ford. Its springs moaned at the arrival of four squaddies from Manchester.

Only the taxi driver seemed happy at the result. He started the engine, still with a smile on his face, released his handbrake and, with a resounding crash, forced the gear into its correct position.

They were off.

'You, ah, not from here, is it?' asked the taxi driver as he crashed another gear.

'No, from Manchester, mate. Best city in the world Manchester is. See this,' Harrison pointed to the fleur-de-lys badge. 'That's the symbol of the Manchester Regiment. Best regiment in the whole wide world.'

'Oh,' said the taxi driver meaningfully. 'You been here long time?'

'We got here five months ago, seems like ages,' said Arthur.

The car went round a roundabout at speed, and they all leant into each other. The taxi driver honked his horn and a rickshaw driver jumped out of the way, mouthing a long stream of unintelligible obscenities at the departing blue smoke of the taxi's exhaust.

'I get you to Tua Seh Kai, no problem.'

'We'd like to arrive alive though, hey.' Harrison elbowed the taxi driver to join in the joke. He gave them a weak giggle and concentrated on the task of driving.

He turned sharply right without signalling and accelerated to a stop.

The taxi driver pointed to the entrance. A large white pillar proudly displayed the words 'Great World' painted in bright red above some Chinese characters. On either side, a crowd of people queued up in front of the ticket booths while hawkers selling all kinds of pungent food weaved between the lines, calling out their wares.

'Okay. You give me the three dollar. Tip too if happy…'

Harrison handed over the money without a tip. 'Well, lads,' he said, 'what are we waiting for?'

They piled out of the taxi, stood outside the main gate to join the queue. Within a few minutes they were at the front of the line with Ronnie taking the lead.

'How many?'

'Four of us.'

'Do you want dancing tickets?'

'Does a Manchester chimney make smoke?'

The woman behind the glass looked at him quizzically.

'How much are the dancing tickets?' asked Arthur.

'One book, one dollar, three dances.'

'Let's get four books then.'

'Are you sure, Ronnie? Seems very expensive to me.'

'Four books is four dollar, plus twenty-five cents entrance equals five dollar total.'

Ronnie handed over the money and received his tickets. They walked under the main arch and were immediately greeted by all the sounds of the funfair; a Ferris wheel, carnival rides, shooting galleries, and games of chance all competed for the money of the crowd. Barkers encouraged everyone to try their luck or try their food.

Off to the right, the discordant sounds of a Chinese opera group clashed with the beating drums of a Malay orchestra. The bright lights of the carousels fought with the dark entrances to the cabarets. The sweet smell of candy floss with the sharp bite of roti prata.

Ronnie grabbed Arthur's arm. 'The girls are this way.'

They walked down the left-hand side, past more Western cabarets and two open-air cinemas showing the latest Leslie Howard movie, to a bright, open dance floor. An orchestra had just started playing Don't Worry 'bout Me as a horde of dancers – mostly young Chinese men in white European clothes with black patent-leather dancing shoes, and girls in semi-European dresses slit at the side – filled the dancing floor. When the dance was over, most of the girls left their partners as soon as the music stopped and went to join other girls in a sort of pen off to one side.

A small, very pale Chinese woman rose to greet them like Stanley greeting Livingstone. 'The Manchesters, I presume.'

'You bet your life, lady,' said Ronnie over his shoulder.

'No, but I'll bet yours, soldier. Come this way.'

She spoke with a perfect English accent. In fact, she spoke more like one of the officers than anything else. They went through yet another doorway and into the bar area itself.

Next to the bar were tables on each of which stood a pile of beer mats and what looked like a votive candle.

'The dancers will be along shortly, gentlemen, or you can go and select the lady you'd like to dance with. Just give her your ticket before the dance. A word of warning: these are dance partners only, no ungentlemanly behaviour will be tolerated.'

Ronnie assumed a look of innocence. 'We're Manchesters, pure as the driven snow we are.'

The woman nodded like she'd heard it all before. 'What can I get you to drink? Beer okay?'

They all nodded in unison.

'Four Tigers, Ah Fai, for our guests.'

With these words, the mama-san departed. Arthur found out later her name was Judy. She'd been born and educated in Guildford, and her father was once a rich merchant who had lost everything in one mad card game in 1935.

She didn't regret anything, though. 'Yuan fen. My fate,' she explained to him one night, when she had drunk too much whisky and sat down briefly at their table. 'My life is what it is, it can't be changed. No use crying over spilt milk.'

He heard later that she died in the bombing of Singapore, sitting at her desk in the dance hall with a bottle of whisky in front of her.

On stage, the orchestra began another song and the dance floor quickly filled up with couples.

The drinks arrived at the table courtesy of the unsmiling Ah Fai.

'Ronnie, you make a toast, you're the one with the words,' said Ted Rogers.

He thought for a moment before saying, 'To us. May we always be the best of mates and the worst of enemies.'

'I'll drink to that,' said Harrison.

The glasses of pale yellow beer rose as one and clinked together, making a noise that resounded with all the clarity of a bell.

'Still miss a pint of Holts. Now that's what I call a pint, not this weak stuff,' said Harrison, staring disappointedly at his glass of Tiger.

'I like it, refreshing it is,' answered Ted.

But before he could say any more, the mama-san, Judy, arrived back with a line of girls trailing behind her.

They peeled off like dutiful chorus girls and sat next to each of the men. One per squaddie.

'Ay up, lads, meat pies have come,' shouted Harrison gleefully in a broad Manchester accent.

Arthur looked up and saw this angelic face looking down at him. He stood up and pulled out a chair for her to sit down.

She couldn't have been more than five feet tall, with a short pageboy haircut, the smallest mouth and the brightest sparkling eyes he had ever seen. She was wearing a creamy flowered cheongsam, which was cut up to the top of her hip to reveal the outside of her thigh. But she didn't look sexy. On the contrary, she looked demure, innocent almost.

'You wanna dance?' Ronnie's girl pulled him up from his chair.

Ted Rogers was already on the dance floor, shuffling around.

'Sure, why not?'

They stepped out onto the dance floor, followed by Harrison and his girl.

Arthur remained sitting, still not saying a word, staring straight ahead.

'You wanna dance?'

Arthur shook his head.

Ronnie gestured to him to join them on the dance floor. He shook his head again and picked up his beer.

'Looks like he doesn't want to.'

His girl shrugged her shoulders and they moved around the small dance floor to Joe Loss. She was a competent dancer, moving smoothly with the minimum of effort.

After three songs and three tickets they returned to the table to rejoin the others, while Harrison stayed on the dance floor. Ah Fai was there again, putting another round of beers on the table.

'Get it down your neck, Arthur,' shouted Ronnie above the sound of Blue Skies Are Round The Corner.

'But I'm still on this one.'

'Get it down your neck, son.'

'You buy more tickets?' asked Ronnie's girl.

The dance floor was full of couples now, all of them shuffling together to the music from the band. None of them able to move more than a few inches before they bumped into the elbows, arms or legs of a neighbour.

At the door, Judy stood guard, occasionally looking at her customers with the jaundiced eye of a recently cuckolded husband.

Harrison came back to the table holding the hand of his girl. 'This one moves like Vera Lynn, smooth as silk.'

The rest of the evening passed in a bit of a blur.

More glasses of Tiger. More shots of a dark-coloured liquid. More dancing. Ted being slapped by his girl. Falling down. Getting up. Harrison vanishing. Arthur sitting there watching everything.

Then they were outside the bar and Ronnie was being sick in the gutter. A deep, deep gutter that separated the front of the shop-houses from the road.

Arthur was still sober. He patted Ronnie's back. 'Get it out, mate. Best that way.'

He waved down a trishaw and told the man to take them back to the camp. He poured Ronnie into the back seat and the trishaw rider began pedalling down the road with all his might.

Arthur was to go back to the Great World many, many times in the time they were in Singapore. It became their place, where most of their money vanished on food, dances, hot sweaty nights at the cinema or gallons of Tiger.

And later, he was to spend far too long there.

But he didn't know that yet.

Not yet.

CHAPTER ELEVEN

Sunday, December 8, 2019
Buxton Residential Home, Derbyshire

It took over an hour for Jayne to make the drive. The A6 was jammed and there seemed to be roadworks around every corner. Even worse, all the traffic lights conspired against her, deliberately turning red just as she approached.

She wasn't in the best of moods as she entered the reception lobby of the Residential Home. It was built from local millstone grit and had all the turrets and angles the Victorians had loved, as well as being surrounded by mature gardens and trees.

It was for this reason Robert, her stepfather, had chosen to live here when his early-onset Alzheimer's made it increasingly difficult to live on his own. He hadn't planned on meeting Vera, though, and now the two had been married for two years, finding love and companionship late in both their lives.

'Are Robert and Vera in their usual corner?' Jayne asked Valerie, the new receptionist. A young girl with hair dyed a bright blue, a nose ring and a tattoo of a jaguar on her neck. But despite outward appearances, Jayne really liked her. She was the most diligent and polite of all the girls who had done the job. Again, it reminded Jayne never to judge people on their appearance.

'I haven't seen them this morning, Ms Sinclair, I think Robert's not feeling too well. You'll probably find them in their suite.'

Courtesy of Vera's money, the two of them had moved into a larger suite together after their marriage. It gave them the privacy they needed as well as the extra space of a small living room. Jayne couldn't guess how much it cost, but Vera always laughed off the expense. 'You can't take it with you when you go, so we may as well enjoy my money while we're alive.'

Jayne walked down the corridor on the right and knocked on their suite door. It was opened almost immediately by Vera.

'I heard Robert wasn't feeling too well,' she said as she walked in.

'Just a cold, I think, but best he stays in bed till he feels better.'

'Is that my Jayne?' a croaking voice shouted from the bedroom.

'It is, Robert.' Vera leant towards Jayne and whispered, 'You'd better go and see him otherwise he'll be moaning for the next couple of days. You know, your dad is the world's worst patient. I used to be a nurse and I would have hated to have him on my ward.'

Jayne smiled and hurried to the bedroom door.

'There you are, I thought you weren't going to come today.'

'How are you feeling, Robert?'

'As right as rain, but Vera insists I stay in bed. I don't know what she's mithering about.'

A bin full of tissues beside his bed suggested Vera was right to keep him wrapped up. 'Vera knows best, you can't be too safe these days. Look at China, there's some virus going around there that's so bad they're even closed off one city.'

'China is miles away and I feel great.'

'Robert Cartwright, you have a temperature of thirty-nine degrees and you've been coughing and sneezing all night. A day in bed will do you no harm.' Vera spoke forcefully while Robert simply raised his eyebrows as if saying, 'see what I have to deal with.'

'Vera's right. Keep yourself warm and wrapped up today.' Jayne saw a half-finished Guardian crossword discarded at the side of his bed. 'You must be ill, you haven't even finished the crossword yet.'

'It's the compiler, Qaos, can't stand his clueing, too many words,' he sniffed, immediately reaching for another tissue.

'Always a sign he's not well when he can't do the crossword.' Vera leant forward and kissed his forehead. 'Still a little bit hot. You'd best stay here for the rest of today.'

'But…'

'I'll be having no arguments from you, Robert Cartwright, is that understood?'

He nodded meekly.

'Right, Jayne, what have you brought for us?'

Jayne dived into her bag. 'All the flights are booked for Perth. It's a long trip even with the extra space of Business Class.' Jayne had decided to treat them both, despite the cost. If they were going to travel halfway around the world to Australia to see Vera's half-brother, they may as well do it in style. 'Now, as we're flying Singapore Airlines from Manchester, I thought we'd break the journey and enjoy a stopover in the city for a couple of days before flying on.'

Vera looked at Robert. 'Why not?'

'Sounds like a great idea, lass.'

She placed some brochures down on the bed. 'They do these special explorer packages. Why don't you choose the hotel, somewhere nice and central.'

'I've never been to Singapore before, it looks very modern.' Robert was looking at the cover of the brochure.

'It will be an adventure, Dad.'

'I hope the food isn't too spicy, you know how it repeats on me.'

She looked across at Vera. 'He is a Moaning Minnie today.'

'What did I tell you? The world's worst patient, that's your dad.'

'I'm still here you know. I may be ill but I'm not deaf. How are the cases going?'

It was Robert who had first introduced Jayne to the joys of family history research. She had been at a low after the shooting of her police partner, Detective Sergeant Dave Gilmour. She had blamed herself for his death even though she was exonerated by the police investigation. Nonetheless, his death had hit her hard, leading her to question herself, her competence as a police officer and her own guilt.

Simply by getting her involved in the routine of delving deep into his Scottish family history, Robert had given her a renewed sense of her own self-worth.

When she returned to work in the police and found she couldn't settle in the job any more, it was he who persuaded her to use her investigative skills to research people's family stories.

She had taken courses at the Institute for Heraldic and Genealogical Studies, becoming certified and joining AGRA, the Association of Genealogists and Researchers in Archives, finally leaving the police six years ago. Since then, she loved her new job and career, investigating the family history of her clients. Nothing gave her more satisfaction than solving a mystery in the past. One of her old cases even involved finding Vera's half-brother, who'd been sent to Australia as a child migrant so many years before. It was this man they were going to visit in Perth.

'I've finished most of the cases now, Robert, there's only one open at the moment. The film actress in LA, but I don't think she'll be going any further.'

'Oh? Why not?'

'I think she was expecting her forbears to have been more aristocratic.'

'And they're not?'

'They're mill workers from Bolton and Manchester.'

'There's nowt wrong with having mill workers in your past.'

'I think she was hoping they would be dukes and duchesses.'

'They still might be, depending on how far you go back.'

'We're in the early Victorian era, at the 1841 census at the moment.'

'You'll have to go back much further using parish registers and the like.'

'I know, but she's put the case on hold.'

'Even if you do go back further, they'll probably be farm labourers.'

'You're right, Dad, but Ronald will handle it when we're away so no need to worry.'

'How is he? I hope he has a better diet these days,' said Vera.

Jayne shook her head. 'Still on the baked beans, I'm afraid.'

'At least he'll always be regular with that much fibre. Now, I was telling your dad…'

'Let's leave my bowels out of this conversation, it's the last thing Jayne wants to hear. Why don't you help me finish the crossword, lass, while Vera chooses the hotel?'

'Good idea, let's stay somewhere special.'

For the next hour, Jayne helped Robert with the crossword. He was right, Qaos was far too wordy. Meanwhile, Vera had found a few hotels she liked. 'Sentosa looks beautiful but it's too far away from town and we're not staying in the Marina Bay area, that's too close to the casinos for Robert.'

'I've got a new system for blackjack, Jayne.'

'Does it involve losing, Dad?'

'You have to speculate to accumulate…'

'Unfortunately, Raffles is closed for renovations,' said Vera. 'So I've selected two affordable places in the centre of town; one old, one new. Goodwood Park or the Orchard Hotel.'

'I'd prefer somewhere with a bit of character,' said Robert.

'Me too,' said Jayne.

'Goodwood Park it is, then. Can you get the travel agent to book it, Jayne? And this is my treat as you're paying for the flights.'

Jayne held her hands up, surrendering to Vera's generosity. 'Now we're sorted, I need to head back to avoid the traffic. This time next week we'll be in Singapore.'

'Isn't it exciting?' said Vera.

'So you'd better look after yourself and get well soon.' She kissed her father on his head. 'Don't take any rubbish from him, Vera,' she said, hugging her stepmother.

'I won't, don't worry.'

'Still here, not dead yet,' came from the bed.

'Mr Grumpy is still with us. Rather you than me looking after him, Vera.'

'Ah,' she said, ruffling his thinning grey hair, 'he's a big softy at heart and I love him to bits.'

He stared up at her. 'You're not bad yourself, Vera Atkins.'

'That's deep praise coming from him. Well, I'll be off, see you in a couple of days. Start packing…'

Jayne waved goodbye and left them both in the bedroom as Vera tucked the duvet around Robert. They were a lovely couple and she was so lucky to have them both in her life.

CHAPTER TWELVE

September 3, 1939
Block 15, Tanglin Barracks, Singapore

They were all clustered around the radio in the corner.

Ronnie was cleaning his nails with a knife. Tommy Harrison was lounging on his back, staring into space. Ted Rogers was reading the Daily Sketch from two weeks ago; somebody must have nicked it from the officers' mess. The rest of the platoon were lounging around on the bunks, blancoing webbing, polishing boots or simply staring into mid-air.

Arthur was sitting at a small desk, writing a letter to Maggie as he always did.

Without exception, they were all sweating.

Just another Sunday in Singapore.

The radio was playing music that droned on – some sort of classical stuff, sounding more like a funeral dirge than light entertainment.

'It's supposed to be Greg Farrell and his orchestra,' said Harrison, checking the schedule in his old paper. 'They've got Dinah Lane as their singer. Bit of a cracker she is, and she can sing. Voice like a turtle dove she has.'

'Don't you mean a nightingale?' said Ronnie, always the clever one.

'She can flap her wings in my direction any time,' answered Harrison.

Most of them were resting their hangovers after the night before. These days, Saturday was always a night down in the Great World. Over the last few months they must have poured gallons of Tiger down their throats, much to the delight of the brewery.

High above their heads the fan turned slowly, barely disturbing the muggy, humid air. Outside the sun was going down on another Singapore Sunday; the geckos were out in force, clicking their ownership of a few square feet of white-washed wall, the grackles squawked their last goodbyes before settling down for the evening, and in the distance, a few pi-dogs squabbled over scraps from the cookhouse.

Harrison was about to twist the dial, looking for something more exciting, when an announcer interrupted the dirge-like music.

'Now, here is an important announcement from His Majesty's Government.'

'Well, who else it would be from with a voice like that,' said Harrison. 'My aunt Sally?'

They all told him to shut up.

'This morning the British Ambassador in Berlin handed the German government a final note stating that, unless we heard from them by eleven o'clock that they were prepared at once to withdraw their troops from Poland, a state of war would exist between us.'

'What?' said Harrison.

'Shhhh,' was the response from a platoon of throats.

'I have to tell you that no such undertaking has been received and consequently this country is now at war with Germany.' There was a long pause. 'Now may God bless you all. May he defend the right. It is the evil things that we shall be fighting against – brute force, bad faith, injustice, oppression and persecution – and against them I am sure that the right will prevail.'

You could have cut the silence with a knife.

Finally, Harrison spoke. 'Does this mean we're at war again? Fighting, like?'

It was Ronnie who put him straight. 'That's right, Tommy, me old son. Finally gonna see some action we are.'

'But I didn't sign on to fight. Just to be a soldier. No fighting. They said nothing about fighting.'

'Are you stupid or what? This is the army, course we're gonna be fighting. That's what we're paid to do. Take orders, fight and die.'

'They said nothing about dying when I signed on. Nothing about that at all.'

'Will you both shut up?' It was Arthur who spoke. 'It looks like they'll send all-us home now.'

Everyone nodded.

'Maggie and the baby boy would have loved it out here. Well, there you go, back to Blighty for us.'

'I don't want to fight,' said Harrison.

Ronnie suddenly launched himself at the man, showering punches, kicks and elbows all over him. Harrison just covered himself up, not fighting back at all.

They all jumped up to pull Ronnie off. It wasn't easy, he was built like a brick Salford terrace. It took four of them to finally drag him off.

'You'll fight, Harrison, don't worry,' he said, jumping in the air. 'You'll fight or I'll kill you myself.'

Harrison was silent. Smart bugger. None of them would cross Ronnie Arkwright if they could avoid it.

'Sod it. If we're going to leave Singapore, we'd better get some drinking time in before we do. Who's off down the Great World with me?'

Ronnie looked around, challenging them all not to go.

Everyone raised their hands. It didn't pay to cross Ronnie.

CHAPTER THIRTEEN

September 4, 1939
Tanglin Barracks, Singapore

She was whispering in his ear. 'Arthur, Arthur, tap your feet together three times and think to yourself, there's no place like home.'

He looked down at his feet and tapped his ruby army boots, whispering the words again and again.

'Let's be havin' you, you shower of Manchester reprobates,' Serjeant Murray screamed in his loudest parade-ground voice.

Arthur opened his eyes. It wasn't Glinda standing next to him with her long auburn hair and silver crown, but Serjeant Murray with a sneer on his lips, and eyes that stared like headlights in a fog.

'But it's still dark outside, Serjeant.'

'You heard the news, get your bags of bones out of those bunks.'

He lifted Harrison's bunk and turned it over, leaving the squaddie sitting on the floor in his vest and undershorts, blinking his eyes rapidly.

'Outside in full kit in five minutes. Anybody late is on a charge.' He strode to the door and then turned back quickly. 'What are you smiling about, Arkwright? Get yourself out of there.'

'Hurry up, Ronnie. We'll all get it in the neck if we're not ready. We're at war now.'

'Yes, Arthur, my boy. Me head's at war, me feet are at war, but I'm not sure if the rest of me has decided to join in yet.'

'You were well gone last night.'

'Aye, it was a great night. A night when the throat was well oiled, the dancing was as elegant as Fred Astaire in a pair of clogs and the women were as beautiful as Stockport on a summer's day.'

He shook his head, trying to remove the cobwebs. 'But I must remember only to drink those Tigers in even numbers. My old dad used to say "Ronnie, my boy, take it from someone who knows. Only drink in even numbers. Them odd numbers are bad for you. Certain to get a bad head and piles if you drink in the odd numbers."'

Arthur was already dressed and staring at his face in the mirror, combing his hair into the regulation arrow-straight side parting. He grabbed his kit, already neatly packed, and his solar topee, fastened the webbing, took one last look in the mirror and rushed out of the door followed by the others.

Serjeant Murray was waiting outside, looking at his watch.

Arthur marched over to him, placed his kit bag down on the ground in regulation position, snapped his body to attention and saluted.

'3524357 Private Horton, reporting for duty, Serjeant.'

'Line up over there, Horton. Get all the others in a straight line.'

Murray marched back into the barracks.

'Get a move on. Anyone who isn't out at parade in thirty seconds is on a charge.'

Murray stepped back as the remaining squaddies all piled out: Ronnie Arkwright, Ted Rogers, Ray Teale, all in their khakis and carrying their battle kit. Harrison, of course, was the last out, still adjusting his uniform.

They lined up in parade ground formation. Arm's length apart, kit in front of them, waiting for inspection.

Murray stood at the end of the line, his hands on his hips, his uniform perfectly ironed, starched and creased.

He moved in front of Arthur and adjusted his solar topee so it was off his eyes.

'You're not Baden-Powell, Horton. This is how you wear your topee. Open your bag.'

Arthur pulled open the regulation knot of the regulation army kit bag and revealed his kit, neatly packed. Luckily Maggie had shown him how to do it before he left Manchester.

'Very good, Horton.'

Murray carried on moving down the line making comments, occasionally grunting. When he got to Harrison the poor man was already shaking.

'Sorry, Serjeant, I…'

'No talking on parade, Harrison.' Murray took one step back and looked the squaddie up and down. Not once. Not twice. But again and again.

'What the…'

'Serjeant?'

'You're on a charge, Harrison. Talking on parade.' He walked closer to the man until his face was only inches away. 'You're not a soldier, Harrison. You're not a man. You're a cockroach. One of those black shiny things I crush under the heel of my boot. What are you?'

Harrison was going to answer but Murray put his finger to his lips to indicate silence.

'You're not going to be in my platoon much longer. You're going to discover the toilets, or the kitchen, or maybe the laundry is in dire need of your services.'

There was a small cough to their left.

'If you will excuse me, Serjeant, I have to make a short statement to the men.'

It was Lieutenant Whitehead, the platoon commander. His uniform was immaculately presented, of course, but somehow it always looked wrong: knobbly knees sticking out from horrendously wide shorts, short arms, and even shorter legs above a large paunch. To all this was added a tiny moustache over a thin-lipped mouth. The moustache looked like two caterpillars had joined hands and danced a wee reel on the man's lip. Above the caterpillars were a pair of horn-rimmed spectacles sitting on his narrow nose.

'Stand at ease, men,' Lieutenant Whitehead announced in his tired, oh-so-well-bred, public-school drawl. 'As you may have heard yesterday on the radio, the Germans have refused to stop their attacks on plucky Poland, so Mr Chamberlain has been forced to declare, um, a war on that said country.'

Harrison coughed, about to say something until he saw Serjeant Murray's eyes staring at him.

'Well, men, it's going to be a jolly little scrap. It probably won't affect us out here in Singapore, but we mustn't let the home team down, what?'

He looked around for agreement from the men.

'Today, we're going to our war positions at Changi. Let's put on a good show. Remember, we're Manchester and Empire soldiers. Carry on, Serjeant Murray.'

With that sterling finale to his speech, Whitehead put his topee on, shipped his swagger stick under the arm and slouched off towards the officers' mess.

After five paces, he stopped and turned around. 'I say, Serjeant, I knew there was something else. We haven't got enough lorries so we've hired an extra Chinese one. This is the one our platoon will use. Make sure the men get all they need from the QM. You know – rifles, socks, those sort of things.'

'How long are we going to be at our position, sir?'

'You know, I never thought to ask. That's a very interesting question, Serjeant. Ask the RSM, he'll probably know.'

'Yes, sir.'

'Carry on, Serjeant Murray.' With a wave of his swagger stick, Lieutenant Whitehead resumed his stroll back to the waiting eggs, bacon and coffee of the officers' mess.

'Save us from idiots.'

'What was that, Harrison?'

'Nothing, Serjeant, just clearing my throat. Dry as a drover's dog it is.'

'Remember, Harrison, they may be idiots. But they are officer idiots. And they are our idiots. Is that clear?'

'Yes, Serjeant.'

Murray continued to examine the kit bag. 'This is a disgrace, Harrison… Arkwright?'

'Yes, Serjeant.'

'Help Harrison sort out this mess.'

'Yes, Serjeant.'

'Right, lads, we've got a busy day ahead of us. Rogers and Horton, you three go to the QM and get the gear. Teale and Arkwright, come with me to the armoury for the Vickers. The rest of you ensure that we're ready to go as soon as the lorry arrives.'

'Yes, Serjeant,' came a chorus of voices. Then another voice, Harrison's, could be heard squeaking across the parade ground: 'But what about breakfast, Serjeant?'

Murray walked up to him and stuck his face two inches away. 'What about breakfast, Serjeant,' he mimicked the man's high-pitched whine. Then his face changed, becoming redder and redder. 'WE'RE AT WAR, SONNY, DIDN'T YOU HEAR?' Spit gathered at the edges of his mouth. A drop landed on Harrison's face and uniform.

Arthur could see Harrison's fingers trembling, itching to go to his face to wipe it off. But he didn't. He let the spittle sit there on his cheek like a single tear.

Murray walked back to his position in front of them. 'The rest of you will eat breakfast after we have requisitioned all the stores. You, Harrison, will ensure the barracks' washrooms and toilets are spotless before we leave today. Is that clear?'

'Yes, Serjeant.'

'Right, jump to it. And don't mess around. The lorry could arrive any minute now.'

That the truck didn't arrive till near eleven o'clock wasn't the Serjeant's fault, of course. As he said, he could have 'built the ruddy thing himself' in the time they had been waiting.

As the rest of the regiment departed in the army lorries, Serjeant Murray stared at the one that had been requisitioned, parked all on its own at the bottom end of the parade ground. 'Well, we've got the truck but the Chinese driver has scarpered, saying it's not his job to drive us all the way to Changi. So, can any of you lot drive?'

Total silence from the ranks. As ever, nobody volunteered for anything in the army.

'Come on, one of you must know how to drive a truck.'

Then Harrison spoke up. 'Ronnie knows how to drive, don't you, Ronnie?'

'Well, Arkwright, do you?'

'Well, Serjeant, it's like this… I've driven a little bit, it was a long time ago. And I'm sure the trucks are different in Manchester.'

'They still have four tyres and a steering wheel, don't they?'

'That they do, Serjeant.'

'Well, then, it's settled. You lot, get all the gear together. Arkwright, come with me and we'll drive the truck up here.'

Ronnie marched off behind the serjeant, throwing his best evil eye at Harrison. He was still cursing his luck when they reached the truck. It was a Ford that usually carried cargo from the docks; open-topped at the back with no shade from the sun.

Along the side were large Chinese characters with a small English translation beneath them: 'Ah Hing Transportation'.

'What are you waiting for, Arkwright? We haven't got all day.'

He got in the cab and handed Murray the starting handle. 'Serjeant, can you start her for me?'

He could see the man weighing up the options in his mind. Finally, Murray came to a decision with a sigh, taking the handle and marching round to the front of the truck.

Arkwright pushed the clutch in and put the truck in gear.

'Ready, Sarge.'

'It's Serjeant to you, Arkwright.'

'Yes, Serjeant.'

He watched as Murray bent over, bottom in the air, and gave the starter a heave.

Nothing. The engine didn't even turn over.

'Are you sure everything is ok with this truck?'

Ronnie pretended to check the dashboard. 'It looks ok here, sarge.'

'That's Serjeant to you, Arkwright. I won't tell you again.'

'Yes… Serjeant.'

Murray bent down once more, this time spitting between his hands and rubbing them furiously. With a fierce grunt, he then grabbed the starting handle in both paws and gave it two almighty swings.

Still nothing. Not even a cough or a splutter.

'Looks like they've give us a duff truck.'

'Keep going, Serjeant, maybe it just needs warming up.'

The Serjeant took off his topee and wiped the sweat from his forehead. Bending down once again, he took the starter handle in the grip of his massive paws and gave it an almighty heave that would have started all the trucks in heaven.

The engine coughed and died.

Sweat was pouring off the poor man now, Arkwright almost felt sorry for him. The sweat was dribbling down his nose and onto the front of his starched, pressed, and oh-so-neatly creased uniform. Beneath his arms, huge, dark, liquid semi-circles had appeared, becoming larger by the minute as he stood beneath the boiling noonday sun.

Ronnie started whistling We're havin' a heat wave, the melody flowing over the sweating Serjeant's face.

'Are you sure the truck's ready to start?'

'Yes, Serjeant,' said Arkwright in the most innocent voice he could muster.

'Here, let me have a look.' Murray marched round to the cab before Arkwright could take the truck out of gear or pull the choke out.

He stepped up onto the running board and his eyes scanned the gears, taking in the gauges, checking the knobs. 'It looks ok to me.'

'See, I told you, Serjeant. One more go should do it.'

Murray strode around to the front of the truck again, still holding the starter handle in his hand like a swagger stick.

Harrison pushed the clutch in and disengaged the gears.

Then, as Serjeant Murray went through his strongman routine: checking his sleeves were rolled up properly, stretching his muscles, spitting between his palms and finally grabbing the starting handle with his two immense paws, Ronnie slowly eased the choke out. Not too much or it would flood the engine and then he'd be badgered.

Murray bent down, sticking his backside in the air, finally giving an immense heave on ether starter handle and the engine coughed into life, running as sweetly as a horse through a meadow

Murray stood up, clutching his back and giving huge boyish grin in Arkwright's direction.

'See, all you have to do is put your back into it, Serjeant.'

The grin vanished from Murray's face. 'Get a move on, Arkwright.'

He put the clutch in, eased the truck into gear, eased the clutch out and the engine put-putter-puttered and died.

Silence.

Murray looked across at Arkwright who simply shrugged his shoulders in response. It wasn't the right time to say anything or make a joke.

He did anyway. 'One more time should do it, Serjeant.'

Murray went through his strongman act once again. He bent down in front of the truck and was about to give the starting handle an almighty heave, when Arkwright spoke again.

'Really put your back into it this time, Serjeant.'

Arkwright could see the man's body tense, his eyebrows giving a tiny twitch of irritation. The Serjeant gave the starting handle a violent twist like he was screwing Arkwright's head off.

The engine kicked into life. Murray ran round the front and jumped into the cab. 'Get a move on, we're late.'

Arkwright put the truck in gear, remembering to double de-clutch and then slowly ease it out, depressing the accelerator with his right foot.

The truck inched forward. They were moving.

They roared up the hill towards the barracks, going at least five miles an hour.

'Have you ever driven one of these before?'

'Yes, Serjeant,' said Arkwright.

'Couldn't we go a bit faster?'

'That we could, Serjeant.' He put the truck into second, easing the clutch out. There was a frightening sound of screeching, grinding metal like a whole orchestra of violins on heat. The truck picked up speed.

'Are you sure it wasn't a horse and cart?'

'No, Serjeant, it had a few more horsepower than that. I used to drive coal from Poynton to Manchester.'

'Wouldn't it have been easier to drive a truck?' said Murray, laughing at his own joke.

'Very funny, Serjeant.'

'Go left here,' Murray ordered.

So Arkwright swung left. A little too sharply maybe, because he went over the white stones and across the edge of the colonel's flower bed.

'Damn,' said Murray, looking behind him at the damage.

Arkwright accelerated away from the scene of the crime with Murray frantically checking if anyone had seen them.

'You'll be the death of me yet.'

'Well, if I am, I'll pray for your soul, Serjeant.'

They braked sharply in front of the barracks and Arkwright remembered to keep the engine ticking over.

Murray hopped out and immediately ordered the men to load up the truck. Arkwright took the engine out of gear, proudly sitting up front as the poor squaddies had to heave all the gear, including the old Vickers and all its equipment, into the back.

'Hurry up, get a move on, put your backs into it,' Murray shouted.

Sitting up in the cab at the front, Arkwright chuckled to himself. It wasn't a bad life really. But you had to take your fun seriously in the army. He might even forgive Harrison for volunteering him.

But not yet.

CHAPTER FOURTEEN

Sunday, December 8, 2019
Didsbury, Manchester

Jayne arrived home, running as fast as she could from her car to the front door to avoid being soaked. Once inside, she was immediately greeted by a miaowing Mr Smith, tail proudly held aloft, intertwining his body between her legs as she struggled out of her coat.

The day that had started so beautifully had ended in an afternoon downpour of biblical proportions. She could have sworn she saw Noah's Ark sailing past the cricket club.

'You're hungry, I suppose?'

To make sure she knew what he wanted, Mr Smith sauntered into the kitchen and sniffed his empty bowl, looking back at her as if she were deliberately withholding food from him.

'Okay, okay, I get the message. You won't get this sort of service at Alice's when you go there.'

She fed him a pouch of lamb's liver in gravy, which he proceeded to devour voraciously as if he hadn't eaten for the last year.

She was about to make herself a cup of tea when the doorbell rang. She switched the kettle on and went to answer it.

Alice was stood outside under a large gold umbrella. 'Sorry, Jayne, is it inconvenient? I saw your car was in the driveway…'

'Not at all, Alice, come in. I'm just making a cuppa, would you like one?'

'I'd love one. I'm a bit parched, it must be all this rain.'

Jayne invited her in, sitting her down at the counter while she made the tea.

'I know it's a bit quick but I was talking to the other ladies at the community centre and I finally told them I was adopted and what we did yesterday. They were so excited for me. I was expecting them to be surprised, but they weren't at all. Even Janet Menton, the snob who lives in the new houses and is always going on about meeting Lord This and Lady That, well, even she was excited for me.'

'You'd like to carry on from where we left off yesterday?'

'That's right, I'd like to find out more.'

'There's only so much we can do until we get your parents' birth and marriage certs from the Registry Office, but we can make a start and who knows, we might get lucky.'

'It sounds so exciting.'

'I'm afraid much of it is looking through old censuses and electoral registers, but we'll see how far we can get.' The kettle boiled and she poured the hot water onto the leaves in the teapot. 'It's PG Tips, but loose leaves not teabags. I can't stand using them.'

'I know what you mean, it tastes so much better with proper tea leaves, doesn't it?'

Jayne carried the teapot over and set out the cups and saucers. 'We'll just let it steep while I switch the laptop on.'

The computer lit up and she entered her password, bringing up Alice's file. She went over to the cupboard and reached up for a pack of Hobnobs. 'Now let's pour ourselves a cup and have a few biccies for an afternoon snack.'

After a few minutes of small talk, it was obvious Alice couldn't wait any longer.

'Shall we get started?' said Jayne. 'I usually like to begin with the male side of the family because the surname doesn't change. Unfortunately, for your father that's all we have, plus the fact he was in the army in 1938. So we'll take a different route and begin with your mum instead, as we know her maiden name from your adoption records.'

Jayne logged into Findmypast. 'We'll try a general search first. We'll enter your mum's married name, Margaret Horton, and see what comes up. Hopefully she used it after her marriage rather than her maiden name. As we don't know your mum's birth date yet, we'll make it five years on either side of 1922.'

'Why that date?'

'Because in 1929, Parliament passed a law making sixteen the legal minimum age for marriage.'

Jayne pressed enter and there were 5,774 possible results. 'Too many. Unfortunately both your mum's Christian and surnames were quite common at the time. Let's narrow our search.'

She typed 'Manchester' in the box marked 'location'. 'She could have been born elsewhere but mobility was far less than it is today. People tended to stay in the areas they were born.'

The results came up: 96 entries.

Jayne took another sip of tea, taking a nibble from a biscuit as she typed. 'Still too many, we need to find a shortcut. We're helped that in 1939, the British government made a census of the population basically to find out who lived where, and what they could do to aid the war effort. People were also issued identity cards and ration books when they registered.'

She brought up the 1939 register and entered the details in the search boxes. 'Now, sometimes they show the maiden names too.' Jayne pointed to the screen. 'I bet that's her. See, she has the same maiden name as on your adoption papers.'

Margaret Horton (Elliot) 1917 20 Prince's Avenue, Old Trafford

Jayne clicked through to the image as Alice watched over her shoulder. 'I'm pretty sure that is your mother. She's living with another older woman with the surname Elliot, who is probably your grandmother.'

'Where am I?'

'Your name is not shown to guard your privacy, but you are probably the third in the column.'

First name	Last name	D.O.B.	SEX	Occupation	Marital Statue
Emma	Elliott	18 Nov 1894	F.	Drafts-woman	Widow
Margaret	Horton (Elliott)	22 Sept 1917	F	Home	Married
This	Record	Is	Still	Closed.	

'This is my family?' Alice asked.

'As it was on the twenty-ninth of September, 1939.'

She pointed to the screen. 'That's my grandmother, Emma Elliot? I like her name.'

'She was a draftswoman, not a common occupation for a female back in 1939. Perhaps, she worked in Trafford Park.'

'There's no mention of my father?'

'He obviously wasn't living with them at the time. Perhaps he was in camp or even in France with the British Expeditionary Force.'

'Where was Prince's Avenue?'

'Close to the cricket ground, I think.'

Jayne pulled up an old map of Stretford. 'There it is, just off Talbot Road. It's where the old Kellogg's offices used to be and is now the new UA92.'

Alice sighed. 'We've seen some changes in our life.'

'There's an old joke that Manchester will be a lovely place to live once it's finished…'

'Shall we find out more?' Jayne began typing again. 'Now we know your mother's birth date and your grandmother's name, we can find out a bit more about the family.'

Alice Taylor rubbed her hands. 'This is exciting.'

'We'll go back to FreeBMD, enter your mother's name and her birth date into the search engine.' She pressed the key with a flourish.

No result.

'Strange. Let's widen the age parameters from 1914 to 1920.'

'Why?'

'Women – and men – sometimes lied about their age or simply couldn't remember the exact dates. Here we go.'

They both stared at the screen, waiting for the results. 'There she is. Born in 1915, not 1917.'

Margaret Elliot   Stevenson   Manchester 9c 238

'We now know your grandmother's maiden name was Stevenson.'

'It's a bit like a jigsaw puzzle, isn't it, researching family history? You find bits of the puzzle and start putting them together so they fit to make a bigger picture.'

'That's exactly it. The job is knowing exactly where to look to find all the pieces.'

'Why did my mother change her date of birth?'

'As I said, lots of potential reasons. She forgot, or did it to hide illegitimacy, or simply vanity.'

'Vanity?'

'Perhaps she wanted to appear younger than she actually was.'

'Why?'

'I don't know at the moment, but perhaps we can find out.'

'Where do we go next?'

'We go back on to Findmypast and see if we can find anything else about your mother now that we know her birth date and maiden name.'

Jayne entered the details into the search fields, narrowing the birthplace to Manchester.

'There she is. Margaret Elliot, born in 1915, which matches the details in the 1939 register. Ooh, that's interesting…'

'What is it?'

'Your mother's name has come up on the National Schools Admission Registers and Log Books record set, even though it's supposed only to go to 1914. The birth date matches: 17 September 1915.' Jayne scanned along the handwritten register. 'She was admitted to Princess Road School, Moss Side in 1920 and was living at 15 Bishop Road at that time.'

'A different address again. She seems to have moved around a lot.'

'Perhaps this explains it.' Jayne pointed to the column for 'parent or guardian'. Only one name was written there: Emma Elliot. 'It looks like her father was no longer with them.'

'Why?'

'I don't know. We can find out later.' Jayne stared at the entry. 'She stayed in school for three years until 1923, and there's a note next to "reason for leaving" which simply states "left district".'

'They were moving around.'

Jayne went back to the original search of Alice's mother. 'Her 1939 records are there, as are her birth registry details. Now, let's dig a little deeper to find your grandparents' wedding. That's what I was hoping for – a marriage in a church.'

Jayne clicked the link.

'It looked like your grandmother and grandfather were married at St Philips in Salford on 30 March 1915.'

First name	Last name	DOB	Sex	Job	Address	Father	Job
George	Elliott	14 Jun 1891	M	Clerk	36 Sidney St	James Elliott	Train Guard
Emma	Judd	18 Nov 1894	F	Trainee	102 Rand St	Thos Judd	Merch-ant

'And there's the name of your grandfather.'

'George Elliot. Sounds like a writer, except this one is a man.' There was a slight pause as Alice checked the notes she had been writing in her book. 'I notice my mother was born only six months later. Do you think it was a shotgun marriage?'

'Possibly. Remember World War One had been going since August 1914, so perhaps your grandfather was going to join up.'

'How will we know?'

'We'll just search for him in the military records, but first I'd like to check the 1911 census for your grandmother and great-grandfather.'

'While you do that I'll make another pot of tea.' Alice picked up the teapot and headed to the sink before stopping. 'I just realised how selfish I've been. You've just got home and I've come round asking for your help to search my records. How thoughtless of me.'

Jayne smiled. 'Don't worry, Alice. For me, this is relaxation. There's nothing more interesting than burying oneself in the records, tracking someone's family. I lose all sense of time and just focus on the task at hand. I love it.'

'You're lucky, Jayne, doing something you love. My husband – my late husband,' she corrected herself, 'he worked in insurance all his life and hated every second of it. The only times he enjoyed were the weekends, when he could work on his motorbikes.'

'And what did you do, Alice?'

'I looked after the home and brought up two lovely children. They're both married and live down south now. I see them occasionally, usually at Christmas.' She turned back to face the sink as her voice broke.

'Do you miss them?'

'Sometimes. I miss the grandchildren more.' She turned back to face Jayne. 'The strangest thing is, and I've never admitted this to anyone before, but I've enjoyed my life far more since John died. Horrible to say, isn't it? But I love working with my church, at the community centre, and volunteering at the food bank. It's like I drifted through the first seventy years of my life and only came alive in the last ten. It's a sad story.' She smiled ruefully. 'I think we definitely need some more tea.'

'Would you like a glass of wine instead?'

'So early?'

'It's nearly six o'clock.'

'What?'

Jayne pointed to the clock as Mr Smith stretched his back legs and wandered out into the hall to find his favourite place to sleep.

'You're right, time flies when you're researching family history.' Alice thought for a moment. 'Why not have a glass of wine? John always disapproved of drinking, so we can toast him.'

'How about a New Zealand Sauvignon Blanc?'

Jayne went to her new wine fridge and brought out a bottle of Villa Maria, pouring two glasses: one for herself and one for Alice.

'Here's to family history.' toasted Jayne.

'And here's to killing demons,' replied Alice. 'Mmm, this is lovely, like a glass full of tropical fruits.' She took another large mouthful. 'I think I could get used to this very easily.'

Jayne nodded at the laptop. 'Shall we get back to the past? Still lots to discover.'

'Top me up and we'll get going again.'

CHAPTER FIFTEEN

September 4, 1939
Changi, Singapore

More by luck than by Arthur's map-reading skills, they eventually found the encampment at Changi, on a spit of land close to the sea surrounded by coconut trees. They had taken at least three wrong turns and had eventually found the bivouac area after being guided in by a RAF officer.

The rest of the company were already there and were setting up the tents.

'You're late, Serjeant Murray,' said RSM Whatmough as they arrived.

Murray glanced malevolently towards Arthur and Ronnie. 'Sorry, the lorry… We got lost.'

RSM Whatmough sighed. 'Get your tents put up. Your officer's been waiting for the last hour.'

Lieutenant Whitehead was standing off to the left, next to the HQ truck filled with gear, tapping the side of his army shorts with his swagger cane impatiently.

Ronnie looked out at the bivouac area. 'This is not a great place to camp, Serjeant.'

'So you're the expert, are you?'

'No, Serjeant, but I know you never camp in a depression.' He pointed towards the low-lying area where the tents were being assembled.

'The army has chosen to camp here, so this is where we will camp,' he snarled. 'Horton and Harrison, you put up the officer's tent. Arkwright and Rogers, you two erect your own section's tent. The rest of you, with me to make the platoon's bivouac.'

'But… but…'

'I haven't finished yet, Harrison. Afterwards, you four can dig the latrines while the rest of us eat. Understand?'

The rest of the platoon were smiling.

'I didn't hear you.'

'Yes, Serjeant,' they chorused.

'Get a move on, we haven't got all day.'

That was the army for you. It was always hurry, hurry, wait, wait, wait.

After erecting the officer's tent, they were ordered to move Lieutenant Whitehead's kit from the back of the Headquarters truck. An extra soft camp bed, sheets and pillows, a table that folded out to the length of a dining table, two folding Hollywood director's chairs, a gramophone with a pile of records, a large mosquito net, his kit bag, spare uniforms, three pairs of shiny boots (non-army issue), a pump lamp and a portable wine box.

'God, I think he brought half of Robinson's with him,' said Harrison. 'Look, this desk set still has the label on it. Thirty-two dollars! Mate, that's more than a month's wages for a couple of pens and a bit of wood. If he'd have asked, I'd have made one for him myself.'

As they finished putting all the furniture in the tent, Lieutenant Whitehead passed by and looked inside.

'Well done, men, well done.' He said it with a peculiar accent, somehow managing to produce the words without moving either of his lips.

'You'll be as snug as a bug in a rug here, sir.'

Lieutenant Whitehead looked at Harrison with all the disdain of someone who has discovered something exceedingly smelly attached to the sole of his shoe.

'Yes, quite, Harrison. You two report back to Serjeant Murray, I believe there are still latrines to be dug. Ask my batman to come and unpack my kit.'

'Yes, sir,' they chorused, saluting him with all the smartness they could fake.

The company's tents had now been erected in the middle of a clearing in a rubber estate about the size of a football field. It sloped away down to a fringe of coconut palms at the bottom. Beyond the fringe of trees was a short, rough stretch of lalang grass, then the beach itself. The other three sides of the camp were surrounded by rubber trees marching away into the distance in long geometric lines.

Lieutenant Whitehead's tent lay at the bottom of the slope about fifty yards away from the tents of 13 and 15 Platoon. It had a wonderful view through the coconut trees to the rolling waves of the South China Sea.

On the left, the sun was going down and the lights of the small boats hunting for squid became bright dots against the far shore.

They had only walked a few steps before Harrison grabbed Arthur's arm. 'I'm gasping for a fag, let's skive off for half an hour and then go back for our tea. I don't want to dig latrines, do you?'

They took one look around and dashed off into the fringe of coconut trees, only stopping when they were out of view, walking through the lalang bordering the beach.

Harrison dropped down beside one of the coconut trees, its creased grey bark stretching above him like an elephant's trunk. He produced two flattened Capstans from the depths of his uniform.

The first drag of the day was wonderful, as the thick blue smoke grabbed hold of their lungs and pounded them into submission like an angry copper with a truncheon.

Harrison coughed twice. 'I needed that.'

They were both quiet, taking in the moment. The sun was deciding whether to set or not, the moon wondering whether to rise. The grey waves of the ocean quietly lapped the shore and a gentle wind crept over the grass and rustled the fronds of the coconut trees.

'My mam loves coconuts,' said Harrison eventually, breaking the silence. 'I remember winning one at Belle Vue fair. Big thing it was. A right sod to open, though. We had to take the axe to it. Split it open and all this water ran out. We threw that away but we ate the white stuff. Just like a coconut macaroon without the macaroon it was.' A long pause as Harrison stopped for breath. 'Arthur?'

'Yeah.'

'Why'd you join the army? I mean, you've got a wife and everything.'

'Same as everyone. No job and no chance of getting one in Manchester and I didn't get on with my mam's new fella, so one day I walked into the recruiting office. And Bob's your uncle, here I am.'

'But you're married now.'

'I tried to get out when I met Maggie but they said I'd signed up for seven years and that was it. Maggie's going to join me soon, though. Major Tudor has said it should happen next year.' He took a long drag on the Capstan. 'Haven't even seen my kid yet…'

Harrison nodded, pushing his glasses back up his nose.

'What about you?' asked Arthur.

'I wanted to get away and see the world.'

'No, really?'

'Really. I wanted to get away. The coppers were after me and it seemed like a good idea at the time.'

'What did you do?'

'A bit of this and a bit of that. Most of it involved breaking into rich people's houses when they weren't there.'

'What are you two likely lads doing here?'

It was Murray's voice. They both struggled to get up, throwing away their fags.

'It's alright, boys. Sure you don't have to get up on my behalf.' They looked behind to see Ronnie emerging from behind the tree.

'You idiot,' said Harrison, 'I nearly died a death. Look, my heart's beating faster than Tommy Dorsey's drummer.'

'Give us a fag, Arthur,' said Ronnie, sitting down.

'What are you doing here? I thought you'd be with the others setting up the camp,' asked Harrison.

'Well, that's an interesting thought. But I'm sure the camp can set itself up perfectly well without my help. And without yours either, I see. Shift your carcass, Harrison. I've seen more life in a corpse.'

Arthur handed him a squashed cigarette. He lit it and inhaled deeply, watching the blue smoke rise toward the sky as he exhaled.

Behind them, they could hear the sounds of music soaring out from Lieutenant Whitehead's tent.

'Sounds like he's wound up his gramophone. Pity he isn't playing a bit of Henry Hall or Victor Silvester.'

'Elgar's "Nimrod", so beautiful. Shhhh, Harrison, and listen.' Ronnie put his finger across his mouth, and stared out across the sea.

Then a strange thing happened. Ronnie stood up, raising his arm and pointing to an electrical storm lighting up the far shore. The colours were beautiful. Reds, greens, electric blues and sudden awful flashes of light that filled the sky with a brilliant radiance.

But there was no sound. No thunder claps. No crashes. No explosions of noise.

Only the sound of Elgar on the wind.

It was then the wind began to gather more strength. A violent rough wind that forced Arthur to lean into it, covering his cigarette with his hand.

His cap flew off and sailed against the trunk of a coconut tree and on back to camp. The sand stung his eyes as it whipped off the shore.

Still Ronnie stood there, unmoving, his arms raised to the light in the sky.

The rain followed soon after. No ordinary rain, but huge gobbets of water that drenched Arthur to the skin within seconds. He stared through the rain, the light and the wind at the one figure standing still, his arms raised to the heavens, a figure framed by the white-capped sea and the charcoal-grey clouds over the distant shore.

Ronnie.

Serjeant Murray ran past, his body bent double against the wind and the rain. 'It's a Sumatra,' he shouted as loudly as he could.

A Sumatra was a sudden storm that came from the Dutch East Indies without warning. Normally, they were safely ensconced in the brick-built comfort of their barracks. But out here, exposed on the tip of the island, there was nothing to protect them.

'Make sure the tents are battened down. I'll check on the lieutenant,' Serjeant Murray shouted, his words whipped away immediately by the wind.

'Yes, Serjeant.'

Arthur turned back to run towards the camp, glancing quickly at Ronnie with his arms raised, his sodden uniform clinging to his body.

Going past the coconut trees, their fronds waving manically in the wind, Arthur could see it was too late.

The tents had already pulled their guy ropes free from the ground. Men were rushing here and here, trying to find shelter from the storm. Others were futilely trying to hold on to the ropes to prevent the tents from blowing away. Still more were trying to trap pieces of kit as it blew past them.

On his right, Murray was vainly trying to help Lieutenant Whitehead save what remained of his kit. A record flew off, sailing over Arthur's head to bury itself in the side of one of the coconut trees.

The hollow where the camp was sited was already under three inches of water, more arriving every second from the sky and from the sea, as the waves broke through the protective barrier of lallang and flowed into the bivouac.

Then, just as suddenly as it had started, the wind died down and the rain ceased.

The Sumatra was over.

Ronnie was standing next to Arthur. How he had got there, nobody knew.

He gazed out at the wrecked camp, flooded with water, and whispered, 'They shouldn't have camped here. I did tell them.'

CHAPTER SIXTEEN

Sunday, December 8, 2019
Didsbury, Manchester

After pouring Alice a large glass of New Zealand Sauvignon Blanc, Jayne went back to her laptop and logged into the Findmypast website, selecting the 1911 census from the list of resources and completing the search form.

'There's George.' Jayne pointed to the second name on the list. 'The family was living in Salford. And that is your great-grandmother Sarah's handwriting. 1911 was one of the censuses where people filled in the forms themselves. I always find it so exciting to see the writing of one of my client's forbears and imagining them completing the form by the light of a candle

First Name	Last Name	Relation	Age	Birth Year	Job	Birth place
Sarah	Elliott	Head	50	1861	-	Wick
George	Elliott	Son	20	1891	Clerk	Salford
Percy	Elliott	Son	17	1894	Fitter	Salford
Angeline	Elliott	Daughter	13	1898	School	Salford
Hector	Elliott	Son	11	1900	School	Salford
Eve	Elliott	Daughter	7	1904	School	Salford

'He seems to have had four brothers and sisters, but there's no father listed and Sarah Elliott is listed as a widow,' said Alice.

'He probably died sometime after 1903. If you look down the list, the daughter, Eve, was born in 1904. She may have been born out of wedlock but I doubt it. Angeline Elliot is also named, she's probably the aunt mentioned in your adoption papers as living in Glossop. What's also interesting is your great-grandmother was born in Wick in the far north of Scotland, it's close to John O' Groats.'

'I wonder how she finally ended up in Salford of all places?'

'We can try to find out about her life later if you want, but let's stick with George at the moment. Let's go back a bit further to the 1901 census.'

Jayne tapped a few keys. 'Luckily your family was still living at the same address.'

First Name	Last Name	Relation	Age	Birth Year	Job	Birth place
George	Elliott	Head	50	1851	Train Guard	Edinburgh
Sarah	Elliott	Wife	40	1861	—	Wick
George	Elliott	Son	10	1891	Clerk	Salford
Percy	Elliott	Son	7	1894	Fitter	Salford
Angeline	Elliott	Daughter	3	1898	School	Salford
Hector	Elliott	Son	1	1900	School	Salford

Alice pointed her finger at the screen. 'That's my great-grandfather, also called George, born in Edinburgh. It looks like I have Scottish ancestors.'

'They may have come to Manchester for work. If you look at George junior's birthplace, it's Salford, so they were in the area at least by 1891. We can take them back earlier through the census and I can access the records from the National Records of Scotland in Edinburgh. But for now let's stick with your grandfather, George, born in 1891. I have a feeling with his age he probably signed up for service in World War One. We can hope his records survived, but many of them were destroyed in a fire in 1940.'

Jayne went back to the military records, entering George's details again. 'There are twelve George Elliots listed but I think this is your grandfather.'

She clicked on a link and an ink-stained page appeared, with the heading 'Short Service Attestation of 13724, George Elliot, 5th Battalion East Lancs Regiment'.

'It's definitely him. Look at the address.'

'Fifteen Dyer Street, Salford,' read Alice. 'And his job is given as clerk, the same as in the census.'

'He signed up on the tenth of April, 1915.' Jayne checked back to her notes on the marriage date. 'Just a few weeks after the wedding.'

'Why did he sign up then? He'd just got married.'

'You have to remember the tremendous societal pressure to join up at this time. There were music-hall recruitment songs, posters with Your Country Needs You on them, plus whole streets joined up en masse to form Pals battalions. Your grandfather seems to have planned it better than most. At least he had time to get married before joining up.'

Jayne clicked to the next page. 'Here we'll find more information about George. His chest measurement was thirty-four inches and he could expand it another two inches.'

'That's smaller than my waist.'

'People were thinner and shorter back then. One of the things they realised at this time was how unfit and unhealthy most army recruits were. A testament to the living conditions of the time and the quality of the food. The good old days is just a myth, I think.'

'There's my grandmother.'

Under a section named as 'Particulars provided by Recruit', Emma Stevenson was listed as well as her address and the date and place of their marriage.

The next page listed George's medical history. 'Probably taken by the Medical Officer in the recruitment centre on Pendleton Road.'

'He was only five feet six inches and weighed just 122 pounds. He was very thin and scrawny, wasn't he?'

'And remember his job was a clerk, so not much physical labour involved. Instead it was probably long hours crouched over ledgers in some office. The MO still wrote that he was of the correct standard and signed at the bottom of the page. They were looking for bodies at the time, they weren't looking for superheroes.'

'Cannon fodder?'

'In 1915, these were recruits for Kitchener's Battalions. The British Army scaled up rapidly in these years in preparation for the big push of 1916.'

'What was that?'

'The Battle of the Somme. Unfortunately the rush to train men and the belief amongst the senior officers that they weren't proper soldiers led to them being instructed to walk slowly across no-man's-land behind a creeping artillery barrage. Nearly twenty thousand men lost their lives on the terrible first day of the battle; the first of July, 1916.'

'It was a terrible time. I hope he didn't die then. In fact, I hope he didn't die at all.'

Jayne clicked on to the next page. It was headed: Statement of the names and addresses of all the Relatives of the above-named deceased soldier in each of the degrees, that are now living.

Below was a list of all George's relatives, including his wife, mother, brothers and sisters.

Jayne glanced up to the top of the page. The name George Elliot was written in big, black, depressing capitals.

'I'm sorry, Alice. It seems he did die. The army was finding out about the relatives, probably for pension purposes.'

Alice was silent for a moment before she asked, 'When did it happen?'

Jayne went to the next page. It was a duplicate of George's attestation papers, except this time the single four-letter word Dead was scrawled across the top in scruffy handwriting.

'They were blunt, weren't they?'

'So many died during the war, about 250,000 men in all. I suppose the clerks who wrote this became inured to death.'

'Can you find out when he died, Jayne?'

The genealogist scrolled through the last remaining papers. 'It seems he was missing presumed dead on the ninth of April, 1918.'

'Presumed dead?'

'Not to put a fine point on it, Alice, but it meant they probably couldn't find his body.'

Tears appeared in Alice's eyes. 'Silly, isn't it. He died over a hundred years ago and now I'm crying for him.'

'It's not silly at all, Alice. I completely understand. The war ended seven months later, in November 1918. If I remember my history correctly, April was the turning point of the war. The Germans' last big attack was winding down and the allies moved on to the offensive.'

'He nearly survived, only seven months left before the end.' There was a long pause as Alice gathered herself. 'I think we've done enough for today, don't you? I don't think I can handle any more heartbreak.'

'We've done plenty. If you want, I can go back over your family tree when I'm free.'

'I don't want to put you to any trouble.'

'Don't worry, I enjoy doing it and anyway, after next week, I won't be able to do anything so it's now or never.'

'Thank you, Jayne. When the birth certificates and the Ancestry DNA results come in, I'll show them to you.'

'Please do.'

Alice stood up. 'I see now why they ask a social worker to interview adoptees who want to discover their family history. It can be quite traumatic, can't it?'

'The past always is, Alice.'

'But it's also liberating too. Knowing where I came from and the struggles my ancestors went through. Somehow, it makes me stronger.'

'I'm glad you feel that way.'

Alice picked up her bag and walked towards the door, stopping as she opened it. 'Something just occurred to me.'

Jayne frowned. 'What is it?'

'We didn't apply for my mother's death certificate. Can we do it now?'

'You're ready?'

Alice nodded. 'I want to know if she was an alcoholic like the Simpsons said. We can't hide from the past simply because we might not like what it shows us.'

'I'll fill in the form for you. With a bit of luck, the GRO will send it all in the same envelope.'

'Thank you, Jayne. Sorry for disturbing your Sunday.'

'Don't worry. Like I said, I love doing this. For me, it's a joy not a job.'

'You're very lucky, Jayne, I wish everybody could say that.' With those last words, she turned and went out of the door..

CHAPTER SEVENTEEN

Block 15
Tanglin Barracks
Singapore
30th September 1939

My darling heart,

So it's started then. You know, I never thought it would come to this. After all, I always believed everybody had their fill of it in the Great War. Uncle Harry and Uncle Fred dying on the Somme and Dad getting a lungful of gas. He was never the same again. Every October, when winter came on, he used to cough up this horrible green stuff from the bottom of his lungs. I remember as kids we were always frightened of Dad when he was coughing. He was like a great big breathless bear.

Anyway, I suppose they know what they are doing, Chamberlain and the rest of them. Herr Hitler has to be put in his place somehow or other. With a bit of luck, he'll realise his mistake and it will all be over by Christmas.

Tell our Harry not to be stupid. He's just got married so he's not to go enlisting. They'll call him if they need him. He's got a wife to look after now. It'll be funny calling Rita Hendricks 'sister'. Her with her posh voice and all that.

The kids must look strange in their gas masks but you should make certain they know how to use them. Also, make sure they know where the bomb shelters are. You can never be too careful with the bloody Germans. Remember what Uncle Tom used to say before he caught it on the Somme?

How is Mary? Does she have a gas mask too? I bet she's growing very quickly. Can you send some photos, I'd love to see what she looks like.

Life here continues on as if nothing has really happened. On the first few days it was-

XXXXXXXXXXXXXXXXXXXXXXXXXXX
XXXXXXXXXXXXXXXXXXXXXXXXXXXXXXX
XXXXXXXXXXXXXXXXXXXXXXXXXXXXXXX
XXXXXXXXXXXXXXXXXXXXXXXXXXXXXXX
XXXXXXXXXXXXXXXXXXXXXXXXXXXXXXX
XXXXXXXXXXXXXXXXXXXXXXXXXXXXXXX
XXXXXXXXXXXXXXX *but that's all there was really. We went back to barracks and back to the old routine.*

We can read all about what's happening, though. The Straits Times is full of it. Poor old Poland seems to be getting a right battering. They are a tough lot though, the Poles, I'm sure they'll pull through.

We've got a new CO who's just arrived. A proper Tad he is, been with the regiment for years. He even won the Military Cross during the Great War. All the lads respect him. Major Tudor says it's too early to bother him about you and Mary coming to live out here. But I will go and see him soon.

Look after yourself now and be careful!!!

Your husband,
Arthur

Censored by Lt. Whitehead

Block 15
Tanglin Barracks
Singapore
10th January 1940

My darling wife,

No, the answer is No. I'm really firm on this. Once you let them send you and Mary to the country, you'll never get back. Look at what happened when War was declared. And what about your mum? Who will look after her? She's not as strong as she used to be.

It's all well and good the Government saying you should go for your own safety, but who is going to feed you? Who is going to clothe you? What about your work?

After all, it's only the Government that thinks the Germans are going to bomb. It's not happened much so far, has it?

So my answer is No. You put your foot down and tell those interfering buggers from the Ministry of Whatever to sling their hook. If you have to go anywhere it should be to your Auntie Angeline in Glossop. I know you think she doesn't want you to stay because she isn't well, but if you explain the situation and twist her arm I'm sure she'll give in.

Enough of that.

I loved the picture of you and Mary which you had taken at Garton's on Oxford Road. She looks like a bonny wee baby with beautiful big cheeks, the spitting image of her mum. How I wish I were back in Manchester holding you both, even with the War and all.

Life has pretty much returned to normal here in Singapore. It's as if the War doesn't really exist. People are still eating and drinking as much as they want. You'll hate me telling you this, what with rationing and everything in Stretford, but here I can buy as much meat, as many eggs and all the flour and sugar I want. A lot of it comes from Australia. Every day I see advertisements in the newspaper from Cold Storage offering fresh lamb, tender beef, succulent chicken and even bloody venison. Pardon my French.

It must be hard for you and Mary living there in Stretford. But keep your chin up, dear. It'll all be over soon, trust me. The French and the B.E.F. will soon teach Mr Smarty Pants a thing or two.

Now have you received the Christmas presents I sent? I hope you got them before Christmas this time. But you can never tell, what with the War and everything.

For Mary, I bought these lovely silk baby clothes. All the children here wear them. I hope they are not too big but if they are, I suppose she'll grow into them.

For your mum, I sent a pair of Chinese slippers. They are very soft and I know she has problems with her feet and her bunions these days.

Now for you, I've got a special present. I'm not going to tell you what it is until you get it. It's going to be a big surprise. Just for you.

Anyway, got to go now. I'm on guard duty this evening. I've agreed to do it for a mate of mine called Harrison. He's got to go into town. I don't mind doing the duty, though. It helps pass the time. It can get so boring out here.

I miss you and Mary all the time.

Your husband,
 Arthur

Censored by Lt. Whitehead

Block 15
Tanglin Barracks
Singapore
15th May 1940

Dear Maggie,

I'm sorry I haven't written to you for such a long time.

You see, I couldn't face writing this letter. I went to see the colonel at the beginning of March. He told me the bad news. Apparently, the War Office has a new policy since Dunkirk. No new married quarters are to be given out and no families brought out to any overseas postings for the rest of the War. The colonel explained it was because of the dangers of German U-boat attacks on our shipping. The War Office, he said, were worried about the effect on morale if soldiers' families were torpedoed en route to joining their spouses.

I tried to explain I had applied over a year ago and it was the army's fault we hadn't been reunited earlier, what with the change of CO and Major Tudor's reluctance to bring up the subject to him.

But he said there was nothing to be done because of the new War Office policy.

End of story.

So that's it, Maggie. I don't know what to do now. You and Mary will never be able to join me here while this War is on. I think the only thing to do is to try to get a posting back to England so I can be with you, it's my only way out.

Lord, I pray every night I can see you and Mary. I pray and pray and pray. But it doesn't seem to do much good. Not any more.

Your husband,
Arthur

Censored by Lt. Whitehead

CHAPTER EIGHTEEN

August 17, 1940
East Coast Beaches, Singapore

'Right then, you lot,' shouted Serjeant Murray.

They all sprang to attention and lined up in the best parade-ground fashion, except their boots were sinking into the soft sand of the beach.

'At ease, men. My name is Captain McLaverty of the Royal Engineers. This morning we're going to start to build the beach defences for this sector of the island. Sergeant Trimble here will show you what to do. If you have any questions just ask him. Right then, Sergeant Trimble, carry on.'

The Engineer's sergeant watched as his officer slipped his swagger stick under his arm and stumbled through the sand back to the main road and his car.

'Right then, lads, we're going to make some offshore beach defences starting from here, and going down to the end of the beach.' He pointed towards the far western end of the beach, where it met a headland on its way to the city. He avoided the majority of the eastern side, which went towards Changi.

Of course one of the lads had to speak, and of course it had to be Tommy Harrison.

'But what about the other half of the beach, Sergeant? Isn't that going to be defended?'

'Not yet, lad. We don't have permission to work on that half of the beach. The civil government is still negotiating with the landowner.'

'Enough questions. Just listen, right.' That was Murray putting Harrison back in his place.

'Right, we'll divide you into two groups. Thirteen Platoon are to start chopping down the coconut trees behind us to clear a field of fire. Fourteen Platoon are to drag the trees here and start sawing them into fifteen-foot lengths. Is that clear? Right, away you go then, lads, step lively.'

'You heard the sergeant, get on with it. Tools are in the trucks back at the road.'

'Building beach defences, would you believe it?' whispered Ted Rogers as they marched back to get the tools. 'Don't get me wrong, I love the army. But we should be training to fight and kill people, not building shore defences – not when there's thousands of bloody coolies on the island, dying for a day's work.'

Within half an hour they were all at work. Arthur had an axe in his hands, flailing away at the trunk of a coconut tree.

'Hey, take it easy. We want to drag this out. If we work too quickly, they'll have us doing this for the rest of our time.'

That was Harrison, looking for a way to skive as usual.

So Arthur went faster, swinging the axe over his head and bringing it down hard on the wood of the coconut tree.

He imagined he was an executioner bringing the axe down on the neck of a prisoner, seeing the head fall in one clean blow, watching the body topple forward, hearing the gush of blood from the severed arteries, the roar of the watching crowd.

But the coconut tree was tougher than a man's neck. Each axe blow merely sent a few splinters flying, hardly disturbing the wood.

'This axe is as blunt as your brain, Harrison.'

The sweat was already pouring off him. He put the axe down and removed his shirt. Sod dressing properly in heat like this. The others followed suit, carefully folding their khaki shirts and laying them down neatly in a pile in the shade.

Arthur spat on his hands. No coconut tree was going to defeat him.

He lifted the axe high and brought it down. Again. And again. And again. A few splinters spat off each time as the axe started to bite into the wood. As he did so, he imagined the faces of all the people who had ever done him wrong.

The man who'd sacked him for being late.

The teacher at school who'd caned him.

The priest who'd told him his father was dead and had gone to Limbo.

The 'uncle' who had beaten him every day with his belt for no reason at all.

And, above all, the stupid officer who'd refused him permission to leave the army.

He imagined them all, smashed into pieces, every time the axe buried itself deep into the coconut wood.

'What's got into him?' Harrison asked Ronnie Arkwright.

'Dunno, why don't you ask him?'

'Not when he's got a great big axe in his hands. I'm no fool…'

'Stop talking and get working, Harrison,' Serjeant Murray screamed from the other side of the beach.

They remained working on the sand until one o'clock. Dragging the newly cut wood into prepared holes and then stacking three logs up into the air, lashing them together at the top.

'What's it supposed to do?' asked Harrison.

'Beats me,' replied Arkwright.

'It's a boat trap, isn't it? Stops the enemy's boats coming up and landing troops on the beach,' said Ted Rogers.

'But the sea doesn't come this far. The tide mark is back there.' Ronnie pointed over his shoulder. 'Plus the waters are too shallow, we should be digging them further out.'

'Right, you lot, back in the trucks for your afternoon siesta back in camp,' shouted Serjeant Murray.

They picked up the tools and trudged up to the main road. Arthur would see the boat traps they had built later when they were stationed on the beaches.

They never were much use.

CHAPTER NINETEEN

Wednesday, December 11, 2019
Didsbury, Manchester

In the days following Alice's visit, Jayne was kept busy with the 1001 things she had to do for the trip. She arranged doctor's check-ups on her stepfather and Vera to ensure they were fit enough to fly such a long distance. He advised them to buy compression stockings to guard against deep vein thrombosis, drink plenty of water before and during the flight, and ensure they never sat for too long but got up and moved around.

There was also a myriad things to buy. On Wednesday, Jayne and Vera went shopping in the Trafford Centre to look for new outfits.

As Vera explained, 'I checked the weather in Perth in December and it's the middle of summer over there.

Usually, temperatures are around twenty-eight degrees during the day but some days can be even hotter.'

'Definitely not woolly jumper weather.'

They ended up spending most of the day there, lunching at Yang Sing and buying anything that took their fancy. Vera even treated herself to a new bathing suit. 'I don't know if we'll swim but I want to look good if we do.'

Jayne had to admit that, for a seventy-year-old woman, Vera took good care of herself. 'Got to, love. Don't want your dad casting a roving eye over the girls in the television room.'

Robert was waiting for them when they returned to the Home. 'Looks like you two bought half of Manchester.'

'Nah, we only bought a third, had to leave summat for the others,' said Vera.

He looked in one of the bags. 'Factor fifty sun protection? Moisturising cream for men? Skin hydration? What's that when it's at home? Soap and water not good enough any more?'

'The air is extremely dry and the sun quite powerful, Dad, you need to protect yourself. We've even bought you a floppy hat.' Jayne plucked it out of another bag.

'It looks like a tea cosy.'

'Just wear it to keep the sun off, Robert, I'll be wearing mine.' Vera held up a matching hat.

Robert shook his head. 'I'll take my flat cap but I'm not wearing no tea cosy.'

Jayne glance at Vera. 'Flat cap it is, better than nothing, I suppose. Anyway, the stopover in Singapore is confirmed, plus all the transfers. I've arranged for an Uber to pick you up here at six a.m. and I'll meet you at the airport before we check in. All clear?'

'I spoke to Harry last night,' said Vera. Harry Britton was her long-lost brother, whom Jayne had found through research after he had been sent to Australia as a young child. 'He can't wait to see you all on December nineteenth.'

'Great, looks like we're all set then.'

'Have you finished all your work, Jayne?'

'Just about. I'm having lunch with Ronald tomorrow to brief him on the outstanding cases.'

'How is he?'

'Same as ever, but he's found a new café on Shudehill that serves beans on toast with cheese.'

'Owned by Gordon Ramsay, is it?'

Jayne laughed. 'Hardly. More like Alf Tupper.' Jayne glanced at her watch. 'Time to go. I'll come back and see you on the day before the flight, just to check everything is A-OK.'

'I can't wait to go,' said Vera. 'Just four more days and we're off.'

'Have you got your budgie smugglers, Dad?'

'My what?'

'Budgie smugglers. It's Australian for Speedos.'

'Speedos?'

'Swimming trunks.'

Her father smiled. 'I think I'll stick with my shorts. I've had them since 1973 and if they served me in Blackpool, they'll work just as well in Australia.'

A look passed between Vera and Jayne. 'Get him some new swimwear.'

'I saw that look and there's no way I'm wearing sparrow smugglers.'

'They're called budgie smugglers. I'll get you a new pair of swimming shorts. If you like them, that's fine. If not, just wear your old ones,' said Jayne.

'But understand you're not coming swimming with me in those tatty old shorts, Robert Cartwright,' Vera added.

He remained silent.

'Right, I'm off. See you in a couple of days.'

'Bye, Jayne, see you soon.'

As Jayne bent down to kiss her father he whispered in her ear, 'Don't make 'em too bright. I'm not as flash as I used to be.'

It had never crossed Jayne's mind that her dad once considered himself flash. True, she had seen an old picture when he was dressed in a tailored suit, brothel creepers and a DA haircut, but he explained it away as the fashion of the time.

'Don't worry, Dad. Navy blue shorts just like the old ones, okay?'

He smiled. 'Thanks, lass, see you soon.'

CHAPTER TWENTY

Block 15
Tanglin Barracks
Singapore
5th June 1940

My dearest Maggie,

I do hope you and Mary are well. It is all the same out here. Nothing really changes very much even though we are at War. We all read the papers and listen to the news. It doesn't sound too good from France now but don't worry your little head, I'm sure we'll push the Krauts back like we did in the First War. It could mean more trench warfare, though. So I'm happy I'm out here rather than over there, if you see what I mean.

Remember how your Uncle Dennis came back from Ypres? Coughing his guts out every night he was. And still coughing ten years later. Poor man. I know it's wrong to say but I'm glad he passed away finally. He had been in too much pain for a long, long time.

As I said, nothing really changes here at all. It's like the war doesn't really exist. You would be shocked at what some of the young ladies get up to here, Maggie, wearing their thin silk dresses and flirting with the officers. It's nothing short of shameful.

I've put on a bit of muscle recently too. We've been building these defences along

*XXXXXXXXXXXXXXXXXXXXXXXXXXXXXXXXXX
XXXXXXXXXXXXXXXXXXXXXXXXXXXXXXXXXX
XXXXXXXXXXXXXXXXXXXXXXXXXXXXXXXXXX
XXXXXXXXXXXXXXXXXXXXXXXXXXXXXXXXXX
XXXXXXXXXXXXXXXXXXXXXXXXXXXXXXXXXX
XXXXXXXXXXXXXXXXXXXXXXXXXXXXXXXXXX
XXXXXXXXXXXXXXX. It ain't half tiring, slogging away in the sun. You'd think they would hire some coolies to do the work for us. But no, they don't. Instead, it's us Tads who have to grin and bear it.*

We've got the Cup Final next week. Us against the Loyals. Ronnie's still in goal for us and playing a blinder. But they've got this ex-professional centre-half who used to play for Blackpool. It should be a great game. I'll let you know how we get on in my next letter.

It's great the allotment's finally sorted out and you're getting some vegetables from it. Dig for Victory, like they say. Just like we have been doing on the East Coast.

Anyway, I've got to go now. I'm doing guard duty again for Harrison. He gives me a few bob for doing it for him. It all helps, especially when I've sent you and Mary presents.

Did you like the special one I got for you?

Give Mary a big hug from me. And give yourself a special one too.

Your husband,
  Arthur

Censored by Lt. Whitehead

Block 15
Tanglin Barracks
Singapore
25th December 1940

My dearest wife,

This is the third Christmas I've been away from Mary and yourself.

It seems for the rest of the year I can forget about it, burying myself in
XXXXXXXXXXXXXXXXXXXXXXXXXXXXXXXXXX
XXXXXXXXXXXXXXXXXXXXXXXXXXXXXXX *which is all we seem to do these days.*

But come Christmas it always seems to hit me hard. I'm sorry to be writing to you like this. I know it doesn't help you or Mary but all I can say is I miss you all so much.

I've been reading about the bombing. It seems to be getting much worse lately. I hope you're not getting hit too badly.

Mr Turner seems to be an awfully good chap, letting you use his Anderson shelter. It must be terrible sitting there below ground as the bombs are falling all around.

How is our Harry doing? He's finally joined up, hasn't he? I knew he'd join the Manchesters as well. He couldn't find a better regiment or a better bunch of lads.

Anyway, I've got to sign off now, love. I'm sorry I wasn't able to send you or the kids any presents this year. I hope you understand. But I'm a bit broke and the cost of sending them is more than it costs to buy them. It all seems a bit stupid to me. When I come home, I'll bring lots with me. I hope you can explain it all to Mary. I'd love to see her now and give her a big hug. But I can't because I'm so far away.

Your husband,
  Arthur

Censored by Lt. Whitehead

Block 15
Tanglin Barracks
Singapore
5th February 1941

Dearest Maggie,

Got your letter last week. I'm so happy your mum is better. Manchester sounds like it's getting a bit of a pasting from the Jer-

ries. I was so worried about you and Mary when I read in the paper about the raid before Christmas. Two of the lads lost their mother in that raid. Sad really, but I know they will get over it. But you should remember to rush down to the Anderson shelter as soon as the siren sounds.

The other thing you could do – and before I write this, Maggie, don't bite my head off – is to send her to your Auntie Angeline in Glossop until the bombing has finished. I know we've talked about this before but I want you to think about it now again.

I couldn't bear it, Maggie, if anything happened to you and Mary while I'm stuck out in Singapore.

Anyway, life goes on here. The days are as boring as ever. We spend most of the day sitting in the barracks. A few of the lads, me included, have taken to napping for a few hours in the afternoon. Nobody seems to mind. I think they all put it down to the heat.

Occasionally, we might do some firearms training or go on an exercise but that's a rare event, and even then the M.O. seems to complain we are all risking malaria.

The war seems so far away from here. Of course, we can read about what's happening in England but it seems not to be real. Here, nobody seems to worry. They go about their lives as they always have done.

A few of the lads wanted to go back to England and fight but the CO soon put them right. We're a regular regiment, he said, our duty is to obey the orders of our commanders. Good man the CO, a 'Tad' through and through, been with the regiment for years. He's always firm but fair.

Sorry for going on about the army. Sometimes I wish I'd never joined up. I've been away from you for nearly three years now and I've never seen Mary.

Your husband,
Arthur

PS: Mr Turner seems a nice bloke, digging a shelter for you. Tell him we'll have a pint in the Bull's Head together when I get back to Salford.

CHAPTER TWENTY-ONE

Thursday, December 12, 2019
Didsbury, Manchester

Jayne Sinclair answered the door as soon as she heard the knock.

Alice was standing on the doorstep. 'I hope you don't mind me calling round so early, but I saw you moving around through the window. They've come.'

'The certificates from the GRO?'

'And the DNA result from Ancestry, but the death certificate for my mother hasn't arrived yet.'

'It'll come soon, don't worry. Come in, Alice. Fancy a cuppa?'

'I'd love one. My heart is racing.' Then she stopped, placing her hand over Jayne's. 'I'm being so selfish. It's ten in the morning, you must have lots of other things to do.'

'Don't worry. I'm having lunch with a friend later but now I'm free. I was going to call you anyway to see if they'd arrived. Come on in and I'll make us a brew.'

Jayne ushered her into the kitchen and put the kettle on. Before long, they were sitting down enjoying a pot of tea together along with a few Jammie Dodgers from the local bakery. Finally Jayne said, 'Which envelope would you like to open first?'

'Which one do you suggest?'

'I would open the birth and marriage certificates first. They should just confirm the details we've already found out.'

'Right, here goes.' Alice ripped open the top of the first brown envelope. Inside was a certified copy of an entry of birth.

Name	Name of Father	Name and maiden name of Mother	Job of Father	Informant	When registered
Mary Emma	Arthur Horton	Margaret nee Elliott	Soldier Manchester Regt	Emma Elliott, grand mother 107 Henshall St.	14 July 1939

'See, we have the right person. My mother is living with Emma, her mother.'

'Your family were living in Hulme at the time, that's why your entry is for Manchester and not Salford, as you thought.'

'She must have moved to Prince's Avenue in Stretford just after I was born.'

'You were right about her moving around a lot. Perhaps she wanted a better environment for you. Hulme at the time was rows and rows of back-to-back houses, many with just outside toilets.'

'I remember them. They were all knocked down in the slum clearances of the sixties.'

'The flats that replaced them didn't last long. They were demolished in the nineties.'

'There's an old joke that Manchester will be a lovely place to live once it's finished…'

Jayne traced along the copy of the birth certificate with her finger. 'Your full name is Mary Emma Horton. You were probably partly named after your grandmother.'

For a moment, Alice was silent. 'I've been thinking about my name. I've known myself as Alice all these years and yet my real name is Mary Emma. I think it's too late to change now. What do you think, Jane?'

'You could change your name by deed poll, but it would mean changing your bank account, pension details and a host of other accounts.'

'A lot of bother. But I would like to remember my mother – after all, she did name me.'

'Why don't you informally start calling yourself Mary Alice? That way you don't have to change any of your bank accounts, but you can still honour your mother.'

'Mary Alice.' She rolled the name between her lips. 'Mary Alice, I quite like that. I could start by asking the people at the community centre to call me that.'

'Good idea.' Jayne returned to the certificate. 'We now also know your father was confirmed as a soldier with the Manchester Regiment. Perhaps he was away, stationed somewhere else in the UK, and couldn't get back for the birth. The informant was your grandmother.'

'I wonder if he was sad at missing my birth.'

'I'm sure he was. Now, you could apply as a next of kin for his army records from the Ministry of Defence. From those, you should be able to find out where he was based at the time.'

'Is it easy?'

'Pretty straightforward. Unfortunately they are not online but we can download the forms and send them off with a cheque for thirty pounds. They are not as quick as the Register Office at replying, though. I've heard it can take some time.'

'Let's do it, Jayne.'

'Okay, but before we do, we can make a quick search on Google to find out where his regiment was based in 1939.'

Jayne logged on. 'It seems there were two regular battalions, the First and Second Manchesters, and two territorial battalions, the Fifth and the Ninth. The First Battalion was based in Singapore and the Second, Fifth and Ninth Battalions were sent to France as part of the British Expeditionary Force, but not until after war was declared on the third of September, 1939.'

'So he could have been in England when I was born?'

'Possibly. If I remember correctly the Manchester Regiment Museum is in Ashton-under-Lyne next to the Town Hall. There's also a library there.'

'Could we go? Perhaps they'll have some records.'

Jayne thought for a moment. Did she have time? She still had to pack for her trip on the 15th.

'Okay,' she finally answered, 'but it will have to be tomorrow. I need to make sure I keep Saturday to do my packing before flying out on Sunday.'

'Why don't I drive you to the airport on Sunday morning? It'll save you calling a taxi and you can drop Mr Smith off before you go.'

'It's a deal. I'll call the Museum and Library to check their records and book a reading table for us both. In the meantime, shall we have another pot of tea before we start on the marriage records and the DNA results? I'm parched. And I think Mr Smith is a little peckish.'

The cat was standing over his empty bowl, staring at it and miaowing disconsolately.

'His highness always comes first,' said Jayne.

CHAPTER TWENTY-TWO

April 1, 1941
Singapore

'That's it chaps, look mean and nasty.'

They were standing up to their waists in this stream while a subaltern from the War Office set his movie camera up on the bank. Next to him, another corporal was contorting himself into the most awkward shapes taking pictures with a still camera, changing the bulb after every flash.

'Now, advance towards me down the stream. No. No. No. John, you there, third from the back.'

'Me, sir?'

'Yes, you, sir.' Of course it was Harrison he was referring to. 'Your eye line is straight ahead towards the enemy.'

'But there ain't no enemy.'

'You know that, I know that. But the British public hasn't got a clue, alright? So look straight ahead.'

'Yes, sir.'

'You know, Major Tudor, the shot lacks something. I don't know what it is. Michael? I say, Michael?'

A young puppy of a lieutenant came bounding up. 'Yes, Trevor, what is it?'

'They need to be more menacing, Michael. See to it.'

'Menacing? Right, Trevor.'

Michael, Lieutenant-what's-his-name, ran back to his shelter under the rain tree. He grabbed a bag and ran back to where they were standing. 'You can come out of the water now.'

Serjeant Murray, Arthur, Ronnie and Harrison stepped out onto the bank.

Lieutenant Michael jumped back in horror. 'Your leg!' He pointed at Murray.

There was a large black leech sitting above the serjeant's knee, calmly sucking his blood. Murray took his knife, dug the point under its mouth, and levered it off.

'Oh, you are a brave man,' said the lieutenant. 'I'll make you look very fierce. Trust me, Michael knows what he's doing.'

He reached into his bag and produced a dark brown compact. He dabbed a powder puff into it and started dabbing Murray's face.

It was now the serjeant's turn to recoil. 'You're not putting any bloody make-up on me.'

'It's just a little tan and blusher. It'll give you lovely cheekbones and highlights for the camera. Think of it as camouflage paint.'

Ronnie stepped forward and said, 'Let him do it to me, Serjeant. Then you can see how it looks.'

'Who's a brave boy then?' He began dabbing Ronnie's face. 'Now when I worked on The Four Feathers with Korda, you would have been perfect. Ralph would have loved you.'

'You used to work in the movies? You've met Errol Flynn?'

'Worked with him in Northampton Rep. Terrible play, all jolly hockey sticks and "what's for tea, Vicar?" Errol was wonderful though, bit of a naughty boy, if you know what I mean.' Here he touched the side of his nose and winked. 'He looks a bit like you. He's an Aussie, of course, but not many people know. Tries to keep it hush-hush, as if anything is ever secret where we come from. Same eyes, though. Wonderful eyes, our Errol.'

Ronnie checked himself in the mirror. 'A little more along the jaw line, I think.'

'Well, we are a pro, aren't we?' said Lieutenant Michael. 'Right, a little extra here and we're done. Next!'

Arthur stared at Ronnie. The brown stain underneath the eyes, along the cheek and shading his jaw line had given his face a fierce resolution, like he'd been up for three days and was ready to fight anybody who dared to challenge him.

He stepped forward. Lieutenant Michael started dabbing his face gently. 'Now keep still, this won't hurt a bit.' It was strange hearing this officer chat to him like he was one of his mates.

When the lieutenant finished, he stared at Arthur before saying 'Private...?'

'Horton, sir.'

'Well, Horton, you might not scare the enemy but you sure scare the hell out of me.'

He adjusted Arthur's shirt, checking him up and down like a knackerman looks at a horse. 'God, I'm a genius. I can make a pig's ear look like a silk purse.'

Arthur took this as a compliment.

'Hurry up, Michael, we haven't got all day. I'm losing the light and Antony wants to get all his stills finished for Picture Post.'

'Ready, Trevor, keep your shirt on. It's not easy working in this heat, you know. My brushes are all sticky.'

He quickly dabbed Harrison and Murray's faces. 'Remember to look fierce, that's my boys.'

'Right, back in the water, chaps. Now remember: you're out on patrol in the jungle looking for the enemy who's lying in wait for you around the bend.'

'If we knew where he was, we wouldn't need to patrol, would we, sir?' Of course this was Harrison.

'Pretend you don't know they are there, soldier.'

'Yes, sir.'

'Right, when I say "action", walk towards the camera scanning the jungle for the enemy. Remember, they're going to see this back at home so put on your fiercest face.'

The other lieutenant looked through the camera. 'I love the look, but could you give that serjeant more tan? He looks a bit white compared to the rest.'

Lieutenant Michael signalled to Murray, who then suffered the immense loss of dignity, having more make-up applied to his manly features.

'They're going to love you down the serjeants' mess tonight. You'll be more popular than Dorothy Lamour.'

'Shut up, Arkwright. Or else you're on a charge.'

'Yes, Serjeant, just a joke, Serjeant.'

'You three mention this to anyone and you're all on a charge.'

'Yes, Serjeant. We mean no, Serjeant,' all three answered in chorus.

'There, Van Gogh couldn't have done better,' said the lieutenant, eyeing his handiwork.

'Those rifles look a little weak, Major Tudor.'

'They're the regulation issue Lee-Enfields. If you want something else, you could try the Thompson submachine gun. We've just been delivered a crate of those. But nobody knows how to use them yet.'

'Oh, a Tommy gun? Like in the movies?'

'I think so.'

'That would be perfect.'

The major turned round to Lieutenant Whitehead. 'Go back to the QM and get a couple of Thompsons, will you? Tell him it's for the shooting.'

'Shooting what, sir?'

'Shooting the film, you ass. Hurry up, we haven't got all day.'

'Yes, sir.'

Whitehead ran off back to the main road about fifty yards from where they were filming.

They were supposed to be in the deepest, darkest depths of the Malaysian jungle. But they were actually just off Holland

Road about a mile away from the camp. Dramatic licence, the director called it. 'The magic of film.'

Arthur and Ronnie had seen exactly the same thing themselves last week at the Capitol. They had gone to see Santa Fe Trail with Errol Flynn and Olivia de Havilland. Of course, the Pathé news was on before the feature like it always was.

There was an announcer rambling on about the brave soldiers from all the world over defending the Empire. This voice ran against footage of some poor squaddies charging up a sand dune with fixed bayonets. They looked bored, hot and tired.

The worst was yet to come. The announcer proudly shouted 'Take that, Fritz' as they watched a Jerry bomber crashing in flames at night in the desert.

Ronnie leant across and said, 'That's not a bomber, it's one of those parachute flares they showed us how to use back at training camp in York. Anybody who's ever served can tell the difference. Do they think we're idiots?'

Arthur stayed silent. What was the point of saying anything?

Lieutenant Whitehead came running back with two Thompsons under his arm. He handed one to Murray, and Ronnie grabbed the other.

'Lovely, lovely,' said the captain/director.

Ronnie took his Tommy gun and, chattering away with his mouth, proceeded to execute all the surrounding ferns and palm trees.

'No. No firing. Remember, you are a very vigilant patrol. Ready. Roll cameras, action!'

He waved his arm and they moved forward through the water, looking aggressively to right and left.

There was a loud splash behind.

'Cut!' Arthur heard the captain shout.

He turned round to see Harrison resurface, spitting water out of his mouth. 'My foot. It got all tangled in some roots. Nearly had me leg off.'

'Okay, return to Position A, people.'

'What?'

'Go back to where you started,' the other lieutenant explained wearily.

'Right you are, sir,' answered Murray.

'Did I look fierce enough, sir?' asked Ronnie.

'You were perfect. In fact, could you swap positions with the serjeant? That's right, you can lead. Now we'll put the man who fell over right at the back bringing up the rear.'

They all changed positions in the stream.

At this point, Major Tudor leant forward. 'But that's not correct, Captain. You see, we wouldn't have a private leading a patrol. That's the serjeant's job. That's the whole point of being a serjeant.'

'Right you are, Major. But this man looks fierce out in front. After all, we want to make your regiment look good on camera. Do you really want to change?'

Major Tudor shook his head.

The captain seemed to think for a moment. 'Silly me, it's so simple, I should have thought of it before.' He looked for the lieutenant. 'Michael, Michael.'

The captain said something to the lieutenant, who ran back to the main road, reappearing minutes later with a pair of scissors, needle and thread.

'Right, cut the stripes off him and put them on that one.' He pointed from Murray to Ronnie.

'But, but, but… Sir?' Murray protested to Major Tudor.

'You heard the captain, Serjeant.'

'Don't worry, this won't hurt a bit,' said Lieutenant Michael.

The lieutenant started to cut away Murray's stripes. His face was getting redder and redder.

'Does this mean they'll be giving me more money, Serjeant?'

'Don't say a word more, Arkwright, or you're on a charge.'

Ronnie looked down at his arm as the lieutenant was sewing the stripes on. 'I think I could get used to these very easily.'

'There you are, all finished, Serjeant.' The lieutenant twisted his head right and left, admiring his handiwork.

Ronnie swaggered around the troop, proudly displaying his new stripes.

'Right, positions, everyone. Remember, think fierce. You're Warriors of the King.'

'Warriors of the King – that's a new one,' said Harrison.

'Right. Ready. Camera. Action!'

They waded through the jungle waters off Holland Road, Tommy guns at the ready and make-up already beginning to drip down their faces onto their uniforms.

'And cut. Print that. Perfect, boys. You've got all your stills, Antony?'

The photographer gave the thumbs-up sign.

'Now we'll go to the next set-up, which I believe is a bayonet charge, isn't it, Major Tudor?'

'That's right.'

'Good, Michael. Oh, Michael…' The captain/director walked off to talk with his lieutenant.

Ronnie turned to Arthur. 'I think I've finally found out what I want to do with the rest of my life. Watch out, Errol Flynn – Ronald Arkwright is coming.'

CHAPTER TWENTY-THREE

Thursday, December 12, 2019
Didsbury, Manchester

After feeding Mr Smith and enjoying a nice pot of tea and a few digestives, they returned to work relaxed and raring to go.

'Shall we look at the marriage certificate now?' asked Jayne.

'Now is as good a time as any.' Alice opened the second envelope. It was titled at the top Certified Copy of an Entry of Marriage.

'It looks like they were married in the same church as your grandparents; St Philips in Salford on 24 June 1938.'

'A summer wedding. But it looks like Margaret isn't telling the truth about her age.'

First name	Last name	Age	Occupation	Address	Father
Arthur	Horton	21	Soldier	14 Pitt St	Thos Horton
Margaret	Elliott	21	Shorthand Typist	108 Rand St	George Elliott

'Probably embarrassed at being older than your father.'

'I understand. I was three years older than my husband. Quite a few of his family were tut-tutting behind their gloved hands at the wedding. He couldn't give a stuff and I used to call him my toyboy.'

Jayne glanced at the woman sitting next to her. There were hidden depths to her and Jayne had only scratched the surface. 'At least we now know your grandfather's name on your paternal side: Thomas Horton.'

'What's a twister?'

'I think it's something to do with the cotton industry. Somebody who twists the raw cotton into yarn. Remember, Lancashire was still the centre of the cotton industry at this time, even though its decline had already begun after the First World War.'

'Right, so are we going back into FreeBMD?'

'I think we can go straight to Findmypast now we know your father's age and where he was living.' Jayne typed the details into the website. They had 2,347 results for the name and year of birth. She then added a place of birth, Salford, and received only 22 results.

They scanned them together, Jayne clicking on two of the results.

'Strange, the marriage comes up in Salford, and your birth, but nothing else matches.'

'What does it mean?'

'It means he wasn't born in Salford but somewhere else. If I widen the search to Lancashire, we get ninety-two results.' Again she scanned the list, clicking some of the options. 'Nothing is coming up which identifies him directly.'

'What can we do?'

'The problem with the surname Horton is that it is such a common name. If we search for his father, Thomas Horton, giving an approximate birth date of 1892, give or take five years, and without a place of birth, we get 19,278 results. Narrowing it to England still gives us 16,308 results.'

Alice looked worried. 'Are we stuck?'

'I don't think so. It's just a question of going through each and every result and cross-checking until we find the right person. We don't have time at the moment but I know just the person who'd love to get his teeth into this problem. Lucky thing is, I'm just going to meet him for lunch. This is right up Ronald's street. And we also know your father was a soldier. He may be in the records held by the Tameside Library. I'll ring them to check what they have and we can visit tomorrow. Don't worry, Alice, all is not lost. Just investigating somebody's past takes time and patience. You have to work around each obstacle as it comes up.'

'Sounds good. Perhaps my DNA records could help?'

'They can't hurt, plus they may be able to narrow down the search area.'

They logged on to Alice's Ancestry account and checked her DNA results.

'According to this, I am 58 per cent Scottish, 28 per cent Irish, 11 per cent Scandinavian and 3 per cent Russian.' Alice looked across at Jayne, 'I'm 3 per cent Russian, wow.'

'This is your ethnicity estimate and, honestly, should be taken with a pinch of salt. To put it simply, our entire DNA is made up of about three billion parts but ancestry companies look at less than one per cent of these parts – about 700,000 SNPs, as they are called – where they know there are differences between humans. Then they compare the patterns of your differences with groups of people in their database to get an ethnicity estimate. The key word here is "estimate" because that's what it is – an informed guess.'

'So not much use then.'

'No, it's useful for backing up traditional research, plus the raw DNA data from the test can allow us to do more.'

'Like?'

'We can use your Ancestry DNA results to find out if you have any matches on GEDmatch.'

'What's GEDmatch when it's at home?'

Jayne logged on to the site as she explained. 'GEDmatch is an online site that allows you to compare your DNA results with those of other people even though they may have tested with a different company. Right, we're in. We've already downloaded your Ancestry results and now we'll upload the data to GEDmatch, but first we'll create an account for you.'

'It all sounds double Dutch to me.'

'What alias would you like? How about MaryAlice?'

'Sounds good.'

At the top right of the webpage, Jayne chose the 'File Uploads' section, selecting AncestryDNA.

'We just have to stay on this page as your data is uploaded. The numbers along the bottom are your chromosomes.'

The page finished loading.

'There's your assigned kit number. You might want to write it down somewhere, because you enter it every time you want to compare your DNA with somebody else.'

'Right.'

'Now, we'll go back to the homepage and log in. See if your data has been uploaded. There are two asterisks next to it which means the batch hasn't been processed yet, so you can't do a one-to-many check.'

'You've lost me.'

'They need to process the information from Ancestry and file it. After about four hours, you can check your data to see if you have any matches with other people. Why don't you come back this afternoon, say around four p.m.? I'll get us some cakes from town for an afternoon tea and we'll check if we can get a match.'

'Are you sure, Jayne? I feel like I've taken up so much of your time already.'

'Remember, I enjoy doing this. If it's okay with you, I'll also brief my researcher, Ronald, to go through the Horton files and see if we can find out more about your paternal ancestors.'

'Jayne, you've done so much already, how can I thank you?'

'Just look after Mr Smith while I'm away.' The cat lifted his head on the mention of his name. 'He's a mean, scrawny, awkward tomcat but he means so much to me. But now I have to get going for my lunch. I'll see you at four and we'll check your DNA matches. Just a warning, you may have none or you could have lots. Serendipity.'

'There's that word again.'

'It happens a lot in genealogy. It's like the man said, success is just a lot of hard work and a little bit of inspiration, with a wee bit of serendipity thrown in to sweeten the deal.'

CHAPTER TWENTY-FOUR

Block 15
Tanglin Barracks
Singapore
7th April 1941

Dear Maggie,

Well, I've been here nearly three years now. So long away from you and I've never even seen our baby, Mary. I bet she's not even a baby any more!!

I miss you all so much. You know, they say the army is one big family but it's not really. I'm not knocking my pals like Ronnie, Harrison, Rogers, and even Teale, but they are not a family. They can't give you love when you need it or let you cry on their shoulder or give you a big hug and tell you to cheer up.

Anyway, enough of me going on, it doesn't help me or you. Life goes on here in much the same way as it always does. There's a lot more troops here now, with more arriving every day. A lot of Australians have come too. Great fellows but they can be a bit rough, if you know what I mean.

Everything else carries on as it always has done, as if there was no war anywhere. It's because Singapore produces all the war stuff England needs to carry the fight to the Germans. That's what Harrison says anyway. I'm not sure if he knows nowt, though.

But you should see some of the carrying on. People drinking and dancing like there was no tomorrow. Nothing is rationed here. You can go down to Cold Storage and buy anything you want. Beef, eggs, chicken, even whisky are all on the shelves. Not that I go down there and buy anything, mind you, me being broke most of the time. But sometimes it's good to wander around and look at everything.

It must be hard for you in Stretford, what with the rationing and the bombing. That butcher seems a real so-and-so to you now. Shame, as he was so kind before, not giving you an extra bit of pork when you wanted it. Why did he change all of a sudden? I hope our Harry hasn't put the kibosh on it.

Good to hear you've found yourself a job in Metrovicks. I'm sure there's lots of jobs now the men have all gone off to fight. I wish it were true before the war, then I wouldn't be out here, thousands of miles away in Singapore. But if you're working, who's looking after Mary?

Time to go now, dear heart. One last message before I sign off.

I love you and Mary. There, I've said it. But I think you've always known it, haven't you, Maggie?

Best regards,
  Arthur

Censored by Lt. Whitehead

Block 15
Tanglin Barracks
Singapore
20th June 1941

My Maggie,

I don't know what to say right now but it looks like the war is coming to us. According to the Straits Times, the Japs are getting closer to the Empire. But don't worry, me and the lads will see those little blighters off. Some of the other regiments
XXXXXXXXXXXXXXXXXXXXXXXXXXXXXXXX
XXXXXXXXXXXXXXXXXXXXXXXXXXXXXXXX
XXXXXXXXXXXXXXXXXXXXXXXXXXXXXXXX
XXXXXXXXXXXXXXXXXX. *But those newspaper Johnnies are always war mongering. I'm sure it's not going to happen at all. More likely, we'll be transferred home*
XXXXXXXXXXXXXXXXXXXXXXXXXXXXXXXX
XXXXXXXXXXXXXXXXXXXXXXXXXXXXXXXXX. *At least if we go there I could be close to you and Mary.*
XXXXXXXXXXXXXXXXXXXXXXXXXXXXXXXX
XXXXXXXXXXXXXXXXXXXXXXXXXXXXXXXX

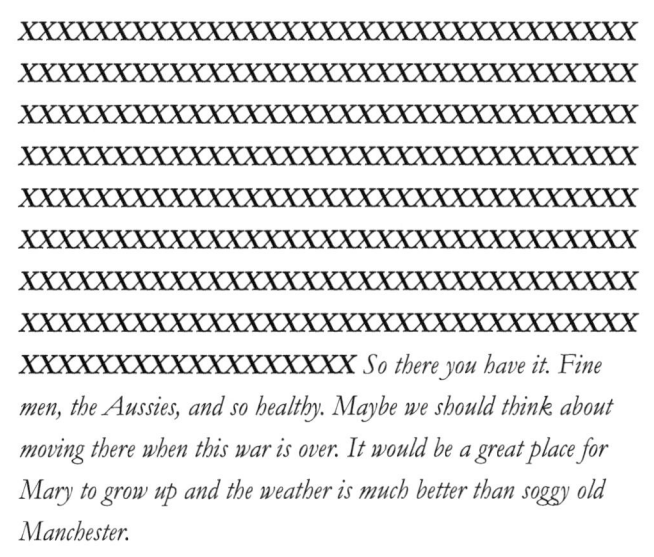

XXXXXXXXXXXXXXXXXXXXXXXXXXXXXXXXXXXXX
XXXXXXXXXXXXXXXXXXXXXXXXXXXXXXXXXXXXX
XXXXXXXXXXXXXXXXXXXXXXXXXXXXXXXXXXXXX
XXXXXXXXXXXXXXXXXXXXXXXXXXXXXXXXXXXXX
XXXXXXXXXXXXXXXXXXXXXXXXXXXXXXXXXXXXX
XXXXXXXXXXXXXXXXXXXXXXXXXXXXXXXXXXXXX
XXXXXXXXXXXXXXXXXXXXXXXXXXXXXXXXXXXXX
XXXXXXXXXXXXXXXXXXXXXXXXXXXXXXXXXXXXX
XXXXXXXXXXXXXXXXXXX So there you have it. Fine men, the Aussies, and so healthy. Maybe we should think about moving there when this war is over. It would be a great place for Mary to grow up and the weather is much better than soggy old Manchester.

And don't you worry your little head about me. If it all comes to fighting, which I don't think it will, there ain't no flies on Arthur Horton. I know how to keep my head down and out of trouble.

Sorry to hear about your mum, she sounds proper poorly. I'm glad to hear that Mary is happy staying at a day nursery run by the Ministry, but I'm sure it would be better if you looked after her yourself. A young child needs her mother, not some stranger. There, I've said my piece, I hope you understand.

It looks like I may be able to sort out a new job for myself. I'm to be batman for XXXXXXXXXX. A batman is a sort of personal servant. It's a really cushy number and I don't mind doing it. Funny though, how you said I was such a messy bugger, pardon my French. Now here I am clearing and tidying up after an officer. The army really is a funny place.

Give my love to Mary and give yourself a specially big hug. You know how much I miss you.

Your husband,
Arthur

Censored by Major R. Tudor

Block 15
Tanglin Barracks
Singapore
2nd July 1941

Dearest Maggie,

I haven't heard from you in such a long time. Are you too busy with your war work at Metrovicks? You must be working so hard at the moment, what with the war and all.

What are you working on? And did your mum help you get the job? I hope she's better now and has gone back to work. It looks like England needs all hands on deck at the moment. But it looks like Mr Hitler may have bitten off more than he can chew with Russia. At least, he won't be invading England any more.

Send me more pictures of Mary. She must be walking now and getting into mischief. Does she enjoy going to the nursery if you are working? As I said last time, I would prefer it if you were staying at home to look after her but, I suppose England needs every worker it has at the moment, even my wife!!!

Please reply as quickly as you can. It's such a long time since I've heard from you or heard any news about the what's going on. It can get awfully lonely out here in Singapore without you and you don't know how much I look forward to receiving your letters with news from home.

Write soon!!!

Your loving husband,
Arthur

Block 15
Tanglin Barracks
Singapore
23rd July 1941

Maggie,

Why haven't you written?
I've sent you three letters now and haven' t received a reply. Is it because you are too busy working at Metrovicks and don't have time? If you don't have time to write, you don't have time to look after poor Mary either!!

Please answer this letter as soon as you can.
I want to hear from you!!!

Your husband (remember him),
Arthur

CHAPTER TWENTY-FIVE

Thursday, December 12, 2019
King Street, Manchester

Jayne parked at the ugliest car park in the world overlooking the River Irwell and walked down Deansgate past Kendals. She glanced across at the big Waterstones on the other side of the street and reminded herself to pop in to check the new arrivals. Over the years, she had spent so much happy time on its floors, discovering books she normally would never have found.

Turning right, she found herself on King Street West. It was one of those streets that reminded her how much Manchester had changed in the last twenty years. A change epitomised by food.

On the left was Bem Brasil, serving chunks of barbecued beef, lamb and pork. On the right, Cicchetti, with their small plates of Venetian snacks, perfect for the ladies who lunch after a hard morning's shopping.

Further on was the Italian restaurant where not so long ago she had met the actress, Rachel Marlowe, on a case. That had been a family journey.

An Indian takeaway on the right, a Korean restaurant on the left, and between them was sandwiched a Greggs. Further on was where she was meeting Ronald.

Essy's. One of the last remaining 'greasy spoons' in the city. Where everywhere else had been taken over by artisan coffee, squashed avocado and toasted sourdough, Essy's had resolutely refused to change, serving builder's fry-ups and all-day breakfasts, and specialising in the culinary delights of the baked potato.

Ronald was already waiting for her inside when she walked through the entrance.

'Sorry, I was starving.'

In front of him was a plate of beans on toast, his staple diet, and a big mug of steaming tea.

'I see you're expanding your menu.' Jayne pointed to the large baked potato smothered in more baked beans and topped off with a generous helping of grated cheese, sitting on a second plate beside him.

'Yeah, I know it's adventurous of me,' he said without a hint of irony – Ronald didn't do irony – 'but I thought, give it a go, what do you have to lose?'

'What indeed. Nothing but your bowels.'

'I thought of them, so I ordered extra beans. Just in case. Can't be too safe, not with the bowels.'

Jayne joined the table and ordered an omelette with a baked potato on the side.

'I never eat eggs. Don't know what's inside.'

'A yolk and some egg white?'

'But what have the chickens been eating? Where have they been kept? When were the eggs laid?' He pointed to his plate. 'Now I know these are from Heinz and they were made just down the road in Wigan. Did you know the world's biggest baked-bean factory is located there, not ten miles from here. The beans come from North America and are rehydrated and cooked in the UK. Three million cans are produced each day. Wigan should be proud.'

'I like omelettes.'

'You might like beans more. It's a Red Indian dish, you know, though Native American might be a better way of putting it. Adopted and adapted by colonists in New England in the seventeenth century. Americans eat them with maple syrup or molasses. Don't like the idea myself.' He picked up a huge scoop of beans and popped them in his mouth.

Despite herself, Jayne asked a question. 'How did they come to England and become part of an English breakfast?'

'Ah, that's the interesting bit. It was an advertising campaign in the sixties that did it. Before that they were considered a bit of a luxury, sold at Fortnum and Mason, no less. You know, there's a baked-bean museum in Port Talbot in Wales. It's my dream to go there one day...'

'I think I prefer cassoulet myself.'

'Now, cassoulet is interesting. Did you know that…'

Luckily, Jayne was saved by the arrival of her omelette and coffee.

'Another plate of beans on toast, Ronald?' asked the owner.

'I think I'll hang on for a while, I've still got the baked potato to get through. I don't want to overextend myself. Busy day ahead.'

Jayne and Ronald had first met last year when they were introduced by an auctioneer. Ronald was a book finder, somebody who discovered rare editions of books and sold them on. Jayne had been commissioned to discover the provenance of one of his books, a first edition of Charles Dickens' A Christmas Carol. It had been a roller-coaster journey and they had stayed in touch, with Jayne occasionally using Ronald's services.

He was particularly good at doing painstaking research in archives and was adept at reading the cursive handwriting of the Victorians, something even Jayne struggled with.

'Busy? What have you found?'

'A rare first edition of Orwell's Animal Farm.' Ronald reached down and pulled a plastic folder from his briefcase beneath the table.

The cover of the book was divided in half diagonally, with light grey and green sections. The words Animal Farm, A Fairy Story by George Orwell were printed on the fronting in an italic typeface. 'Not in great nick but it should be worth a few bob. There are a lot of collectors of first Orwells out there.'

'But isn't this book quite recent?'

'August 1945, to be precise. Only 4,500 copies were printed because of World War Two restrictions and paper shortages. This one has the original dust jacket printed on the blank side of an unrelated Searchlight Books jacket to comply with restrictions. And the publication was delayed from May until August of 1945, even though it says "First Published May 1945" on the half-title verso. Shame about the foxing and the tears to the jacket. They'll bring down the price.'

'Where did you find it?'

'In a job lot of books from a house clearance in Withington, cost me a fiver for the box.'

'And how much is it worth?'

'In this condition? Between four and six thousand quid. Lot of collectors in America and the UK for an Orwell.'

'How much did it sell for new?'

'Six bob from Secker and Warburg.'

'I'm in the wrong business.'

'But you've got to know what you're looking for, Mrs Sinclair.' He tapped the side of his nose. 'I smelt this Orwell as soon as I entered the house. The owner was a university lecturer who'd lived there all his life. I knew this, or something like it, was going to be there.'

Jayne knew what he meant. There was always a point in her genealogical research when she imagined herself living and experiencing the life of the ancestor. It was then she knew she would find the truth.

'So, let's get to business, shall we? I'm afraid our Hollywood actress is having cold feet about discovering her past.'

'Shame. I was looking forward to going through the parish registers.'

'She may change her mind, but I don't think so. I do have a new job for you, though.'

'Interesting?'

'I think so. An adopted eighty-year-old woman looking to research her birth family.'

'She's started a bit late.'

'It's not when we start, but the fact we start that is important.'

Jayne thought of herself. She still hadn't researched the maternal side of her own family. She wasn't ready to open that particular can of worms yet, but she had to do it one day. Preferably before she was eighty.

Jayne took Ronald through her research on the family so far.

'So you have a minor brick wall at her father?'

Jayne nodded. 'There are just too many Hortons.'

'No worries, I'll plough through them all, looking for possible matches.'

'I may be able to get you more information after we visit the Tameside Museum tomorrow.'

'No worries, I'll do it tonight. Should be able to let you know tomorrow morning.'

Jayne forgot that Ronald didn't sleep very much when he had a job to get his teeth into.

'Usual terms, Mrs Sinclair?'

'I'm doing this one pro bono, Ronald. Alice is looking after Mr Smith while I'm away.'

'Oh, okay – then there'll be no charge. With the little Orwell I don't need money at the moment. And I forgot to tell you I'm doing an online course with the Society of Genealogists.'

'They are good, you'll learn a lot. Set yourself up in business soon.'

'I don't think so, Mrs Sinclair, I'd have to deal with people every day. Too complicated. I much prefer my books and my archives. They speak to me, people are too difficult to understand.'

'We understand each other.'

'Ah, but you're different. We only ever talk about work, nothing else.'

She realised it was true. Jayne had a totally transactional relationship with Ronald. Feelings or emotions never intruded on their business. Since she had separated from her ex-husband Paul, she'd only had one relationship which was non-business related. He was a lecturer at the university but they quickly realised they were better as friends than lovers. Emotions clouded judgement and got in the way.

Was she becoming more like Ronald? Avoiding emotional attachments completely? But she realised that wasn't true. She had a strong attachment to her stepfather and Vera. Strong enough to go on holiday with them to Australia. It was romantic attachments she avoided.

Had her marriage to Paul burnt her so badly?

'Hello, Mrs Sinclair…?'

'Sorry, Ronald, I was miles away.'

'I do that all the time. On the spectrum, they called it. I think I just couldn't be bothered listening to their voices. Anyway, as I was saying, you buy lunch and we'll call it a deal. Deal?'

'Lunch is less than twelve quid, Ronald.'

'But it's worth it. I might just expand my repertoire to baked potatoes with cheese and baked beans. Now I just have to learn how to cook it.'

'You could even experiment with different kinds of cheese…'

'Don't want to take it too quickly, Mrs Sinclair. I've got a sensitive stomach. Lancashire will do me, thank you very much,' he said putting an end to the discussion.

CHAPTER TWENTY-SIX

August 28, 1941
Tanglin Barracks, Singapore

It was hot, with a strength-sapping humidity that only Singapore could deliver.

That morning they had a perfunctory roll call lasting twenty minutes, followed by callisthenics with Serjeant Caldwell, the PE instructor. Of course, Ronnie had managed to get out of it, claiming he had bunions and had to see the MO.

Afterwards, they had slumped back to the barracks to lie on their bunks. Above Arthur's head, the fan hung down from the ceiling and whirred slowly, stirring the warm, damp air but not providing any relief.

'Lord, how I wish it would rain.'

'You and me both, Arthur,' answered Ronnie, now back from the MO and no longer wearing his boots but a pair of plimsolls.

'A long drizzle like we used to get in Salford, when the rain creeps in, makes itself comfortable and stays all day like an unwanted guest.'

'Here the heat sucks you dry like a straw emptying a glass. I mean, I just stick my head out of the barracks and walk across the parade ground and by the time I get to the canteen on the other side, I'm already soaking wet, dripping from head to toe.'

'Even the officers seem to have got it all worked out. After breakfast, they vanish back to their rooms or their houses for a long nap.'

'Except the stupid ones. They play on the golf course in front of the officers' mess every afternoon, chasing a small round white ball into a hole. They never seem to catch it, though.'

'A-ten-shion!' someone shouted. Immediately twenty bodies snapped rigid like tin soldiers.

'Stand easy, lads, stand easy.' It was Regimental Serjeant Major Whatmough who spoke, followed into the barracks by Serjeant Murray.

The RSM was an old Tad who'd been decorated for leading a charge against a machine gun on the Somme. The regiment had lost 400 men, killed or wounded, out of a total of 700 who had left the trenches that morning. Whole units, whole families, whole streets of Manchester were wiped out.

Not RSM Whatmough, though. Legend had it the man was so hard the bullets bounced off him. And looking at him, Arthur believed it.

As the lads ran to stand in front of their beds, Whatmough strode purposefully to the centre of the room. In a voice used over many parade grounds in countless different outposts of the Empire, he announced to all the lost souls of Block 15, 'Men of the Manchesters, occasionally my position gives me the odious job of delivering sad news…'

He spoke like some biblical prophet, his voice deep, profound and leaving no opportunity for argument, no opening for questions, no possibility of error.

'Unfortunately in war, and in this war against the evil that has invaded our German brethren, there will be casualties and victims.'

It was then he produced a brown envelope from behind his clipboard.

They all knew what they were. Every soul was praying he wasn't going to receive one. A mass whispered prayer of 'Let it not be me. Let it not be me.'

Arthur hoped for it not to be Maggie or Mary. Just give me this one chance, this little hope, and I won't go down to the Lady Bar or Great World any more, he thought. Just one chance. He crossed his fingers as they hung at attention down the seam of his khaki trousers, hoping Whatmough didn't notice.

The RSM looked down at his clipboard and Arthur knew it was going to be him before the man even read out his name. '3524357 Private Arthur Horton.'

He marched one step forward from his bunk. 'Sir.'

The RSM marched up to him, stiff as a pole, clipped moustache greased and edged perfectly. Holding the brown envelope up, he said, 'I'm sorry, son.'

Arthur took it and held it in his hand, feeling its crisp brownness like a knife designed to stab him through the heart with a few cutting sentences.

'You need to read it, son.'

'Now?'

The RSM nodded.

Arthur unsealed the back of the envelope, taking out the single sheet of thin onion-skin paper within.

The Home Office regrets to inform you of the death of your wife, Margaret Horton nee Elliot. STOP. And of daughter, Mary Horton, in an air raid in Salford on the night of 21 June. STOP. Please accept our heartfelt condolences. STOP.

CHAPTER TWENTY-SEVEN

August 28, 1941
Tanglin Barracks, Singapore

After receiving and reading his letter, he was marched in to see Major Tudor.

The officer was sitting behind the large desk in the Adjutant's Office. On his left stood RSM Whatmough, with Serjeant Murray on his right. In front of him were a large stack of papers and an unfinished crossword.

Arthur Horton stood to attention in front of the officer.

'Stand at ease.'

Arthur shuffled his feet open, his hands clasped behind his back. He didn't know what to think. Was Maggie alive? She couldn't be dead.

The major coughed, stroking his moustache. 'I believe you have received some disturbing news this morning, Horton.'

'Yes, sir. A telegram saying my wife has been killed in an air raid. But what I don't understand, sir, is the telegram says she died on June twenty-first, but that was over two months ago. Why have they only just told me?'

The major shrugged his shoulders. 'I don't know, Private. I suppose they must be frightfully busy in Manchester.' He looked down at his desk and picked up a sheet of paper. 'We have some more details, if you would like to hear them?'

'Of course, sir.'

The major coughed again, clearing his throat as he began to read. 'Apparently, your wife, Margaret, was visiting her mother in Salford Royal Hospital on Chapel Street. The Germans launched a raid on the docks and unfortunately some bombs went astray, killing your wife, her mother and your baby daughter…' He searched around for a name.

'Mary, she was called Mary.'

'You will address the officer as "sir",' RSM Whatmough ordered.

'Sorry, sir, my daughter was called Mary.'

'Apparently, she died in the raid too as did seven other patients and fourteen nurses.'

'Permission to speak, sir.'

Major Tudor looked up from his papers and eyed Arthur over his glasses.

'I'd like to apply for emergency leave to return to England. Compassionate leave, sir.'

Major Tudor sighed and took off his glasses. He rubbed his eyes and refocused them on the desk in front of him. 'You know the rules, compassionate leave is not permitted at present.'

'But my wife and daughter have just died, sir.'

He held his arms out to his sides. 'I'm afraid the rules are very clear. No compassionate leave for serving soldiers in a theatre of war.'

'But we're not at war here, sir.'

'This is still classed as a theatre of war, Horton.' He looked down at his papers and began shuffling them nervously. He refused to look at Arthur as he spoke. 'We have an important job to do, defending the Empire, defending the Singapore fortress. We can't have all the soldiers up and going when they feel like it, can we?'

'Well, no, sir,' he agreed reluctantly. 'But my wife and daughter have just died.'

'I'm sorry, Horton, there is nothing I can do. The rules are the rules.'

'I'd like to appeal to the colonel, sir, I'm sure he would understand.'

Major Tudor glanced sideways. 'You shouldn't disturb the colonel, Horton, he is a busy man and he would give you exactly the same decision as I have done. There is no compassionate leave at present.'

'But sir…'

'Permission denied.'

'But sir…'

'I said permission denied, Private.'

'I don't think you understand the situation.'

He looked down at his papers once more and said, 'Escort this man from my office, Serjeant Murray.'

'But sir…'

Serjeant Murray laid his hand gently on Arthur's shoulder. 'The interview is over, Private Horton.'

'You heard the officer, Horton. Permission is denied,' RSM Whatmough said.

He stared at Major Tudor, his shiny head bent over his paper like some balding monk.

'Atten-shun. About turn.'

Arthur couldn't force himself to salute. It was as if the backbone had been sucked from his body. His legs almost buckled before Serjeant Murray grasped him under the arm and whispered, 'Keep yourself together, Arthur.'

He stood up straight and marched out of the office.

He wasn't going to give Major Tudor the pleasure of seeing him collapse to the floor.

CHAPTER TWENTY-EIGHT

Thursday, December 12, 2019
Didsbury, Manchester

Jayne knocked on Alice's door as soon as she arrived back from lunch with Ronald.

After they had finished lunch, Jayne had spent a happy hour browsing in Waterstones and then went to Hotel Chocolat near the Royal Exchange to pick up some Rabot Estate Marcial 70% dark, a single estate chocolate she had always meant to try.

Marks and Sparks was next, for a ready-to-eat carbonara as she didn't feel like cooking, a couple of bottles of wine, some cakes for afternoon tea, as well as pouches of cat food for the perennially hungry Mr Smith. She would go to the local supermarket to buy his food in bulk tomorrow to make sure Alice had plenty in stock while she was gone.

The old lady opened the door immediately, holding up an unopened envelope. 'The postie delivered it after you'd gone, found it at the bottom of his bag.'

'It's the death certificate for your mum?'

'I think so.'

'If you're ready, GEDmatch should also have completed its data processing by now.'

'I can't wait.' Alice put on her coat and hurried across to Jayne's home.

The house was nice and warm with Mr Smith fast asleep in his favourite place – on the windowsill above the radiator. When they came into the kitchen he studiously ignored Jayne and went straight to Alice, winding himself around her legs as she stroked his back.

'That cat would sell his soul for an extra bowl of lamb's liver. He's shameless.'

'Don't speak like that, Jayne, he's such a lovely cat, so loving.'

'Not to me, he isn't. Spends his time either ignoring me or demanding food.'

'You'll miss Jayne while she's gone, won't you, Mr Smith?' Alice cooed as she stroked his fur.

The cat simply responded by purring loudly.

After making a cup of tea and feeding the insatiable Mr Smith, the two women settled themselves in front of the computer.

'The certificate or the DNA comparison first?'

Alice touched the envelope. 'I'd rather get it over and done with.'

'Right, here goes.' She opened the envelope, bringing out a single piece of paper and laying it out on the table so Alice could see.

It was headed *1941, Deaths in the district of Salford in the county of Lancashire.*

When and where died	Name	Age	Occupation	Cause of Death	Signature of Informant
21 June, Salford General Hospital	Margaret Horton nee Elliott	25	Factory Worker Metrovicks	Injuries from bombing of SGH 21/06/41	Stephen Carter Surgeon SGH

'What? I don't understand. She died from injuries in a bombing. She wasn't an alcoholic?'

Jayne quickly googled the date, adding the name of Salford General Hospital. 'It looks like there was a raid on Manchester that day and the hospital was bombed. She must have been one of the casualties.'

Alice was shaking her head. 'All these years I thought she was an alcoholic. Why did the Simpsons tell me she died from alcoholism?'

'I don't know. I suppose we'll never know. Perhaps they were told that by the children's home or by Margaret's aunt.'

'I've lived the last forty years believing I was given up for adoption because my mother loved drink more than me, but it wasn't true. She died in a German raid.'

Alice looked devastated, her whole life being relived and reassessed as she sat next to Jayne.

'Do you want to go on or shall we stop now?'

Alice shook her head. 'We must go on, we've come too far.' Then she stopped for a moment. 'I must go on.'

Jayne switched on the computer and logged into GEDmatch.

'Ready?' asked Jayne.

'I suppose so. There can't be anything worse to find out.'

'What we're going to do is run a one-to-many search on GEDmatch.'

Alice looked at the screen quizzically.

'Other people have loaded their DNA results into the GEDmatch system. If we do a one-to-many search it will show us if there are any matches to your DNA results from other people who have also submitted their DNA.'

Jayne entered Alice's kit number into the search field, set the filter for autosomal results with a limit of fifty and a cM size of seven. She then pressed enter and sat back.

'What's a cM when it's at home?'

'It's a unit of genetic measurement, describing how much DNA and the length of specific segments of DNA you share with other people. Put simply, the more centi-morgans you share with someone, the more closely you are related.'

The computer responded almost immediately with a table of numbers, names and email addresses.

Kit	Name (alias)	Email	Age (days)	Total CM	Gen
WCA3476	Henry	HenryXtan798@yahoo.com.sg	33	970.4	1.56
PCB2398	*norma	Norma @ hotmail.go	648	38.8	4.27
HAD0674	*famhis	Famhis678 @internet	343	37.5	4.29
FGS289	Louise	Llol@intermail	1006	36.1	4.31
GMP3256	Bob South	RSReas @ BTintermail	855	27.3	4.52
HJO7591	*Terry	Terrytoo @ interweb	2365	26.9	4,.53
BND 9768	Aiden Mac	Aiden6597 @ dis .co	478	26.9	4.53

Jayne stared at the screen and her eyebrows rose. 'Oh, that's interesting.'

'What does all this mean, Jayne?'

'It's a lot to take in at first glance, Alice, but there are just a couple of columns that are really important when you are looking for close relatives.' She pointed to the top result. 'This is the really interesting one. See the number of cM is high and the generation number is low?'

Kit	Name (alias)	Email	Age (days)	Total CM	Gen
WCA3476	Henry	HenryXtan798@yahoo.com.sg	33	970.4	1.56

'You've lost me, Jayne.'

'Reading from the left are the kit number, and a name or alias used by the person who uploaded the DNA results. The third column is an email address for that person.'

'So does that mean we can contact them?'

'Yes, but they may not reply. Some people do, others don't. The fourth column is the number of days since they first uploaded their DNA to the site. In your case, on the first line, Henry uploaded his kit thirty-three days ago. In GEDmatch terms, he's quite a noob.'

Alice raised her eyebrows and sighed.

'A noob or newbie,' Jayne explained. 'It means he hasn't been on the site long.'

'All these terms. It's a whole new world, Jayne.'

'Don't worry, it's easy enough once you get the hang of it. The next two columns are interesting for us. The rest of your results are relatively low in centimorgans but this person is very high at 970.4.'

'You said the more the more centimorgans I share with someone, the more closely they are related to me. So that means…?'

'All the others may be related to you but in the relatively distant past. But this person…' She pointed to the line with the kit number WCA3476,'…has 970 centimorgans which suggests quite a close relationship. The site gives an estimate of the number of generations between the two of you in the next column. It suggests a generational number of 1.9.'

'What does that mean?'

'In genealogical generations, you are zero, your parents are one, and an uncle or a nephew is approximately 1.5 and a grandparent is two.'

Alice pointed to the first line. 'So if this person has 970 centimorgans, what's his relation to me?'

'Ah, there's a lovely website that will help us with that.' Jayne opened a new tab and logged on to the Shared cM Project. 'This was made by a man called Blaine Bettinger.

He created a chart using the average and the range of cM numbers for each relationship . See, you are in the centre under SELF.' Jayne's pen followed the numbers across the chart. 'Well, according to the this, with a cM number of 970, this Henry is either your first cousin, great uncle, or first cousin, once removed. And if we go to the left, he could be your half-nephew, half uncle or half-cousin, once removed.

'It sounds awfully complex, Jayne.'

'The one thing to take away is that the science doesn't lie. This Henry is a close relation of yours. Now we have to work out the relationship.'

'How do we do that?'

'We send an email and hope he responds.'

'Can you do it?'

'Send the email?'

Alice nodded.

'No problem.' Jayne opened her Gmail account and typed in Henry's address.

'What's dot-s.g.?' Alice asked.

'A Singapore address. Perhaps he lives there now.'

She then began typing.

Dear Henry,

My name is Jayne Sinclair. I'm a genealogist representing my client, Alice Taylor. Recently, Alice uploaded her DNA data to GEDmatch and your result came up as a close match. We'd love to know how yourself and Alice are related.

Her GEDmatch number is GA4348B, if you would like to check the results.

Thank you in advance for your response.

Best regards,
Jayne Sinclair

'Shall I send it?

Alice sucked in her breath and finally nodded.

'It's on its way. I'll contact you as soon as he responds.'

'I can't wait to find out.'

CHAPTER TWENTY-NINE

November 23, 1941
Boat Quay, Singapore

For the last two months, Arthur had walked around in a sort of daze.

He was a ghost in a uniform; wearing his khaki, doing guard duty, saluting the officers and saying, 'Yes, sir. Three bags full, sir. Anything you say, sir.'

But his heart wasn't in it any more.

He'd thought about deserting, but where would he go? Stuck out on a tropical island, surrounded by jungle, miles away from Manchester – how could he get home from here?

He'd tried to find out about more about what happened to Maggie but nobody seemed to know anything. He'd sent telegrams to the authorities, but received no reply. He'd written letters trying to find out where she had been buried and who had paid for the funeral, but no information came back to him. He even wrote to his local MP, but nothing came of that except a mimeographed form letter two months later, explaining that the MP was unable to answer as he was busy with important war work.

All he had left now was a tiny photograph of his wife and baby, taken in a studio in Manchester. He would spend hours staring at the photo, not speaking to anyone, not saying a word.

The rest of the platoon began to avoid him. They had asked him to go out with them but he had turned them down again and again, until they stopped asking.

Only Ronnie still spoke to him. 'Arthur, mate, you can't mope around for the rest of your life. Come on out with us.'

'No, Ronnie. I'll stay here, get an early night.'

'Suit yourself, but you can't sleep your life away.'

The problem was he didn't sleep at all. Each night, he lay on his bunk staring up into the rafters of the barracks, watching the fan turn lazily in the moonlight. Thinking of Maggie, imagining her lying there next to him, her skin soft and warm, her breath hot against his chest.

He'd never seen his daughter. Never held her in his arms. never heard her cry. Never heard her laugh.

He'd taken to going into town on his own when he had time off. Just wandering the streets, having no plan and nowhere to go.

It was the only time he felt alive.

Last week, he had walked along the Singapore River, past Anderson Bridge and the godowns lining the waterway.

All around him was the hustle and bustle of purposeful activity. Rubber being loaded. Planks of wood being stacked. Bales of cotton being shifted. Machinery whirring. Waves lapping. Men grunting. And always, the staccato beat of bare feet against the pavement giving the city its rhythm.

Somehow, he had come to love the smell of the river. Its sharp odours of dying fish, old durian, human waste, sticky mud and – hanging over it all like a shroud – the stench of money.

He could see the fat Taipans in their white suits sweating as they gave the wrinkled coolies orders, mopping their brows and dreaming of the cool of indoors.

That day he walked down the river, alone as usual, nobody paying attention to him, when he came across a crowd of people.

He pushed to the front and at the centre was an old blind man. The storyteller was talking in a quiet, almost whispering voice, the sounds going up and down as he played with the melody of his story.

In his right hand, he held a hollow bamboo tube which he would occasionally bang on the pavement to emphasise some important point or to signal a change in character.

Arthur didn't understand a word he said, but he could follow his story and be entranced by the sound of his voice. It was like music without lyrics, without a melody, and without any chorus.

He looked around at the assembled faces. The children were sat at the storyteller's feet, the men and women stood with their arms folded, straining to hear every word, leaning forward, afraid to miss a sentence.

Occasionally, the crowd would laugh out loud. The storyteller must have told a joke or passed a witty remark. Arthur didn't understand. He wasn't supposed to understand.

After about ten minutes, a young boy came round holding a red tin cup. He jingled it in front of the watchers' faces, hoping to shame them into giving money.

Most gave something. Some walked off before he got to them, their meanness ensuring they didn't hear the rest of the story.

Then the young boy passed in front of Arthur, waving the cup in his face.

'You're supposed to give him something. It doesn't have to be much.' The voice came from a Chinese girl standing next to him.

'How much should I give?'

'Most of the others give ten cents, but as you're a Hung Mo Gwei, they will expect fifty cents from you.'

'Hung Mo Gwei?'

She laughed. A pretty laugh, like the tinkling of a piano. 'Literally, red-haired devil. It's the local name for foreigners. I think the first arrivals here must have been from Scotland and had ginger hair. We Chinese have no choice, our hair is always black.'

She touched the side of her short hair.

The boy rattled his red tin cup again.

Arthur dug into the pocket of his khaki shorts and found some coins, dropping them into the cup. The young boy bowed deeply and moved on to the next watcher.

'You gave him too much, over a dollar.'

'I didn't look.'

'Ah, you must be rich not to care about how much money you give away to blind storytellers.' She was teasing him. 'We don't get many soldiers here, most tend to stay around the dubious delights of Lavender Street or Great World, with the officers preferring their clubs or Raffles.'

'I like coming here, walking around this area.'

'Why?'

He thought for a moment. 'Honestly, I don't know. I think it's because everywhere seems so alive.'

'I know what you mean. My mother doesn't like me coming, she thinks it's not suitable for a young woman.'

'But you come anyway.'

She smiled again. 'I do, parents should be sometimes listened to but not heard.'

Around them the crowd was drifting away as the old man packed up his stand and grabbed his stick, leaning on the young boy's shoulder as they began their journey home.

'You speak good English.'

'Thank you, courtesy of Singapore Girls' School. What's your accent?'

'Manchester. It's where I'm from.'

'You must be one of the Manchester Regiment. I keep reading about your colleagues in the Straits Times. Last week, it was stealing cars.'

'They're bored, I think.'

She looked up at him out of the corner of her eye. 'But you… you, I think, are different.' She smiled again as if thinking of an idea. 'I have to go somewhere else, would you like to come?'

He checked his watch. 'I don't know, I have to be back in camp by six.'

She took his arms. 'Come on, it's not far.'

They walked away from the river through the narrow streets of Chinatown.

Above his head, long bamboo poles festooned with wet washing extended from windows. Street hawkers sold all manner of fresh and dried foods. A man carved a melon into neat slices with one sweep of his parang. Another shop had barrels full of different kinds of rice, and next to it, trays of dried fish and shrimps, stinking in the sun.

And always people, so many people.

As far as the eye could see there were heads, all intent on going about their business. Some were shopping. Others carrying two heavy loads balanced across their shoulders on a bamboo stick. Still more shouting their strange wares from the stalls lining the street.

Most just standing, watching and waiting.

The girl stopped and pointed to a temple set back from the road. 'See, I told you it wasn't far.' She stepped over the low entrance wall and into the first courtyard. Around him, women struggled to get past, not paying any attention to the figure in khaki.

As Arthur followed her into next courtyard, the smell of thousands of burning joss sticks assaulted his nose, reminding him here was the East, here was something foreign he neither understood nor needed to understand.

Ahead of him lay the main building of the temple, surrounded by a vast throng of worshippers.

'This is a very popular temple, particularly today. It's a good day to ask the gods for a favour. That's why I'm here.'

She strode across the courtyard, entering the main body of the temple. The garish altar, covered in a long-faded gold cloth and rows of statues of fierce red gods, dominated the rear walls.

In front of the main god – an evil-looking carved wooden piece about two feet high, with fierce glowing eyes, dark tattered hair and a streak of some dark gooey substance on his face – old women were bowing down, mumbling some incantation.

The air was stained with smoke from the joss sticks of the worshippers and from six huge cylindrical temples of incense that looked like immense mosquito coils. They were suspended from the ceiling, their smoke fighting with the rays of the sun to create dancing motes in front of his eyes.

Around him, the prayers of the worshippers merged to form one long drone of sound, like an infernal choir. For a moment, he wasn't certain whether this was heaven or hell.

The girl – he didn't even know her name – presented him with a bunch of joss sticks, gesturing to him to follow what she did.

She approached the altar, dipping the ends of the sticks into a flame and, clasping her hands together as if in prayer, swayed backwards and forwards, chanting in a strange tongue.

He wasn't sure what happened next. One minute he was standing watching the girl and the old women around her, the next he was with them on his knees in front of their smoke-eyed god.

Still the voices droned on around him, ignoring his presence, as if having an English soldier praying in their temple was the most normal thing on earth.

He felt the girl nudge him with her elbow. She stood up, bowed three times, then placed her still-burning joss sticks into a bronze ewer.

He followed her moves exactly, but bowing lower than she did.

Then she backed away, her head staring down at the floor, out through the other worshippers and into the relative quiet of the courtyard again.

'How do you feel?' she asked.

'Okay, I think. A little woozy, though.'

'It's the opium they use, it'll soon pass. You've just prayed to Guan Gong, the God of War, for good luck. I hope you get it.'

'I certainly need it.'

'I think you will when the Japanese get here.'

'The Japanese? Why would they come to Singapore?'

She shrugged her shoulders. 'Many reasons – rubber, tin and oil to name a few. But mostly, it is in their nature to conquer. Anyway, I have to go now. I hope you enjoyed yourself, Tommy.'

'My name's Arthur, not Tommy.'

'Arthur? Like King Arthur and the Knights of the Round Table?'

'Same name, different job title. It's Private Arthur Horton of the Manchester Regiment.'

She put out her hand. 'Nice to meet you, Private Horton.'

He took her hand in his, feeling the cool softness of her fingers. 'And your name is…?'

'Just call me Ah Mei.'

'And what do you do, Ah Mei?'

'I hope you never need my services, Private Horton. I'm a VAD at Alexandra Hospital.'

'A what?'

'A nurse working for the Voluntary Aid Detachment at the new military hospital.'

'Then, I also hope I never need your services too.'

She smiled and pointed over her shoulder. 'I need to go now. Can you find your own way back to the river?'

He looked past her. 'I think so.'

'You can pick up a trishaw back to camp there, but don't let it cost you more than thirty cents.'

He laughed.

'Anyway, nice to meet you, Private Horton… Arthur.'

'And you, Ah Mei.' Arthur paused for a moment before taking the plunge. 'Could we meet again? I'd love to understand more about Singapore.'

She smiled and stared over his shoulder for a moment, before answering. 'Why not? I'm here most Saturday afternoons, it's my day off.'

Then she turned and vanished into the crowd. He watched her go, wondering if they would ever meet again.

Two weeks later the war came to the island.

CHAPTER THIRTY

Friday, December 13, 2019
Didsbury, Manchester

Friday morning, and Jayne was up early. Outside it was still as dark as Bury black pudding, and a crust of frost rimed the grass of her small lawn. To think, in two days' time she would be on a plane heading to the warmth of a winter down under. She couldn't wait; the long dark days of December in Manchester were beginning to drain all the energy and life out of her.

She checked around the kitchen and in the hall. Mr Smith still hadn't returned from his nightly wanderings. Perhaps he was staying with Alice?

Jayne switched on the Nespresso machine and selected the strongest pod of coffee she had. As the machine buzzed, whirred and brewed, she booted up her laptop.

The first sips of strong coffee surged through her veins and she began to feel vaguely human again. Her email list was full of the usual promotional messages, adverts, and newsletters from websites she had clicked on long ago. Ronald had emailed her very late last night with a confirmation that he had found the Arthur Horton they were looking for.

Dear Mrs Sinclair,

Attached find the birth details of the correct Arthur Horton. He was relatively easy to find. It was just a question of going through the documents. Here's the volume and page numbers if you want to order the birth certificate.

JULY-SEPT 1917

Arthur Horton   Gormley   Manchester   4b 107

Would you like me to research into Mr Horton's family tree? Please let me know.

I remain your obedient servant,

Ronald

Her friend was as efficient as ever. She would check with Alice if he should proceed.

Scanning the rest of her inbox, about halfway down, she noticed an email from Henry Tan.

Hi there,

Great to hear from you and lovely to finally make contact through GEDmatch. You are the first person who has ever emailed me.

I checked Alice's GEDmatch number with my own and we do seem to have quite a close match.

A few details about myself. My name is Henry Tan and I was born in Singapore in 1970. I am Singaporean Chinese but it appears my grandfather was British. His name was David Stephens. Does Alice have anybody with that surname in her family tree?

I would love to get in touch with your client, is it possible to get her email? My mother died last year and that spurred me on to find out about my past and whether I have any relatives still living in your part of the world. I am so excited that I do.

*Best regards,
Henry*

'Well, that's a turn-up for the book,' Jayne said aloud. 'Alice is related to a Chinese man who comes from Singapore.'

As she was speaking to herself, Mr Smith squeezed his body through the cat flap, miaowing loudly.

'The conquering hero returns, finally. Have you spent the night with Alice or is the tabby at number nine taking up more of your time?'

The only answer was another loud miaow and a poignant stare at his empty bowl.

'Alright, alright, I get the message.' Jayne went to the fridge and took out one of his sachets of cat food: liver and onions in a meat sauce.

'You eat better than I do.' She spoke as she emptied the pouch into his bowl and added some dry cat food to it, stirring the lot together to mix it properly.

She had no sooner placed it on the floor, when he pounced and began eating.

'Must have been a busy night.'

Jayne went back to her laptop. She pulled up Alice's family tree but there was no one with the surname Stephens on it. She might have missed one of the relatives but she didn't think so. None of Alice's forebears had a lot of children. She checked the possible relations given the number of cMs that linked the two GEDmatch numbers.

She couldn't find any possible link.

Had she missed something important?

CHAPTER THIRTY-ONE

December 08, 1941
Tanglin Barracks, Singapore

Last night, war began.

They had been expecting it for a couple of days but had been given no news. But squaddies were always good at reading the signs; the officers no longer played golf in the afternoon. Stores were being distributed. Orders were given to break down and clean the Vickers. A company was sent out to their positions on the beach at Changi.

They all knew something was coming, it was just a question of when.

The when happened at 4.00 a.m. in the morning on December 8th. They had been sleeping in the barracks as usual when, from the direction of the city, they heard the drone of aircraft engines followed by the soft sound of muffled explosions.

They all rushed outside.

'Hear that sound? Those are bombs dropping,' said Ronnie.

A brief flare of orange light from the direction of the docks, followed a few seconds later by the sound of an explosion.

'Why are all the lights in the camp still on?' Harrison was pointing upwards towards the lamppost outside their barracks.

'They're still on in the city too.'

'You'd have to be blind to miss them from the air,' said Ronnie.

More explosions, more flares of light. Somewhere off in the distance the wail of a fire engine siren.

'What happened to the air-raid sirens?'

Nothing.

The aircraft engines were becoming duller now, moving away from the land. From their position, they could see an orange glow lighting up the sky from the area around the city and the docks.

Arthur remembered his walk through Chinatown with Ah Mei. All those people living cheek by jowl, how would they survive?

Serjeant Murray appeared from the direction of the serjeants' mess. 'Looks like it's started, lads. I've heard reports of landings in Thailand and Malaysia by the Japs.'

'We're at war, Sarge?' asked Harrison tentatively.

'That we are.' He slapped the young soldier on the back. 'If the Japs come here, we're going to have to push them back into the sea. Better get a good night's sleep, lads.'

'Are we going to our positions on the beaches tomorrow, Serjeant?' asked Arthur.

'Not us, Horton. According to Major Tudor, we've been tasked to help the civilian authorities clean that up.' He pointed to the orange glow haloing the city centre.

As he did, the drone of more bombers passed over their heads, going towards the city. Instinctively, they all ducked except Serjeant Murray, who stood up straight and unwavering.

'Why don't they turn out the lights, Sarge? Isn't there supposed to be a blackout?'

Murray shrugged his broad shoulders. 'Your guess is as good as mine, Harrison. Anyway, I'd get some shut-eye if I were you. By the looks of those fires, we're going to be busy.'

'What if the Japs bomb the camp, Sarge?'

'Well, Harrison, I suggest you follow standing orders and head for the bomb shelters.'

'But we don't have any, Sarge.'

'That's our second job tomorrow. You likely lads are going to start digging.'

A loud groan came from the platoon, accompanied by the sound of more explosions in the city.

'Looks like they're not interested in us tonight, Harrison. It's those poor sods who are getting the pasting.'

But none of them went back to sleep that night, they all stayed where they were. The orange glow in Chinatown gradually become brighter and brighter as fires took hold, fingers of flame occasionally reaching up to touch the stars.

Arthur stayed where he was, listening to the drone of the bombers as they passed overhead and the sound of the explosions as the bombs landed.

Was that what Maggie heard in the last seconds of her life?

CHAPTER THIRTY-TWO

December 10, 1941
Central District, Singapore

It was strange how dead bodies didn't look like people.

Arthur stood there, the roasting smell of flesh, cordite and wood barbecuing together assaulting his nostrils.

In front of him, one of the shop-houses had been hit directly by a bomb. The outside walls had collapsed, revealing the inside of a room. The wallpaper was still there. A picture of some long-forgotten ancestor. A small altar, joss sticks still burning next to a bowl of fruit. A charred rafter lying across a table, chairs still placed as if the occupants were about to start their evening meal.

Instead, the occupants, six of them, were stretched out at his feet. They looked like mannequins; waxy skin, dust-covered hair, sightless eyes. There were no marks of an explosion though, no loss of limbs. Just a terrible, sightless lack of life.

Arthur knew they had once been full of lusts, tears, love, hate and despair. Now they were twisted rags of clothes, discarded like some child's doll.

The ARP men had formed long lines to remove the piles of debris engulfing the shop-house. Searching for life, finding only more dead bodies. A young child here. A broken woman there.

Overhead the sirens were now wailing, heralding another bombing raid. The ARP wardens simply stood still for a few seconds, gazing up into the sky, shielding their eyes from the sun. Then it was back to work again, searching for the still living, listening for breath, fighting for life.

Arthur leant back on the open door of the three-tonner. They were at the corner of Middle Road where, before the war (how strange to think of a time before the war), they had searched for bargains in the shop-houses lining the road.

Now, the ARP searched for life in the same intense manner they had once burrowed deep into the oddments bins for cheap socks and shirts.

He tried to think back to a time before war. That was another life; a lazy, past life. War was the only thing existing now. The terrible beauty of war.

'Right, lads, I've just spoken to the head of the ARP. He says we can't be any more help here. He suggests we go back to camp and wait for instructions.' Serjeant Murray was looking as spruce and proper as ever, as if he had just stepped off a parade round after being reviewed by a general.

'Don't they need help with those?' Arthur indicated the bodies lying at their feet. An old couple, two young children and a man and his wife, still holding hands in death, her dress obscenely torn.

An ARP warden came over and looked at the couple. Slowly, he covered her face with his jacket. Then he walked away again to rejoin the line.

'Not our job, the mortuary men will move them eventually. Arkwright, you're driving. The rest of you, in the back.'

Ronnie was standing at the front of the lorry, eating a sandwich.

'There's nothing to be done here, Arthur. It's time we were off,' he said between mouthfuls of bread and egg.

Arthur took one last look at the bodies. Another had been added to the line by the ARP warden. A small body, that of a young child.

He climbed in the rear of the lorry, hearing the engine start and feeling the vibrations through the wooden floor.

Ronnie crunched the gears and they moved away from the smoke and the smells and the sounds of death.

War had begun.

CHAPTER THIRTY-THREE

December 17, 1941
East Coast Beach, Singapore

Their platoon had been sent out to the beaches at Changi after a few days of digging and constructing air-raid shelters in their barracks area and helping the ARP clear the bombed areas of the city.

They had been there almost a week already, lulled into a false sense of security by the gentle breezes through the palm trees, the lapping blue waters and soft sand. A welcome change from the fires, charred remains and dead bodies of the city.

'I think we'll listen to Frenesi now, Horton.'

'Yes, sir.' He picked up 'Artie Shaw and his Orchestra' and laid him down on the turntable, working the handle until the speed was correct, and lowered the needle.

Instantly, the tent filled with the clarinets and trumpets of the big band.

Major Tudor was sat in his armchair drinking tea and reading the Straits Times. The war wasn't going well. Last week, when they were still sleeping in their barracks, they heard about the loss of two big ships.

Arthur was sitting, having a cigarette with Ronnie Arkwright when he heard the news.

'The bastards have sunk the Repulse and the Prince of Wales.' It was Harrison doing his impression of a headless chicken as usual.

'Rubbish, they couldn't have done.'

'Heard it myself on the radio.'

'It's just Jap propaganda.'

But it wasn't, it was true. They found out later from the paper. 'Over 2,000 naval survivors – official,' said the headline. It was only when they read more did they learn the two ships had been sunk.

'Didn't we only watch your men sail out a few days ago with their flags flying, the sailors cheering and those big guns pointing toward the sky?' said Ronnie.

The article said the ships had been sunk somewhere off Malaya.

'They don't even know where the ships were sunk,' shouted Harrison.

Ronnie sighed. 'It's put like that so as not to reveal the position to the enemy.'

'But don't the enemy know where they are? After all, they have just sunk the things.'

Arthur remembered going drinking with a sailor from the Repulse. Proud of his ship he was. Proud of her guns and her speed, and her sleek lines. 'A racehorse with tiger's teeth,' he'd called her.

Well, now she was well and truly nobbled.

Arthur hoped he was still alive, though. A good man, from Dukinfield. Arthur didn't know what he was doing in the navy. Dukinfield was miles from the sea. Poor lad had probably never even seen the sea before he signed up. Except at Blackpool on Wakes week, maybe.

The situation from Malaya wasn't any better. He could see they were trying to put a positive gloss on what was happening, with talk of strategic retreats and fortified positions and consolidating the lines. But any old idiot who could read a map could see that the Japs were advancing on all fronts.

'Looks like Penang has fallen, Horton.'

He was dragged back to the present by the major's words. 'Yes, sir.'

Major Tudor stood up and went over to the map stretched out on his campaign table. He pointed to the island, on the west coast of Malaya. 'Looks like the Japs have turned our positions on the west and are advancing down the coast road in the east. If I were Percival, I'd hold them at one of the rivers. Either at Kampar or on the Slim River. That's where we'll stop the little blighters.'

'Yes, sir.'

Tudor put his pipe in his mouth and lit it, puffing out a small cloud of smoke.

'The east coast is a problem, though. It doesn't look good at all…' he said to himself.

'What would you like for lunch, sir? The mess sergeant says there are some sandwiches or tinned bully beef if you want something hot.'

'Sandwiches will be fine, and see if you can rustle up a fresh brew. Afterwards, go down to the beach and check on the positions with Serjeant Murray. Make sure the men have eaten.'

'Yes, sir.'

Arthur had resumed his cushy number as batman and runner for Major Tudor when they had moved out to guard the beaches. It was a quiet posting, far away from all the fighting. The radios had packed up pretty quickly in the salt air, so his main job was to look after the comfort of the major and to wander down to the pillboxes and slit trenches along the shoreline to check their reports.

As he walked to the officers' mess to get the major's lunch, the weather was hot and clear, with a blue cloudless sky streaked with contrails. Unlike last time, there were no Sumatras, no downpours and no high winds.

Only the occasional drone of bombers high above their heads going to attack the city disturbed the peace and indicated there was a war being fought.

He picked up the lunch from the mess corporal and a flask of hot tea, before delivering them back to the major.

'You'd better be off and check the posts. Tell everyone to sit tight until we get orders.'

'Yes, sir.'

Arthur stepped out into a beautiful Singapore day. In the distance, the screams of children and the raucous squawks of their scrawny chickens from a village of Malay huts.

He ran off in the direction of the beach posts. He did take this company runner job seriously, even though after a hundred yards, he was huffing and puffing worse than an old steam train.

Up ahead, he could see the tall towers of the Lloyd lights and beyond them the grey sea, the waves coming in one by one by one by one.

No more barracks now. No more canteen. No more film shows. No more beer. No more nights out at Great World. No more afternoon naps.

This was it. This was real. This was what they were paid to do. This was what they were meant to do.

It had been another mess, moving here. You would think the army had learnt its lesson over the years. But not a bit of it.

There wasn't any transport as usual, so they'd had to steal a truck from the engineers. Gave it back, of course. Major Tudor was in a right blue funk when he found out.

'It's just not cricket, Murray.'

'But sir, we needed to move the men, the lights and the generators out to the beach. How were we going to do it without transport?'

'Find a way, Serjeant. That's your job. But don't steal other units' equipment.'

'They weren't using it, sir. And anyway, we didn't steal it, just borrowed it for a short time. The keys were even in the ignition…'

'Well, Serjeant, now their CO has complained to our CO and he needs me to write a complete explanation before four p.m. this afternoon.'

Murray shrugged his shoulders like he always did when faced with the strange breed of man known as an officer. He had found a way to get them out there. With all the Vickers and the Lloyd lights and the generators and the ammo and the grub and even a few bottles of Scotch to keep them warm on the long nights looking out at the sea.

The beaches they had spent preparing for the last two years lay in front of them. The fields of fire calibrated. The range of the guns set at 400 yards. They had enough ammo for the Vickers to last them into the next century. Even the Lloyd light and its generator were working.

It always seemed strange to Arthur that here they were, staring out at the open sea, when the Japs were behind them in Malaya. But theirs not to reason why. The brass must know what they were doing.

'Horton, orders from the major?'

Serjeant Murray had appeared out of nowhere, surprising him. 'Not really, Serjeant, he just says to sit tight. He asked me to check if the men have eaten.'

'Cook came round half an hour ago with bully beef. Any news?'

'Not a lot. We're consolidating positions, apparently.'

The serjeant didn't answer, just stared out at the sea.

Arthur decided to ask the question. 'It's not going well, is it, Sarge?'

For once, Murray didn't rebuke him, just shook his head.

'I don't know, Arthur. I just don't know.'

CHAPTER THIRTY-FOUR

Friday, December 13, 2019
Didsbury, Manchester

When Alice came round later that morning, Jayne showed her the email from Henry Tan.

'I don't understand, Jayne. There aren't any people with the surname Stephens in my tree, are there? And I'm certainly not Chinese.'

'We haven't found anybody with the surname Stephens. When I read this, I went back over our research, looking to see if I had missed anybody, but it doesn't look as though I did.' Jayne scratched her head and stared at the laptop. 'The number of centiMorgans would seem to indicate we have missed a close relative.'

'But how could that be? The Simpsons told me I was an orphan when they adopted me, and the documents confirm it – both my mother and father died. And we didn't find any Chinese relations, did we?'

'Any Chinese ethnicity would have been picked up by the Ancestry DNA test.' Jayne frowned. 'We need to dig more. I'll ask Ronald to check it out. He's already discovered your father's birth date and index references.'

'That's quick.'

'It's Ronald, he's punctilious in his research. Shall we order the birth certificate?'

Alice nodded.

Jayne went back into GRO and completed the form. 'It will arrive after I leave, but if you have any questions, you can send me an email or message Ronald directly. I'll ask him to check if Arthur had any brothers or sisters. They may have been responsible for the closeness of your relationship with Henry Tan. But normally the centiMorgan number wouldn't be so high. It just doesn't make sense.' Jayne scratched her head. 'By the way, I checked and unfortunately the Museum of the Manchester Regiment is closed at the moment. It used to be in Ashton Town Hall along with the local studies library, but they are remodelling the Town Hall.'

'That's a shame, I was looking forward to going there.'

'But not to worry, they transferred all the archives for the regiment to the Local Studies Archive and it's now just around the corner on Cotton Street.'

'That's a good name for that area.'

'I rang them this morning and booked a space for both of us.'

'What are we waiting for? Let's get going.'

'Before we do, you know we might not find anything? We certainly won't find records for your father. World War Two service records are still kept by the Ministry of Defence.'

'I know, Jayne, but if we don't look, we won't find.'

'True. Before we go, shall we respond to Mr Tan?'

'I'd like to find out more from him. Do you think we could ask for more information, like a picture or a wedding certificate for his grandmother?'

Jayne smiled. 'If we don't ask, we won't get. I'll also give him your email so you two can chat directly. Is that okay?'

'Not a problem, I'd love to hear from him. But I'm not very good with emails. The hands don't type so quickly these days.'

Jayne quickly sent a message to Henry Tan.

Dear Henry,

Thank you for replying so quickly, it was great to hear from you.

Alice would love to get an email from you. Her address is alicesmith380742@gmail.com.

Could you give us any more information about yourself and your family? It would be great to work out how you were related as, through GEDmatch, it does seem to be quite close. Alice was told she was an orphan and you are the first living relative she has found in her family history search.

Thank you in advance for your answers.
Have a great weekend.

Best regards,
Jayne Sinclair, on behalf of Alice Taylor

Alice rubbed her hands. 'This is so exciting, Jayne. I've learnt more about myself in the last two weeks than I have in the last seventy years.'

'Let's go and see if we can find out more.'

CHAPTER THIRTY-FIVE

January 17, 1942
Tanglin Barracks, Singapore

The lads were stretched out beneath the coconut trees when Harrison began to sing.

'It was Christmas Day in the harem
The eunuchs were standing around,
And hundreds of lovely ladies were stretched on the ground.
When in strode the big, bad Sultan,
Surveying his marble halls, saying
"What do you want for Christmas boys?"
And the eunuchs answered...
Tidings of comfort and joy, comfort and joy,

Oh, tidings of comfort and joy.'

The last two lines were sung by everybody as Harrison continued on with the song, each verse becoming bawdier and bawdier.

Arthur was sitting slightly apart from the others, smoking a cigarette. He already served Major Tudor his Christmas lunch. The mess serjeant had done his best with what was available; tough chicken, boiled carrots and some sort of Chinese vegetable they'd bought off the local villagers. There had been Christmas pudding though. Apparently, the stores had three tons of the stuff.

The same lunch had been delivered to the squaddies down at the beach and now everybody was relaxing, full of village chicken, Chinese vegetables, Christmas pudding and good cheer.

'Give us another song, Tommy,' shouted Ray Teale as Harrison finished his song.

'Maybe later, when I've had a rest. Pass the bottle, Ray.'

Ronnie had managed to buy three bottles of warm Tiger from the villagers and they shared these around as they sang.

'I could murder a pint of Boddies right now,' said Ted Rogers, 'we always used to go down the pub on Christmas Day, come home at 3 pm, well leathered and then eat whatever mum had made. Then after a quick kip, we'd be out again to round the night off. I used to love Christmas, me.'

Arthur thought back to his childhood. Christmas spent in bed trying to keep warm. His mum in the kitchen hunched over a dying fire, stirring the constant pot of tea she kept stewing. Dinner was a slice of bread and dripping and, if they were really lucky, a bar of Fry's chocolate as a treat.

He always remembered the smooth, sugary taste of the chocolate. He used to hold it as long as he could in his mouth, waiting for the chocolate to melt over his teeth, before he swallowed, feeling the softness melt down his throat.

That bar of Fry's used to last hours on Christmas Day. It was the only thing that kept him warm.

Harrison had started singing again. Another bawdy song, this time involving reindeers and elves.

Arthur stopped listening to the words and thought about Maggie and Mary. He'd never had a Christmas with them. He'd never see Maggie in the silks he had sent her. Never see Mary in her little Chinese dress. Never see either of them again.

They were dead and he was stuck out here in the back of beyond.

Tears began to sting his eyes and he quickly wiped them away with his sleeve before anybody saw.

Arthur stood up and brushed the sand off his trousers.

'Going back to Major Tudor?' asked Ronnie.

'He needs his afternoon tea, drinks gallons of the stuff.'

'Merry Christmas, Arthur,' he said gently, adding, 'Don't think about home, not today.'

'What else is there to think about?'

And with that he strode off back to the command post, the voices of his friends gradually fading away until he could hear them no more.

Christmas Day 1941. He couldn't wait for it to end.

CHAPTER THIRTY-SIX

January 17, 1942
Tanglin Barracks, Singapore

Spit and polish. Spit and polish. If he had to do this webbing one more time, he'd throw the stuff against the wall.

Arthur checked out the other squaddies. They were relaxing on their bunks; some reading, some sleeping and some just staring up into the rafters. The only difference from before was that they were all tanned now. Three weeks at the beach out in Changi would do that for anybody.

At least they were back in camp and not living in tents any more. The brass had put another company out on the beach, watching the sea. Poor blighters.

The lads were still taking a beating in Malaya. The papers were full of strategic retreats and well-organised withdrawals. Arthur was no soldier but even he knew that if you were retreating you were not winning the battle, whatever they might say at HQ.

Serjeant Murray strode into their barracks. A few of the lads half-heartedly rose from their bunks.

'At ease,' Murray shouted. 'His lordship would like to see you, Horton.'

'What is it now?' Arthur mumbled under his breath, putting the webbing down on a sheet of newspaper with a large headline shouting 'Strategic retreat at Slim River. Kuala Lumpur under threat'.

He laughed. Major Tudor had told him that KL fell to the Japs nearly a week ago.

'Hurry up, Horton, the major wants to see you now.'

'A woman's work is never done,' said Ronnie out of the corner of his mouth. 'Perhaps he needs his underpants ironed.'

Arthur ignored them and stood up, adjusting his uniform and grabbing his tin hat from the table at the side of his bunk.

'At the double, Horton.'

They both ran down to the canteen, which now doubled as an operations room.

'Ah, Private Horton, the radios are on the blink again. I need you to take this message up to Command on Fort Canning.' Major Tudor handed across a tightly folded message sheet.

'Do get a move on, it's quite urgent. You can use Corporal Anderson and the Ford.'

A surly-looking corporal was standing nearby.

'Right, sir, am I to wait for a reply?'

'Only if they want to give you one.'

'Yes, sir.'

He saluted and marched out, followed by the corporal.

'We'll hurry to Fort Canning, and then I have to pick up something on the way back from the market at Cold Storage.'

'Right, corporal.'

He started the engine and they were off. Down Holland Road, past the Botanical Gardens, to the bend at the top of Orchard Road.

Arthur stared out of the windows. There was little sign of bombing out in the suburbs. It was the docks and the built-up areas that had taken more of a pounding.

They accelerated down Orchard Road. Shop-houses lined either side, selling anything and everything. It was only when they reached Dhoby Ghaut that it became more crowded with buildings. Here there were a few more signs of bombing, and an ARP warden directed them around a burst water main next to a collapsed house, the ruins still smoking.

'Rather them than me,' said the corporal coldly.

The same dark sheets that Arthur had seen before were stretched out in front of the building, the shape of bodies lying beneath them.

They drove up to the road to Fort Canning Hill and were forced to stop near the top by sentries.

'No entry,' one of them announced gruffly.

'But I have a message for Command from Major Tudor.'

'I don't care if you have a message from the King, no vehicles allowed in.'

'I'll park here and wait for you, Horton. But don't take too long.'

'Yes, corporal.'

Arthur stepped out of the car into the heat of the afternoon and began to trudge up the hill. It wasn't that steep but still he felt his lungs gasping for air. Since Maggie had passed away he'd been smoking far too much, lighting one after another after another like an Indian chief with too much to say.

He turned right, walking past the main building to get to the Command Post in the rear. He'd been there before, delivering messages. HQ Company of the Manchesters had the task of guarding it and he saw Tommy Halford and Wesley Valentine standing smartly to attention, stiff as pokers in the hot afternoon sun.

'How do?' he said to Halford.

'Oh, you're back again, Arthur,' he answered. 'You'd better be quick, there's a bit of a flap on.'

Just then a whole pride of colonels walked out from the dark entrance. Halford, Valentine and Arthur snapped to attention and whipped out the smartest salutes at the assorted array of brass hats and red tabs.

They ignored them.

One rabbit-like man brought up the rear. A small caterpillar of a moustache, a sharp angular nose, jug-handle ears and a small smiling mouth all led down to the absence of a chin. His uniform was sweat-soaked, damp with long hours of tedious discussions and debates.

He walked straight past Arthur on his own, his eyes darting from wall to wall, soldier to soldier. Finally, he remembered to return the salute and did so with a casual tip of his swagger stick on his topee.

It was only the commander of the Allied Forces, Lieutenant-General Percival, waiting for his car. His shoulders were slumped, his body sagged. Only his eyes jerked around, constantly watching, constantly looking for something that obviously wasn't there.

The staff car arrived and, like an old man, he climbed into the back alone.

'Was that who I think it was?'

'Yeah, our Lord and Master.'

'Does he always look so shattered?'

'Sometimes he looks worse. I don't think it's going well, Arthur, not well at all.'

He left Halford and walked down the slope and underground, through the blast doors of the Battle Box.

A row of electric lights guided his way for about fifty yards before he reached another blast door painted green. A soldier checked his ID and opened the door. A wind of stale air, even staler sweat and the indescribable smell of fear rushed out at him.

'Get a bloody move on so I can close the door,' said the soldier on guard.

Arthur stepped inside, holding his breath. On the left the constant jingle of phones and operators sang like a chorus from some ancient opera. He walked straight on to find the brigade major, who was attached to the general commanding the Singapore Garrison. First left, second right, second left.

He passed an open ops room. A group of WAAFs were moving tiny wooden shapes across the top of a map of Singapore.

'Twenty-seven bandits at 13,000 feet,' one of them intoned in a peculiarly mechanical voice into the microphone. Then she listened. 'No, no, no – Tengah. Twenty-seven bandits at 13,000 feet heading east south-east. Repeat, east south-east.'

Around her, people shouted into other microphones, phones rang, men swore, officers ran in with more messages.

In the corner, two men lay sleeping on miniature camp beds. They looked peaceful, their faces blessed with the sort of innocence that only comes from sheer exhaustion.

Arthur found Major Davies and handed him the message. He took it without looking up.

'Any reply, sir?'

'No,' was the curt answer.

He left the way he had come. Dodging the runners in the corridors, ignoring the smells of rotten food, stepping over the sleeping bodies and out into the bright, bright light of a beautifully sunny Singapore day.

He felt like he had been let out of prison.

CHAPTER THIRTY-SEVEN

Friday, December 13, 2019
Ashton Local Studies Archive, Manchester

Ashton-under-Lyne was in the eastern half of Greater Manchester, part of that long tranche of mill towns that reached out with their iron fingers into the foothills of the Pennines. The local studies archive was located in the back of an old building which proudly proclaimed in carved golden letters in the granite that it was the 'Heginbotham Technical School and Free Library', opened in 1891.

As they entered, Alice whispered, 'I love these places.'

'I think this one was the old Ashton Library, part of the desire to educate people back in the day.'

'I spent my youth in libraries. There's a certain smell about them that takes me back all those years ago.'

'Me too. I know what you mean, it's almost as if you can smell the learning.'

Jayne strode up to the librarian's desk. 'I wonder if you could help us?'

The woman looked up and smiled.

'We've booked two seats and would like to look into the Manchester Regiment archives.'

'And your name is?'

'Jayne Sinclair.'

The librarian checked the reservation page on her computer. 'Your down in the book. The local studies section is around the back of this building. Just go out the door, take the first left and it's on your left about eighty yards down.'

'Thank you.'

They followed the instructions and found themselves standing outside a modern brick extension to the library. A large sign indicated it was the Tameside Local Studies and Archive Centre, opposite a car and motorhome sales forecourt.

They entered through a nondescript green door and walked up to the counter, repeating the information they had given earlier.

'I'm afraid the archivist is off today, but I'm happy to help,' said the librarian.

'We're particularly looking for information regarding one of the soldiers in the Manchester Regiment, an Arthur Horton, who served somewhere between 1936 to 1942.'

The woman frowned. 'I'm afraid we don't keep the service records of individual soldiers here…'

'We think he was my father,' interrupted Alice.

The woman smiled again. 'But we do have some records for the Manchester Regiment during that period. The First Battalion was based out in Singapore from 1938…'

Jayne glanced at Alice.

'…while the Second and Fifth Battalions were with the British Expeditionary Force in France, escaping from Dunkirk.'

'I think we're more interested in the First Battalion, the one based in Singapore.'

'Right.' The librarian stared at her computer. 'I'm just checking the catalogue. We have the Roll of Honour for the Regiment in World War Two.'

'What's that?'

'It's a list of people who died whilst serving,' answered Jayne.

'There are the enlistment books, which are catalogued by army number or surname. They might be useful. Plus, quite a few of the serving soldiers or their families have donated personal records and belongings to the archives.'

'Could we look at the Roll of Honour and the enlistment records? I'd also like to take a look at the catalogue.'

'I'll get the first two. You can check the catalogue on the computer over there. Good luck with the search.'

Jayne and Alice took their bags to the table. Logging on to the catalogue, Jayne went through the listing of items linked to Manchester Regiment and Singapore. Most were newspaper cuttings or personal papers. She created a list of possible items which she thought might be relevant.

'Why did we just ask about the First Battalion and not the others?'

'I think it's too much of a coincidence that Henry Tan is your closest match and he lives in Singapore. My bet is that your father was with the First Battalion out there.'

'But what if he wasn't, Jayne?'

'Then we expand our search, but if we don't focus at the beginning we'll simply be overwhelmed by the magnitude of the task.'

Alice frowned. 'Looking for a needle in a haystack?'

'Not that bad. At least we have some clues to work with. The Singapore link seems important to me. Last night I researched the fall of the city during World War Two. Churchill called it "the worst disaster and largest capitulation in British history". And the Manchesters were in the thick of it, being based there from 1938. Nearly 100,000 troops surrendered to an invading force of Japanese. Afterwards, many were forced to work on the death railways in Thailand.'

The librarian appeared next to them, interrupting Jayne.

'Here are the enlistment books for the period 1920 to 1942. These ones are listed by regimental number, and these ones by surname. I'll bring you nominal rolls and the Roll of Honour in a jiffy.'

Jayne gave her the short list of numbered records she had chosen.

'You'd like these as well? It'll take me a while to find the oral history recordings, but the others are shelved in the regimental section. I'll get them for you.'

Jayne picked up the enlistment books catalogued by surname and quickly found G–J. 'Are you ready, Alice?'

'As ready as I'll ever be.'

Jayne opened the book and found that each individual's surname had been handwritten, along with a printed service number that always seemed to start with a 35. She turned over the pages, looking for Arthur Horton's name.

'Hooton, Hornblower, Horner… Horton. Here he is.' She pointed at the entry.

3524357 Horton, Arthur. Pte.

Jayne ran her finger along the entry line. 'There are more details. He enlisted on the twenty-second of March 1937 and was aged twenty, giving his trade as clerk.'

'That's him, the age is correct,' said Alice.

'In a different handwriting, there is a next of kin listed and it's Margaret Elliott as his wife. It's definitely your father. There's one other record. It says he was transferred to the First Battalion and disembarked for Singapore in 1938.'

'So that's why he wasn't in Manchester when I was born. Anything else, Jayne?'

'That's it, I'm afraid.'

Alice lowered her head towards the book. 'I've waited for so long to find out who he was, it's a bit overwhelming.'

'We can stop if you want, Alice.'

'No. We're here now, let's carry on. What's next?'

'Shall we look at the nominal roll? It might tell us what happened to him.'

This time the soldiers weren't listed by surname, but by company and serial number. Jayne went back to the enlistment book and made a note of Arthur's number and rank.

'Ready, Alice?'

This time the older woman simply nodded.

Jayne opened the book.

CHAPTER THIRTY-EIGHT

January 27, 1942
Yishun, Singapore

All the regiment's radios had finally packed it in. They had known all about this since the first exercise in 1939, the heat and humidity affected the valves. Not very useful when they were trying to tell HQ they'd seen a whole formation of Jap bombers heading straight for the city.

Anyway, the major had heard on the grapevine there were some replacement sets available, so he told Arthur and Ronnie to get up to Yishun quickly and get them before the rest of the army heard about it.

Well, they were too late.

They had driven with Corporal Anderson from Tanglin up past Adam Park and on to Thomson Road. Of course, they had kept their eyes peeled for any Jap bombers or fighters prowling about. But that day they seemed to be having the afternoon off. Maybe it was the Emperor's birthday or Japanese Christmas or whatever.

Well, it didn't really matter because they had a lovely clear run. They were driving down Thomson Road, getting close to the camp, when they saw a long line of three-tonners queuing up outside the gates.

'It looks like half the army is after them radios,' said Ronnie.

'We'd better join the queue. Let me off here and I'll go and see what's happening.' Arthur jumped down from the running board of the three-tonner and ran to the front of the camp.

There were about five drivers arguing with a supply sergeant.

'I know, but orders is orders.'

'But don't be a daft chough. We're here now and you've got the radios, right?'

'Right, but my commanding officer's orders says we can only start issuing them at oh-nine-hundred hours tomorrow.'

'Get the wee radge to change his mind.' This came from a small Gordon Highlander wearing a kilt.

'Listen, chief, if I don't get the radios ma sergeant is gonna have ma guts for garters.' This was from another Scot to the left.

'Orders is orders. Come back at nine tomorrow.'

'Ooh, away to hell, we're no' going back without them.'

It was then they first heard the sound. A drone of an engine, and then another, and another, getting louder and louder. Immediately, all of them looked up at the sky, searching for the source of the noise.

It was the Scot who spotted them first.

Arthur looked to where he was pointing. Three small Japanese planes were banking round about a mile away. He could see the round red circles against white painted on the green of their wings. He even imagined he could see the small grinning eyes behind the goggles of the pilot.

Then the planes straightened out and began to dive directly towards them.

Arthur started to run back towards Ronnie and the car. All around him he could hear shouts and screams as men dived for cover or fought to get out of the comfortable seats of their trucks and into the safety of the ditch.

He heard the sound of bullets exploding around his feet.

A scream. A shout. A truck exploding. And then the whine of the engine as a plane passed over. It almost felt as if he could reach out and touch its undercarriage.

Then more bullets exploding on the ground. He saw a ditch to his right and dived in, burying himself deeper, deeper, deeper into the mud.

The two other planes passed over his head. He waited for the crump of the exploding bombs.

He waited, waited, waited.

Nothing.

He looked up over the top of the ditch. Seven or eight bodies lay back on the road to the camp gate. He could see the small Gordon Highlander lying motionless on the tarmac, his kilt around his waist.

The supply sergeant was still guarding the gate but now he lay against the wire mesh, his left leg a tangled mass of bone, sinew and blood, stretched awkwardly beneath him.

Arthur looked down the long line of trucks. One or two were burning, the rest were deserted, their doors thrown open.

The Jap planes were banking round again, coming in for another run.

Then he saw him, sitting on the roof of the car, Lee Enfield pinned tightly to his shoulder, aiming at the oncoming Jap planes.

'Ronnie, get out of there,' Arthur shouted.

He looked back at the Jap planes. The first one was firing now, its bullets throwing up plumes of dirt on the left.

He looked back at Ronnie. He was calmly working the bolt of his rifle, aiming and then firing. The Jap planes still came on, for some reason concentrating their fire on the seated soldier.

He never flinched, calmly aiming and firing his Lee-Enfield.

Then, for no reason, the Jap planes broke off their attack and peeled away to the right, back towards the north.

Arthur climbed out of the ditch, mud clinging to his uniform, and walked back to where Ronnie was still sitting on top of the car.

'Frightened them off, I did.' A slight pause for effect. 'Where's the corporal? Let's get those radios before the rest of this mob wake up.'

CHAPTER THIRTY-NINE

February 1, 1942
East Coast Beach, Singapore

Arthur stood looking out across the sand to the point where the waves greeted the shore. The wind was blowing through coconut palms, the trunks creaking as they swayed before its strength.

Down on the beach, at the edge of the water, he could still see the wooden poles they had built guarding the beach. One or two had already fallen over. How much sweat and graft had they put in? Now they were useless: a waste of time, energy and wood.

He heard footsteps behind him.

'How's it going, Arthur?'

A cigarette appeared next to his face, held by nicotine-stained fingers.

'Okay, Ronnie.'

He took the cigarette and lit it from the dimp handed to him.

'Any news?'

Arthur was still the company runner for Major Tudor and, as such, found out everything before anybody else.

'The siege has started, that's what the messages are saying. I was talking to a corporal up at HQ, apparently the Japs pushed the Argylls back onto the island yesterday. They crossed the Causeway with a lone piper playing "Highland Laddie".'

'Is help going to arrive soon?'

Arthur shrugged his shoulders. 'Major Tudor seems to think so but I'm not so sure. I mean, it's not like another siege of Ladysmith. There's miles of ocean between us and any rescue. He thinks we'll fight to keep the Japs off the island.'

Ronnie looked back towards his sandbagged position. The muzzle of a Vickers machine gun was poking out between some palm fronds.

'How long are we supposed to last out?'

'To the last man, according to Churchill.'

'He always was careless with other people's lives. My dad was at Gallipoli in the first war with the Lancashire Fusiliers. Never spoke about it, but he lost a lot of good pals at that hellhole.'

Ronnie lit another cigarette. 'I've been doing a lot of thinking while staring out to sea, in between the sweating. You know, in the three years we've been here, I've never actually fired that Vickers. It's just like new, fresh out of its crate, the oil from the factory coating its levers and the stamped letters of its makers as clear as tram tracks on the side of its barrel. I'd love to fire it. To feel its jerk and stutter. To watch the long belt of 303 bullets vanish into the machine, to emerge hot and deadly out of the spout. To watch them hit home, lines of charging Japs falling like waves vanishing in the sand.'

A long inhale of the cigarette followed by a cloud of smoke embracing his face. 'It always amazes me the commandment says "Thou shalt not kill", but we men have always been able to add a few exceptions to that simple instruction. Thou shalt not kill unless the person is of another religion. Thou shalt not kill unless it has been sanctioned by a higher authority. Thou shalt not kill unless it is the duly ordained revenge of the law. Thou shalt not kill unless one has been paid to do so by His Majesty's Government…'

'We're soldiers, Ronnie, it's our job.' Arthur said been his breath.

His friend stopped talking, smiled and then patted him on the shoulder. 'That we are, Arthur. We're Manchesters, the best bloody regiment in the British Army. If Tojo or his mates dare to set foot on this beach, we'll throw him back all the way to Nipland or wherever he comes from.'

Arthur smiled back.
But he wasn't so sure.
Not any more.

CHAPTER FORTY

February 4, 1942
East Coast Beach, Singapore

'Looks like the city is getting a bit of a pasting.'

Arthur, Ronnie and Harrison were sitting on the beach looking west towards downtown, smoking their Capstans. Beneath their feet the waves lapped on the shore, adding a background sound to the occasional thumps, bangs, rumbles and thuds coming from the city.

Lights flashed orange and yellow against the night sky, occasionally brilliant, at other times a dull glow. The drone of the bombers heading towards the city had been almost continuous for the last hour.

Arthur was on his nightly rounds on behalf of Major Tudor, checking on the posts arrayed in front of the shore. They were on an alert but still found time to take a break from the stuffiness of their positions.

Harrison pointed towards the north. 'There are more flashes over at the Causeway. Looks like artillery to me.'

'What would you know about artillery, Harrison?' Ronnie said roughly.

'Me dad, he was in the trenches. Said he could handle the rats and the rotten food and the lice, but when the guns went off that's when he was on his knees praying for his soul.'

'He was a religious man?' asked Arthur.

'Nah, but he said when the shells were landing all around them, everybody in his dugout discovered God.'

'What do you think it means, Ronnie?'

'Looks like the Japs are preparing to attack, using artillery to soften up the defences. Luckily it's on the other side, not on ours.'

'You reckon they'll come here?'

'Maybe, maybe not.' Ronnie took another long drag from his cigarette and flicked the end off into the darkness where it glowed for a second before finally going out.

'It's not looking good, is it?' asked Harrison.

'Major Tudor thinks help is on its way. All we have to do is stick it out for a few more days till the reinforcements arrive.'

A loud explosion illuminated the sky about a mile off to their right, close to Katong. They all flinched, covering their heads – all except Ronnie, of course. He just sat there smoking his Capstan, as unperturbed as ever.

'A stray one, that was close,' said Harrison.

'Too close for me.' Arthur stood up, dusting the sand off his tunic.

'I reckon I should get back now, the major will be waiting.'

Ronnie remained seated. 'Look after yourself on the way back.' He lit another cigarette, the match glowing in the dark in a brief respite from the bombing. 'Don't do anything stupid.'

At that moment, Arthur knew it was all over. He didn't know how he knew, perhaps it was the flashes in the sky or maybe the deep sense of despair that seemed to emanate from every bone in Ronnie's body. But Arthur knew, and strangely enough, he didn't care. Not any more. Their world was finished. Maggie and Mary were dead, there was nothing left for him any more. Just these men, this platoon, his company and the regiment.

'Look after yourself too,' he finally answered. 'See you soon.'

'Not if I see you first,' replied Ronnie, looking up at him with a half-smile on his face.

They would see each other again often over the next three days.

But in the end, Ronnie would be dead.

CHAPTER FORTY-ONE

Friday, December 13, 2019
Ashton Local Studies Archive, Manchester

Jayne took a deep breath and opened the book. The catalogue had been clear in its description.

The nominal roll of the 1st Battalion Manchester Regiment showing the location and movement if alive, and date, cause, and place of death if dead. Also contains information regarding the movements, where known, of those held as prisoners of war (POWs) at Changi by the Japanese following the Fall of Singapore.

'If Arthur had served in the Manchester Regiment in Singapore this roll would give his details. The book was laid out by company and the men were listed in alphabetical order.'

Jayne began with company A, following the list of names with her fingernail. She was surprised how many had died. It looked as if almost half had passed away. Most had a date and place handwritten next to their rank and name.

Service Number	Name	Rank/ Unit	Date of Death	Cause of Death	Place
3517231	Dawson M	Pte/ MR	07.03.43	Cholera	Rin Tin Camp, Thailand
3528978	Stubbs T	Pte/ MR	15.07.43	Typhoid	Nikha Camp, Thailand
3532376	Hart S	Pte/ MR	23.03.42	Enteritis	Changi Camp, S'pore
3519087	Collins F	Pte/ MR	04.04.45	Malaria	Kinkseki Camp, Formosa
3520346	King P	Pte/ MR	15.11.43	Dysentery	Nakhon Pathom, Thailand
3539933	Lowe E	Pte/ MR	25.05.43	Dysentery	Nam Chong Yai, Thailand
3526004	Swazy T	Pte/ MR	07.11.44	Indigestion	Nikha Camp, Thailand

'So many passed away, Jayne.'

'Most of the names seemed to be in Thailand. They were obviously part of the prisoners of war sent to build the death railway. Many POWs died, a lot of them from Manchester.'

'It looks so sad, Jayne. I don't know if I want to see any more'

'I understand, but if we don't look now, you will never know.'

Alice nodded her head. 'I've waited so long, it's time I found out.'

It wasn't until they reached Company D that they found Arthur Horton's name.

Service Number	Name	Rank/Unit	Date of Death	Cause of Death	Place
3524357	Horton A	Pte/MR	15.02.42	Wounds	Alexandra Hospital, S'pore

Alice gripped Jayne's hand. 'It's him, my father.'

'The service number and rank matches. I'm so sorry, Alice.'

The old woman bowed her head and then slowly raised it. Her eyes were glassy when she spoke. 'It's silly, I never knew who he was but I can't help but be emotional. It's as if he's reaching out from the grave to talk to me.'

'If I remember my research correctly, Singapore surrendered to the Japanese on the same day, February 15th, 1942. It looks like he was wounded in the fighting and then died later in hospital.'

'At least he didn't have to go through the horrors of the death railway in Thailand like the others.'

Jayne paused a moment before saying, 'Would you like to see his grave site?'

Alice frowned. 'You know where it is?'

Jayne took out her laptop. 'If he died during the war, the Commonwealth War Graves Commission will have kept a record of his death and created a memorial for him somewhere. All we have to do is search on their website.'

She went into the CWGC website and entered Arthur's name in the search area. Immediately his details came up.

There were two records that appeared on the screen, both with the same details: a grave registration and a Schedule A form.

'Shall we download his certificate from the Commission?'

Alice simply nodded.

Jayne pressed the button and a full colour PDF appeared on her screen.

In Memory Of Private

ARTHUR HORTON
Service Number: 3524357

1st Bn., Manchester Regiment who died
on 15 February 1942
Remembered with Honour
KRANJI WAR CEMETERY
Coll. Grave 38. D. 43

Immediately as she saw it Alice began to sob. Jayne put her arm around the old woman's shoulders, holding her as tightly as she could.

'Shall we go for a cup of tea?'

'What about the records?' Alice whispered through her tears.

'They can wait. They've waited nearly eighty years, after all. They'll still be here when we come back.'

CHAPTER FORTY-TWO

February 10, 1942
Changi Beach, Singapore

The waves were still flowing onto the beach, past the shore defences.

Arthur had been watching them for the last hour after delivering his message from Major Tudor.

'What did you say?' shouted Ronnie.

Serjeant Murray was staring right at him.

'It's... orders,' Arthur stammered.

'Orders from who?'

'F-f-from Major Tudor.'

'You mean to say after two years of building these pillboxes, stringing out this wire and erecting those boat traps, we're going to pack up and go? Here you are, have this beach, we don't want it?'

He nodded. It seemed the only thing to do. 'Apparently the Japs have landed on the north-east of the island and are pushing towards the city, everybody's pulling back.'

'Let me read it.' The serjeant spoke softly.

Arthur handed over the paper. He knew it well; Army Form C2136, size large, pads of 100 requisitioned from the quartermaster at intervals of not more than three months.

Serjeant Murray scanned the In and Out lines with their times for the signals. He saw Major Tudor's neat block capitals written, as always, in aquamarine ink from his beloved Parker pen. He read his own name with his rank missing, of course.

Down past the message instructions with its bold number four, indicating there were four copies of this order, across the security classification – in this case, secret – and on to the originator's number, which in Tudor's case was 05, a number of which he was very proud.

'Near the top of the classification, Horton. Promotion soon, wait till you see.' Tudor said the same thing every time he gave him a message.

'Yes, sir,' Arthur always answered, 'I'm sure you'll get what you deserve soon, sir.'

Murray took a long time to read the message itself, as if he were reluctant to understand his orders. Then finally he read them out loud, stumbling over the words. 'Strategic Withdrawal to new positions. D Company to cover withdrawal at Tampines, Tanah Merah Besar junction on

Changi Road. Withdrawal to begin 0400 hrs, 11th February. All company commanders and CSMs to report to Company HQ at 2130hrs, 10th February, for briefing.'

He looked down and saw Major Tudor's scrawled signature along the bottom of the order.

'You'd better get on back, Horton. Tell Major Tudor I'll report to HQ at 2130 hrs.'

'Yes, Serjeant. Tomorrow I'm to report back to Thirteen Platoon.'

'Lost your cushy number, have you, Arthur?' said Ronnie.

He looked down at the floor of the pillbox. A pile of seashells lay in the corner, put there like a child had collected them after a long stroll down the beach in Blackpool.

'Oh, Arthur, don't mention anything you've heard here. This is between us. It's not for their ears.'

'Yes, Serjeant. I mean no, Serjeant. Well… You know what I mean. Serjeant.'

'Yes, I know. You'd better get back now.'

'Yes, Serjeant.'

Perhaps it was the heat in the pillbox or just because Murray suddenly called him by his first name. But whatever it was, he did something that surprised himself. He asked Murray a question. 'We're losing, aren't we?'

The serjeant looked down at his freshly polished boots and wiped away an imaginary piece of dirt lying on the surface. Then he looked up at Arthur. The late afternoon sun streamed in through the firing slit of the pillbox, catching his face, dividing it into two. A light half where the mouth was and a dark side, behind which lay his eyes.

'I don't know, Arthur. I don't know any more. But we're going to fight. That's what we're here to do. Fight.' He turned away to look through the firing slit. 'You'd better go back to the Command Post.'

'Yes, Serjeant.'

But he didn't go back straight away. Instead, he hid in the shade of one of the coconut trees, staring out at the sea.

Behind him, he could hear the sound of the Vickers and the lights being stripped down, the grumbling of the men as they lifted the heavy gear, the shouted orders of Serjeant Murray as he organised the withdrawal.

The beach was still there. The waves were still rolling in. The coconut palms still swaying like the dancers down at Great World.

They'd spent hours on these beaches, staring out at the sea, waiting for the Japanese. They had come alright, but on the other side of the island.

Now, their platoon was pulling out.

He didn't think the beach would remember them. Would anybody?

CHAPTER FORTY-THREE

Friday, December 13, 2019
Ashton Local Studies Archive, Manchester

Jayne escorted Alice out of the Local Studies Archive, and searched for a local café nearby. There was a small one about 100 yards away. After ordering a pot of tea for two, she sat down next to the old woman, taking her hand in her own.

'I am sorry, Jayne.'

'What for?'

'Not like me to get emotional, especially over somebody I never knew.'

'He was your father, Alice, it's natural. And you've only just discovered some unfortunate news about him. I would be far more surprised if you weren't emotional.'

'Does it happen often?'

Before she could answer, the café owner came with a tray and the pot of tea, placing the cups down in front of them.

'Anything else I can do for you?'

They both shook their heads.

After Jayne had poured the tea, she answered the question. 'Discovering your family history is always a journey. Sometimes it turns up things that have been hidden for a long time, whether through shame, ignorance or simply because it was too painful to discuss. In my own family, I discovered my father had been imprisoned for murdering somebody.'

'Really?'

'It came as a shock. But it led me to discover a secret about his family that had been buried deep for many years.' Jayne took a deep breath. 'The past is always with us, Alice, even though we prefer to ignore it. What happened and how it took place can often determine the fate of generations in the future. Our ancestors made us who we are.'

'Just as the death of my parents made me who I was.' She paused for a moment, staring at her cup of tea. 'I spent my life looking for security, Jayne, finding it with my adoptive parents and then with a man I didn't really love. It's only since he died that I feel I have come alive.'

Jayne lifted her teacup and toasted Alice. 'Here's to living life to the full.'

Alice smiled and raised her cup in return. 'Is that why you're going to Australia?'

'It's one of the reasons. It's been on my bucket list for years. Things to do before you die.'

'If you don't mind me asking, what happened with your husband?'

Jayne put the cup back down on the saucer. 'It was just one of those unfortunate things; we grew apart, wanting different goals and aspirations for our lives. When he was posted to Brussels for work, it emphasised how far we had split apart. He's re-married now and I think he's happy.'

'I used to wave to him from my bike. He seemed a nice man.'

'He was. It was just time to part ways.' A long pause. 'The more time we spent together, the more we grew apart.'

Alice smiled. 'I know what you mean. I wish I'd had the courage to do it.'

'A different time with different expectations for women. But I think the point about understanding the past and our family history is to live better lives now, in the present. We can't escape what has already happened but we can embrace it, understand it, and move on to do what we want.'

The cup of tea came up again. 'So true, Jayne.' She took a sip and then asked, 'Do we have much research left to do?'

'Not much. There are a couple of diaries and oral histories from soldiers who served in Singapore that I'd like to go through, but if you'd rather we stopped…'

'No, I'd like to find out more if we can.'

'Shall we have something to eat and then go back?'

'The scones look good and I could murder another cup of tea.'

'A bacon and sausage barm cake is calling my name. Researching family history always makes me so hungry.'

CHAPTER FORTY-FOUR

February 13, 1942
Paya Lebar Road, Singapore

They were setting up the Vickers again exactly as they had been taught in training; two walls of sandbags built to exactly four feet in height, an aperture in the front and left-hand walls of exactly one foot, and the ammo boxes placed exactly two paces behind the firing position, perpendicular to the left-hand sandbags. Finally, the Vickers' base was placed on the firing platform and the barrel attached to the base.

When they had finished, Arthur looked over the top of the sandbags. They were in the eastern edge of the city, at the junction of MacPherson and Paya Lebar Road.

In front was nothing but lalang grass and an old quarry with a disused railway. To their right, the road stretched on towards the coast and the Chinese Swimming Club. On the left were a few deserted godowns.

They had done this four times now, after each strategic withdrawal back from the defences towards the city. But still they hadn't fired the Vickers, nor seen any of the Japs that were supposed to be in front of them.

Major Tudor came down to the position, followed in his wake by Lieutenant Whitehead.

He took out his measuring tape and began to lay it across the top of the position.

'I'm getting them to rebuild it, sir, it's not right.'

'Damn bad show...' He looked at Whitehead like he was a piece of chewing gum on the end of his shiny brogues. 'Do it again, and do it properly this time. We can't let standards down at a time like this. Not in the Manchesters, we don't.'

The major scanned the horizon. 'What's to our right, Whitehead?'

'It's supposed to be the Gharwalis, sir, but we haven't seen them since we got here. And the patrol we sent out couldn't find them either. Our flank is open as far as I can see.'

'Send someone out again to check where they are, will you? I'm sure they are over there somewhere, otherwise HQ would have told us they weren't. Stands to reason, doesn't it?'

'Yes, sir, but suppose—'

'Signs of movement behind us on the right, sir.' Ronnie Arkwright pointed out the small figures that were barely visible about 300 yards away at the side of the road. 'Shall I open fire, sir?'

'No, wait a moment. Lieutenant, where are my bloody glasses?'

'Here, sir.' Whitehead handed them over.

'Looks like Japs. They are setting up some sort of position. But the Gharwalis should be over there. Whitehead, where are the Gharwalis?'

'I don't know, sir.'

Major Tudor started to walk towards the Japs, thought better of it and rapidly walked back to the wall of sandbags. From there, he looked through his glasses again. 'We're going to have to retreat. Our flank has been turned. Whitehead, organise a few men to clear the way for our lorries.'

'How should I do that, sir?'

'Simple man, do I have to think of everything? Fix bayonets and charge them, what else? Clear the little men away from here. I'll follow up with the lorries.'

'But it's an open road, sir… Wouldn't it be better to flank them over there?' Whitehead pointed to a track through the lalang grass, leading behind the Jap position.

'You have your orders, Whitehead. Clear them away from our line of retreat.'

CHAPTER FORTY-FIVE

Friday, December 13, 2019
Ashton Local Studies Archive, Manchester

On their return to the Local Studies Archive, Jayne found a note from the librarian on top of a small stack of papers and books.

Here are the requests you made. I'll look through the rest of our collection and see if there is anything else you might find interesting.

Beneath the note were a few documents and two ledgers. Jayne went through the first, it was a list of troop movements of the First Battalion throughout the 1930s. The Manchester Regiment had spent the years before their arrival in Singapore in Palestine. From the tenor of the attached report, Jayne had the impression it wasn't a happy stay in the Holy Land for the soldiers; being policemen separating two warring communities was not their strength nor were they give any training on how to handle the situation.

Alice read the report but it was obvious her mind was elsewhere. Jayne glanced through the rest of the documents. There was nothing here that shed any more light on Arthur Horton or his death on February 15th, 1942.

'Would you like to go, Alice? It looks like we've been through everything they have here.'

Alice sighed. 'I suppose we've done enough. I thought finding the date of my father's death would be the end of my research, but I'm realising it's only the beginning. I need to discover more about what happened and why Singapore fell so easily, sacrificing the lives of so many brave men.'

'I could ask Ronald to create a reading list for you. Would you like that?'

Alice nodded and then asked. 'Is it always like this?'

'What do you mean?'

'Family history. It's like we discover one secret only to find there are three more hidden away too. It's never-ending...'

'It often happens. I always feel that family history is like peeling back the layers of an onion – you eventually get to the centre only to discover there are still more layers to go. I think that's why people can spend thirty years doing the research and we haven't even hit a brick wall yet.'

'Brick wall?'

'When there are no documents or we can't find the documents we need. Or perhaps an ancestor changed their name or their identity. That's when I think the real work begins.'

'I hope that never happens to me.'

'So you want to carry on researching the rest of your family history.'

She nodded again. 'It's addictive, a bit like a drug, there's always one more secret to discover.' A long pause. 'But not today, I think we've done enough for today, don't you?'

'I agree. I'll drive you back and we can get some cat food for Mr Smith. He's going to eat you out of house and home while I'm away.'

'Don't worry, Jayne, I love watching him eat. It's obvious he really enjoys his food.'

'But you haven't discovered how picky he is yet. Only the best liver or lamb for his Highness.'

Jayne began to put her laptop and notepad back in her bag. As she was doing so, the librarian approached them carrying two box files.

'I thought you might like looking at these documents I found in the archives. They are personal accounts of two soldiers of the Manchesters during the period you are researching. Shall I leave them with you?'

'Actually, we were just leaving, but thank you for the work.'

'No worries, I'll take them back. I hope you found what you were looking for.'

'We did, thank you.' Jayne glanced across at Alice. 'Unfortunately, it wasn't such a happy discovery.'

'I'm sorry to hear that.'

The librarian was about to turn away when Alice spoke.

'It's only two files, Jayne. Let's go through them, it won't take us long. I'd hate to think we came all the way to Ashton and then didn't look at everything.'

'If you don't mind, Alice.'

'Let's do it.'

The librarian placed the two files down on the desk. 'Can you return them before you leave? One of them is an aural recording. The tape player and headphones are in the corner. We haven't digitised this record yet.'

'Thank you,' said Alice as the librarian returned to her desk.

'I wonder what we have here?' Jayne opened the first box file and peered inside.

CHAPTER FORTY-SIX

February 13, 1942
Paya Lebar Road, Singapore

'Right, Serjeant Murray, are the men ready?'

Arthur could see Lieutenant Whitehead was nervous. His left hand lined up with the seam of his trousers in regulation pattern, but the index finger beat a constant tattoo on his leg.

Serjeant Murray adjusted the chin strap of his helmet. 'Thirteen Platoon all present and correct, sir.'

Arthur looked across at the platoon: Ronnie, Tommy Harrison, Ted Rogers, Ray Teale and the rest were lined up like marathon runners at the start of a race. He brought up the far left-hand side.

'Fix bayonets, men.' Lieutenant Whitehead whispered the order.

Fifteen bayonets rasped out of fifteen scabbards and Arthur heard the click of the locking socket as they were fixed into place at the end of the Lee-Enfields.

Harrison was still messing about with his. Serjeant Murray walked over and watched his hands shaking as he tried to attach the bayonet to its locking lug.

'Can't make it fit, Serjeant, maybe it's broken.'

Murray snatched the Lee-Enfield from Harrison, slotting the bayonet into place with an easy, satisfying click. He tossed it back to Harrison, who dropped it on the tarmac of the road.

All the others looked around as the rifle clattered to the ground.

'Quiet, that man,' shouted Lieutenant Whitehead.

Harrison bent down and retrieved his rifle. 'Sorry, Serjeant, sorry…'

Lieutenant Whitehead looked down at the line of men. 'Right then, when I blow my whistle at…' he looked down at his watch, 'exactly one thirty, we are going to take the position with a bayonet charge.' He pointed down the road, about 300 yards away. 'It's time to chase the little men off, chaps.'

Arthur followed his arm to where it pointed down the road. The Japs were in behind them. Not in force yet though, he hoped.

'Ready, men. Steady, men.' Lieutenant Whitehead raised the whistle to his lips.

A drop of sweat dripped from Arthur's nose onto the road where it splashed and sizzled on the hot tarmac. So this is it, he thought. What you've waited and trained and wanted all your life to do.

'Men, I suggest we walk for the first hundred yards and then when I blow my whistle again, we will charge. Twelve Platoon and the Vickers will be laying down covering fire so the little blighters should be keeping their heads down.'

Unholstering his Webley, he sucked in a vast balloon of warm air and blew his whistle, striding forward.

Arthur followed, looking down the line to check all the others were moving too. They stretched out in a line across the road, bayonets at the ready, striding forward like they were on the parade ground at Tanglin. Even Harrison looked like a soldier right then.

Another drop of sweat fell from Arthur's nose. He stared at the Jap position. There was no sign of movement yet. Nothing to show anybody was there at all. Maybe they had decided to run when the platoon was forming up?

He didn't know and didn't care.

He glanced at the wonderful straight line stretching across the road, the hobnails of the men's boots beating a staccato rhythm as they advanced. Next to him, Ronnie had a strange smile on his face, almost happy, like they were back at Great World and they had just ordered a large round of Tigers. Harrison was gripping his rifle tightly, as if afraid he would drop it. Ted Rogers and Ray Teale were the next in line, behind the lieutenant, each one staring ahead, looking for any signs of movement.

Serjeant Murray was on the far side looking after the rest of the platoon, still as dapper as ever.

And then a wave of pride washed over Arthur. This was his family now. Maggie and Mary had gone, and this was all he had left.

A long, dusty road stretched out in front of him and he knew then that this was what he'd been born to do.

CHAPTER FORTY-SEVEN

February 13, 1942
Paya Lebar Road, Singapore

Arthur heard the second whistle blown by Lieutenant Whitehead and broke into a jog. The others followed him, running with their packs banging against their backs. He looked across the line, it was more ragged now.

'Keep the line straight, lads. Come up, Harrison,' shouted Serjeant Murray.

Arthur looked ahead to where the Japs were supposed to be.

Still nothing.

To the left, the sound of firing. Who from?

Tiny spurts of dust from the road up ahead. It was the covering fire from Twelve Platoon and the Vickers.

Stupid idiots couldn't hit a whale from two yards away. At least it seemed to be keeping the Jap heads down.

Lieutenant Whitehead was firing his Webley. God knows what he was doing. He was still miles away from the Japs and there was nothing to fire at anyway.

Ronnie was next to him, jogging easily, hardly out of breath.

Then Arthur could see what the lieutenant had been firing at. A squad of Japs were moving off to the right into the lalang grass. They were pulling out. They had chased the little men off.

Lieutenant Whitehead started running faster towards them, still firing his Webley, screaming at the top of his voice. Serjeant Murray also began wailing like a banshee and suddenly they were all running as fast as they could.

Arthur found himself running too, his pack banging against his back, the rifle pointing forward, bayonet glistening in the sun.

And then it all slowed down.

Arthur's hands clammy on the stock of the Lee-Enfield. The blurred presence of Ronnie running next to him. The whoosh of a bullet whizzing past his head. The mechanical tap-tap-tap of a machine gun on his right.

He saw Lieutenant Whitehead running in front of them. He heard the Webley firing. He smelt the acrid aroma of cordite.

But everything was slowed down, moving as if swimming in clear treacle.

And then Lieutenant Whitehead went down.

Ted Rogers ran over to help him to his feet and he fell over too.

There were other bullets hitting the road around their feet. The machine gun was louder now. The Japs in front had vanished. One minute they were there and the next minute they had gone.

The platoon was still running, though, past Lieutenant Whitehead and Ted Rogers.

Serjeant Murray shouted, 'The right, watch the right…!'

But nobody reacted. They just kept running towards the Jap position. Ray Teale had fallen now too. Nobody was helping him, though.

Arthur saw Ronnie was in front of him. Still strong, still defiant, still with the smile across his face. Harrison was on the other side of Ronnie, screaming at the top of his voice, but Arthur could not hear anything. The man's mouth was open but there was no sound coming out.

And then Ronnie stopped like he'd run enough and couldn't run any more. He just stopped there, in the middle of the road. His knees sagged and his body went loose and he collapsed to his left.

Arthur saw his arm reach up towards the sky. Then it fell to one side and he didn't move any more.

'Fire into the lallang on the right, there's a Jap machine gun there!' shouted Serjeant Murray.

Arthur felt a blow on his shoulder, like somebody had pushed him. His body suddenly went weak, he had no strength to run any more, no feeling in his legs.

The grey tarmac rushed up to meet him and his head hit it hard, but he felt no pain. He saw his helmet on the road three feet away from him.

How did it get there?

He tried to shout to the platoon. His mouth was moving but no words were coming out.

Harrison's face appeared above him, a long way away, silhouetted against the clear blue of the Singapore sky.

And then it all went dark, and he could see and hear and feel nothing.

CHAPTER FORTY-EIGHT

Friday, December 13, 2019
Ashton Local Studies Archive, Manchester

Inside the first box file was a small handwritten diary. Jayne checked the listing on top of the diary.

'It's an account written by one of the officers of the Manchester Regiment about his escape from Singapore in February 1942.'

They both stared at the diary before opening the pages and seeing the writing beginning to fade. At the bottom of the box file was a typed transcript.

'Perhaps, it would be easier to read this,' said Jayne.

They both began reading, turning the pages slowly as they finished. The diary was from a Lieutenant Clavell Spanton and it detailed his amazing escape from Singapore in 1942 by sailing a boat across the Indian Ocean, surviving attacks from the air, encounters with Japanese vessels and a shortage of food or water. While it was fascinating to read the incredible bravery of this man, it advanced nothing about their knowledge of what had happened to Arthur Horton.

'Let's listen to the tape,' said Jayne.

They walked over to the tape player, slotted the cassette into the machine and put on the headphones. Immediately a voice began to speak.

'This is a recording of Thomas Harrison made on April fourth, 1988, recounting his experiences of the Manchester Regiment during the period before the Fall of Singapore and his subsequent imprisonment and work on the death railway in Thailand. It ends with his experiences in the mines of Japan and liberation in 1945.'

There was a slight pause and then a different voice came on. This one was older, huskier, and spoke with a broad Manchester accent.

'I joined the Manchester Regiment in 1936. There wasn't much work in Stockport at the time. The mill where I was working had closed down the year before. I'd tried looking for another job but there wasn't anything. I weren't married then, and one day I was walking past the recruiting centre on Oldham Road and I just decided to go in and sign up. I didn't plan it at all. My mam was a bit upset but my new stepdad was quite chuffed. It was one less

mouth to feed, you see, and he wasn't getting much work as a painter and decorator himself.

'*So off I went to the training camp and three months later, we were shipped out to Palestine for a couple of years. I didn't like the place at all – too hot and dusty for me – and we were just policemen there really, trying to keep the people from killing each other.*

'*I were glad when we were moved and shipped to Singapore. I loved the place. We had a good barracks and life was pretty easy. The local colonial population treated us pretty badly, they saw us as the lowest of the low, like bits of mud on their shoes. But the locals were good and as long as you kept your nose clean, did what the NCOs said, it was a pretty good life. Lots of dancing, the food was good and we didn't have to do much. I used to play a lot of sport back then, football and the like. It was a good life.*

'*And then the Japs invaded. We were sent out to the beaches out near Changi. We sat in the pillboxes looking out over the water with our Vickers and our lights waiting for them to come, but they never did. All the time we were hearing about the fighting in Malaya and how it seemed to be getting worse and worse.*

'*It wasn't till near the surrender that we saw any fighting ourselves. We had been ordered to pull back from the beaches to a road on the eastern edge of the city. Somehow the Japs had got behind us and we were ordered by the major, he was a veteran of the first war and a bit old-fashioned in his ways, to charge with our bayonets and clear them out. I'll always remember that day; charging down that road, shouting at the top of my lungs. The Japs just melted away from in front of us, but a machine gun opened up and my mates began to fall…*'

A long pause as his voice stopped and there was a loud sigh.

'Lost a lot of good mates that day. Ted Rogers, Ronnie Arkwright, the lieutenant, Ray Teale. I lost my best mate Arthur, too. He was shot through the shoulder and we loaded him on a truck with the other casualties to go to the hospital. I remember watching the lorry slowly move away down the road, back towards the city. Looking back to where we had begun our charge, it was empty. No soldiers. No Japs. No sign we had ever been there. Just a road, somewhere in the east of Singapore... I...'

Another long pause.

'I never saw Arthur again. I don't know what happened but after the surrender, I heard there had been a massacre at the hospital. Perhaps Arthur was killed there. I'll never know. I can never forgive the Japs for what they did to me and my mates. I know everybody says forgive and forget, the war's been over for years. But I can't, I still can't. I think about Arthur and Ronnie and Ray and all the others every day...'

The other voice came in.

'Would you like to take a break, Mr Harrison?'

Jayne stopped the machine.

'Do you think this Arthur could be my dad?' asked Alice.

'It's possible. The nominal roll said he died at Alexandra Hospital on February 15th, 1942.'

'At least I know now,' Alice said quietly.

'I'm sorry you had to find out this way.'

'So I was an orphan when I was adopted by the Simpsons. I've tried to remember my mum and my dad, even the time at the orphanage, but there's nothing. It's like my life started when I was three and a half years old.'

'And it did, Alice. You were lucky; a lovely, loving family adopted you and gave you a wonderful life.'

Alice slowly nodded her head.

'Shall we listen to the rest of the tape?'

'Would you mind if we didn't, Jayne? I don't think I can bear listening to what this poor man went through on the death railways. I'd like to go home now. I have lots to think about.'

'Let me just rewind the tape and return the documents to the librarian and then we can be off.'

'I'm sorry, Jayne, but part of me wishes I'd never started this journey. I was happier when I didn't know anything. It seems my birth parents lived such sad lives. War is so cruel.'

CHAPTER FORTY-NINE

February 14, 1942
Alexandra Hospital, Singapore

Arthur slowly opened his eyes to find Ah Mei watching over him.

'Is that really you, Ah Mei?'

'Yes, it's me.'

'What are you doing here? Is this a dream?' He tried to sit up but a sharp pain shot through his arm and beneath his shoulder.

He felt her hands pushing him gently back onto the white sheets.

'Where am I? What happened? Why…?' he babbled.

'Shhhh, rest for a while. You've been shot but you were lucky – the bullet went through your back, grazed a rib and came out beneath your arm.'

He focused past her face. He was in a small room with six other beds, each with a soldier lying on it. Between the beds, other mattresses on the floor had soldiers lying on them. Next to him, a man seemed to be mumbling deliriously, his body shaking and his hands trembling.

'You're in Alexandra Hospital. The doctor has already looked at you and I bandaged you up.'

For the first time, he noticed white bandages stretched tightly around his chest and across his left shoulder.

'What are you doing here?' he mumbled.

'Remember I told you I was a VAD? Well, this is my hospital. Luckily, I spotted you as you were being triaged by Colonel Craven.'

'I thought you were a dream.'

'I'm not, as real as you are.' She touched the back of his hand. 'But you were given morphia after you were shot…'

He remembered now, the charge down Paya Lebar Road. Lieutenant Whitehead falling first, followed by the others, all lying stretched out on the tarmac. Then the push to his shoulder and he was falling, falling, falling…

He tried to get up. 'Where are my clothes? My wallet? My identity tags? I need to go back to the regiment…'

Again the hands pushed his shoulders back into the softness of the bed. 'You're not going anywhere. The surgeon had to cut your uniform off you, we'll find you a new set soon. Your identity tags and wallet are there.' She pointed to the small table separating the beds where his

dark green and red tags lay in a heap next to his wallet.
'For this moment, you need to sleep.'

'How long have I been here?'

'You were brought in by a truck along with three of your comrades. I'm afraid your lieutenant didn't make it.'

'What happened to the others?'

'I don't know, but I can check for you, if you like. But as you can see, we're a bit full at the moment.' She indicated to the patients lying on mattresses between the beds on the floor.

A pale orderly came up to her and whispered something in her ear which Arthur couldn't catch.

'I'll come back and see you later, but I have to go now. There are more new arrivals from surgery. You need to sleep.' She stood up.

'Strange we should meet like this again.'

She smiled. 'Perhaps it was fate.'

And then she was gone.

Arthur was left alone in his bed, staring up at the white-painted ceiling. Next to him the delirious mumblings of the man became louder, the words clearer.

'Don't do that. Over there to the left! Go that way, man, quickly. Have to get out of here… Don't do that.'

On and on it went, a constant barrage of words without gaps for sentences or meaning.

He zoned the man out and noticed different noises. The crump and thump of artillery – or were they mortars? They sounded far off, somewhere in the distance. He tried to shift position to look around the small room but as he did so another sharp pain shot through his shoulder. He ignored it and lifted his head. There were no windows in his ward, instead shelving lined the walls, against which the beds were pushed. This had obviously been a storage area before the war and was now converted into a ward. He could see army clothes neatly folded at the head of each bed, jackets hanging from hooks screwed into the walls. Next to him the man babbling deliriously was an officer, beyond him was a sergeant from the Loyals, judging from his badge.

The pain became too much and Arthur's head fell back against the soft pillow. He lay there, listening. The artillery sound was louder now, closer. And occasionally the steady sewing-machine rat-tat-tat of a Lewis, he'd recognise the sound anywhere.

The fighting was still going on and seemed to be much heavier here than over in the east with the Manchesters.

The soldier next to him had finally gone silent.

Arthur's eyelids were heavy and he fought against their weight to stay awake.

Then it became dark.

CHAPTER FIFTY

Friday, December 13, 2019
Didsbury, Manchester

Jayne arrived home feeling emotionally and physically drained. During the drive back to Didsbury, Alice had not said a word. It was only when they arrived outside her house that she finally spoke.

'I didn't mean what I said earlier, Jayne, about wishing we had never started. I'm glad we have. The past is part of me, I can't change it. My mum and dad's deaths were so desperately sad but I'm glad I've found out all about it. Things start to make a lot more sense now.'

'In what way?'

'Why my adopted mum never told me. Why she kept it a secret for all those years. I suppose she thought it would be all too painful.'

Jayne nodded in agreement. 'Sometimes the past is painful. Would you like me to ask my friend Ronald to continue researching your family? He could find out more about them? So far we've only gone as far back as your great-grandfather.'

Alice thought for a long while before answering. 'I don't think so, Jayne. I found out enough now. I'm happy with what I know. Thank you.'

Then she opened the car door and hurried into her house.

Back at home, Jayne fed Mr Smith, who was as voraciously hungry as ever, and poured herself a large glass of good Australian Shiraz. She needed something big and bold to relax with.

Something at the back of her mind was nagging her. What was it?

She thought back over the day and checked her notes. There it was, underlined and in block capitals. The words **ALEXANDRA HOSPITAL** followed by three exclamation marks.

Wasn't that where Arthur Horton died? She vaguely remembered something about the place in the research she had done before.

She went over to her laptop and switched it on, googling the name of the hospital and adding the date of February 14, 1942.

Immediately the Imperial War Museum website came up with a private paper entitled: 'History of the Massacre at the British Military Hospital, Alexandra, Singapore on 14–15 February 1942'.

Unfortunately the paper was not available online and Jayne didn't have time to go to London to check out the original.

Further googling revealed a host of articles about the massacre on the BBC and historical websites. The event was shocking. Japanese troops invaded the grounds of the hospital on Valentine's Day 1942 and began butchering the medical staff and the wounded as they lay in their beds. Even worse, more soldiers and staff were placed in three rooms and led out to be executed in cold blood in a nearby field. The total number of deaths was unknown but estimated at over 250 people.

Was Arthur Horton one of those killed?

Probably, if his death was recorded at the hospital on February 15th.

Jayne sighed. Should she tell Alice?

It was just one more terrible event in a very sad history. Her father was being treated for his injuries and then was probably executed as he lay in his bed. Wasn't it enough that she knew he died on that day? Did she have to know the exact details?

Jayne took a large swallow of her Shiraz and clicked off the website. She would sleep on it tonight and decide tomorrow.

One last look at her emails before closing the computer for the night.

There was a reply from Henry Tan.

Dear Alice and Jayne,

Great to hear from you. It is wonderful that you got back to me so quickly.
Here are the details you asked for.
I was born in 1970, the first son of Wong Ching Kin and Mary Stephens. My father's parents were both Peranakan from Malacca, Wong Siu Kin and Chen Lan Ching.

Jayne quickly googled Peranakan and found it meant the Straits Chinese, who were born in Malaya and adopted both Malay and Chinese customs. She carried on reading.

My grandmother's side of the family is probably where the link to Alice lies.

My grandmother married a British soldier, David Stephens, in 1946. My mother, Mary Stephens, was born two years after the marriage in 1948. Three other children were born; Margaret in 1950, Ronald in 1952 and Thomas in 1954.

Unfortunately, my grandfather David died in 1972, shortly after my birth. My grandmother, Chen Siu Ping is still alive, though, and a sprightly 94 years old. I have asked her about my grandfather's family but she doesn't remember much.

It is wonderful to know we have relatives on the other side of the world. Perhaps we could meet up one day? I travel to the UK often on business.

Could I get some details of Alice's family? It would help immensely in constructing the British line of my tree.

Thank you for getting in touch.

Best regards,
 Henry

Jayne read the email again. It didn't make any sense.

How could Alice and Henry Tan be related, unless Arthur Horton had a relationship with a woman in Singapore?

She checked it one more time. Henry's mother wasn't born until 1948, six years after Arthur had died in the massacre at Alexandra Hospital.

None of it made any sense. But one thing she was sure of – the science didn't lie. Somehow, Henry and Alice were related.

CHAPTER FIFTY-ONE

February 14, 1942
Alexandra Hospital, Singapore

'Wake up, Arthur, wake up.'

'What, what...?'

He found a small hand being clamped over his mouth. 'Be quiet and listen. The Japanese are in the hospital.'

Arthur listened. There was the sound of shouts and screaming nearby, followed by two loud rifle shots.

'We need to go, now. Get up and get dressed.'

Ah Mei left his side and went to the delirious soldier in the next bed, trying to wake him. Arthur raised himself onto his elbows. Another orderly was also going round the room, trying to wake the sleeping patients. Most were not responding, only a few were sitting up.

'Arthur, get up,' Mei hissed at him, throwing the uniform from the officer's bed to Arthur. She went to the closed door and listened.

There was more shouting coming from downstairs. Harsh, guttural shouts.

Arthur sat up and began to put the jacket around his shoulders. Pain shot down his spine and he grimaced. The orderly was helping two slightly wounded soldiers from their beds and into their clothes. Next to him, the delirious soldier was quiet, his mouth open and his eyes staring glassily into space.

'He's already died, poor soul,' said Mei, covering his face with a sheet.

She then helped Arthur with the jacket, draping it over his shoulders, pulling back the bed clothes and swinging his legs over the edge of the bed to help him put on the trousers.

Then she stopped.

The sound of heavy leather boots on the stairs outside, running down the corridor. Doors crashing open, screams and then gunshots.

She began to slip his right arm into the sleeve. It was an officer's uniform, a captain from the three pips on the shoulder.

'I can't wear this, it's an officer's.'

More screams from outside, further away now.

'No time, come on.' She helped him to his feet, placing his arm around her shoulders. He let go for a second, snatching his wallet from the bedside table.

The orderly was already at the door listening, two soldiers in pyjamas standing behind him. He cautiously cracked open the door, staring out into the corridor. Outside was quiet and empty.

He signalled the soldiers to follow him and they stepped out into the corridor.

Mei walked with Arthur leaning heavily on her. They had just walked out of the door and moved towards the stairs when a group of Japanese soldiers appeared from a ward at the end of the corridor, led by a sword-wielding officer.

Mei pushed Arthur through a small door on the left, closing it behind her and turning the lock. They were in some sort of cupboard. Clean linen lined shelves on one side of the small room, and a large canvas basket full of bloodstained clothes and sheets stood at the end against a wall.

Outside, the sound of raised Japanese voices.

They heard the orderly say, 'This is a hospital. These people are my patients.'

More shouting in Japanese.

'It's okay, take my watch, I don't need it. But these men are wounded…'

The words were cut off in mid-sentence as Arthur heard a loud scream, followed by the sound of a bayonet being stuck into a body again and again and again.

Mei turned over the basket, emptying the dirty linen onto the floor. Then she took the clean sheets and opened the neat packets, scattering them everywhere.

'Quickly, under the basket.'

Arthur did as he was told, climbing under the sheets and into the upturned basket, the officer's jacket slipping from his shoulders onto the floor.

A pounding on the door, followed by shouting.

Sheets were thrown over the basket and a few seconds later, Mei climbed in next to him.

The pounding on the door continued. The wood split and the door crashed open.

Mei stared at him, her finger across her mouth.

Arthur held his breath.

Outside, silence.

The stench of blood and dirt and decay filled their hiding space.

They heard the sound of boots enter the room, followed by more guttural shouts. Somebody was kicking the sheets away.

Mei hunkered closer to Arthur. He was expecting the basket to be thrown off them any second to reveal a Japanese soldier, bayonet raised ready to stab them.

More sounds of the sheets being kicked. The corner of the basket shivered. Mei closed her eyes.

A grunt followed by a bayonet slicing through the wickerwork of the basket and stabbing down between their faces, its steel smeared with blood.

Then, a Japanese voice and the sound of a command. The bayonet was pulled out and the hobnails of the boots echoed down the corridor.

They both breathed out, listening for fresh sounds.

Nothing except the sound of machine guns in the distance.

'What do we do?' whispered Mei.

Arthur thought for a second. 'We stay here. We're safe here for now.'

The pain in Arthur's shoulder was a dull ache, his wound forgotten in the adrenalin of the moment. Now it began to throb.

'Your shoulder, it…'

'It's fine,' he whispered. 'Let's just stay here.'

So they lay together for the rest of that day, holding each other, hidden beneath their shroud of stained and bloody linen.

CHAPTER FIFTY-TWO

Saturday December 14, 2019
Didsbury, Manchester

The following morning, Jayne went straight to her computer.

The night's rest had given her a few ideas for research and she was determined to pursue them before getting on with her packing for the trip.

She spent the next two hours going through the research while Mr Smith dozed happily in the corner, dreaming his cat dreams of world domination. She brewed herself a strong cup of espresso, working out what she was going to say before going to see Alice.

Just as she was about to leave, the doorbell rang. Jayne opened the front door and Alice was standing there.

'I'm sorry, Jayne, I know it's your last day before you leave tomorrow but I just had to come round and see you.'

'Come in, I was just going to see you. I presume you saw the email from Henry?'

She stepped across the threshold. 'That's why I've come across. I don't understand it.'

They moved into the kitchen, sitting down at the table.

'Would you like some tea?'

Alice shook her head. 'What does it mean?'

Jayne took a deep breath. 'I'm not certain, Alice, but the DNA doesn't lie. Henry says his mother was born in 1948. The father was a former British soldier, David Stephens.'

'Does it mean I'm also related to this man?'

'It looks like it.'

'This morning I researched the war history of David Stephens. Luckily there are extensive records of his service and being a POW at the National Archives which have been transcribed by Findmypast.'

'Why?'

'I think the Japanese were avid record-keepers, plus the soldiers who became POWs wanted to keep records of those who died in Thailand and elsewhere. These were collated after the war by the various tribunals investigating war crimes.'

'So what did you find?'

'Captain Stephens was an officer in the Royal Engineers who was made a POW in Singapore. He wasn't held at the main camp in Changi but at another camp in a place called Great World, a former amusement park apparently. From there, he was sent to Thailand where he was imprisoned at a place called Chungkai. This was mainly a hospital and receiving camp for those transported from Changi to work on the death railways. The prisoners were sent from Singapore on long train journeys to Thailand, where they disembarked and were forced to march to the slave labour camps further out in the jungle.'

'I remember reading about this. They died of cholera, typhoid and dysentery. It sounds a terrible place to be.'

'It was, but their nightmare didn't end there. Many were sent to labour in other countries. David Stephens was sent to Taiwan for a short while and then transferred to another camp in Japan at Osaka, where he worked in a mine. He was eventually freed after the dropping of the atomic bombs on Hiroshima and Nagasaki in August 1945, and transported to Singapore where he demobbed in October of that year. Somehow he managed to survive everything, many others did not. There are no more army records after that date. But going from Henry's account, David Stephens married his grandmother in 1946 and remained in Singapore for the rest of his life.'

'But how am I related to him?'

'That is the 64,000-dollar question, Alice. I have been through our research again and again, and I can't find a relative we have missed.'

'I don't understand. I thought it would be easy…'
'But I do have an idea.'
'What's that?'
'I'm convinced the answer lies in Singapore. Well, I'm going there tomorrow and I'll be in the city for three days. Perhaps I can meet Henry and see if he can tell us any more?'

'But I can't ask you to do that, Jayne, it's your holiday. And besides, your parents will be with you.'

'I don't think either Robert or Vera would mind too much. It would only be a couple of hours out of my trip. I need to know the answer to this puzzle myself. If you agree to me meeting him, we may find the solution. I'm sure the answer lies in Singapore and what happened there during the war.'

Alice thought for a moment and then nodded her head. 'Do it, Jayne, as long as you don't mind.'

'Let's write back to him now.'

Jayne opened her Gmail account and composed the message.

Dear Henry,

Thank you for your email.
It seems to have raised a lot of issues which we don't understand.

I am going to be making a short trip to Singapore, arriving on December 16 and staying for three days. I wonder if we could meet up? I can then show you Alice's family tree and ask you a few ques-

tions about your family. Alice is happy for us to talk. Is the timing convenient for you?

Best regards,

Jayne Sinclair

CHAPTER FIFTY-THREE

February 14, 1942
Alexandra Hospital, Singapore

Arthur slowly opened his eyes. Where was he? And then he remembered the screams and the gunshots and the shouting of the Japanese as they butchered his comrades.

He reached up with his right arm and gently pushed over the wickerwork basket. A faint light streamed in through two ventilation holes at the junction of the wall and ceiling. Occasionally, the night sky flashed orange and yellow as the thump, thump, thump of artillery sounded in the distance.

Mei was still sleeping, her head resting on his chest, her arm on his stomach. He listened to the gentle sound of her breathing, resting his hand for a second on her jet-black hair.

Outside, all was quiet. There were no screams, nor shouts nor gunfire. It was as if the whole world had gone to sleep in the middle of the war.

Mei stirred, mumbling something in her dreams. He shifted slightly to check the time on his watch and a sharp pain shot through his left shoulder, forcing him to groan loudly.

Instantly she was awake. 'Are you okay?' she whispered.

'It hurts when I move.'

She sat up and began checking the bandages in the half-light from the ventilation holes. He could see a round, dark patch where the blood had seeped through from his wound.

'We need to change these bandages soon and clean the wound, otherwise it could become infected.'

'I can't hear anything outside.'

'What time is it?'

He tried to turn his wrist to check his watch. Again, a groan issued from his lips.

'Stay still, you'll open the wound.'

She took his hand and looked over at the watch.

'Twelve twenty-five. Past midnight, perhaps they are all asleep.'

Arthur listened again. There was no local sound of gunfire. Indeed, the loudest noise was that of a gecko on a nearby wall, looking for its prey.

'We have to get out of here before it's light. What if they start searching all the wards again?' said Mei.

Arthur thought for a moment. Should they stay here? Hide until everything had blown over? At least they were safe for the moment. But what if they came back like Mei said? They wouldn't survive for one minute. What should they do?

Mei made the decision for both of them. She stood up and, stepping over the sheets she had scattered around the small room, edged towards the door. One central panel was missing where the Japanese soldier had smashed it with his rifle butt, but the rest was intact.

She peered through the missing panel. 'It's still quiet,' she whispered. 'We should leave now.'

She walked back to Arthur, moving the soiled clothes basket to one side and helping him stand up.

For a second, the room started to spin and he nearly collapsed, leaning on Mei's shoulders.

'Are you okay?'

'Fine, just dizzy for a second. Fine now.'

'We need to get you some clothes.'

He looked down. All he had on was a pair of striped flannelette pyjama bottoms, definitely army issue.

She picked up the officer's jacket from where it had fallen to the floor and helped him put it on, sliding his right arm into the sleeve and draping the rest of the jacket across his left shoulder. A bloodstained pair of army shorts lay in the corner. She eased off his pyjamas and, leaning on her shoulder, he stepped into them.

'Are you ready? We should go now.'

He nodded.

She crept over to the door again, peered through the missing panel and slowly eased it open.

It gave a loud crack as the hinges splintered from the wood.

She froze, body stiff, and her ears listening for the sound of leather boots against polished wood.

Silence.

She breathed out and stepped into the corridor, gesturing for Arthur to follow.

The bodies of three soldiers lay in front of the stairs. The orderly was lying on his front, blood soaking his white jacket from three bayonet wounds. The other two were lying on their sides, still wearing their army issue pyjamas, as if they had fallen asleep

The floor beneath Arthur's bare feet was sticky. He lifted them up and found them covered in blood.

Mei was kneeling down at the feet of the orderly, pulling off his slippers. 'Sorry, Joe.'

She passed them to Arthur and gestured for him to put them on. Then she stood up and went to the banister of the stairs, leaning over to listen for noise from the floor below.

Still quiet.

She waved her arm and began to walk down the stairs, her eyes staring forward onto the ground floor.

He followed in her footsteps, keeping his back to the wall. His wound throbbed and every movement made his chest heave as it gasped for air, but still he kept going. He had to keep going.

They reached the bottom of the stairs. The long corridor on their left was empty, save for two dark lumps lying on the floor. As artillery fire flashed in the distance, the lumps resolved themselves into human beings, one of them wearing the white coat of an army doctor.

Mei touched his arm and pointed off to the left.

'We can get out through the kitchen,' she whispered.

She started off keeping to the left-hand wall, ducking down below the sill each time she came to one of the windows.

He followed her, his senses alert for any noise, half expecting a whole company of Japanese soldiers to suddenly appear at the end of the corridor.

She approached another door and listened for a second before pushing it open. Light streamed in through the large sash windows, illuminating the dead bodies strewn like discarded puppets across the worktables and the floor.

Mei pointed to an open area that led to an outside courtyard. Stepping over one of the bodies, she crept towards it and froze.

A Japanese voice off to the left.

Arthur stayed where he was, his foot raised in mid-stride.

Somebody was singing. A plaintive song full of longing for home and family. A drunken voice shouted loudly and the singing stopped.

Mei glanced back at him and continue to creep across the courtyard.

She quickly peered around the wall and stopped, allowing her eyes to focus. She pointed to a row of traveller palms lining a narrow road.

'We cross over there and then bear right to Alexandra Road,' she whispered. 'It'll take us back towards the city. Are you ready?'

The air was heavy with the stench of burning oil. A fire in the depot behind the hospital drew an eerie orange glow in the night sky, silhouetting the palm trees.

Arthur nodded.

They ran out across the lawn, Arthur expecting to hear a Japanese shout, followed by the loud bang of a rifle.

But nothing.

They reached the safety of the traveller palms and stopped. Arthur was gasping for breath, clutching his shoulder.

'Can't go on…'

'You must,' urged Mei. 'Lean on me.' He felt her body lean into his, supporting him. 'There's a ditch that will give us cover to the road.'

They staggered out and tumbled into the dry ditch at the bottom of an embankment.

'Where are we going?'

'To my home further up Alexandra Road. My father is a doctor. Unless we get you to him…'

She didn't finish her sentence, but Arthur understood what she wanted to say. He leant on her, stumbling forward.

Behind them, an explosion in one of the oil tanks sent fingers of orange, yellow and green flame shooting into the night sky.

To Arthur, it looked like a painting of hell.

CHAPTER FIFTY-FOUR

Monday, December 16, 2019
Changi Airport, Singapore

The heat struck Jayne as soon as she stepped out of the airport. Waves upon waves of hot air, as if coming from some hidden volcano.

The last day in Manchester had been a rush. Last-minute shopping at the Trafford Centre, driving out to Buxton to check on Robert and Vera, making sure Mr Smith – along with all his toys, blankets, baskets and food – was safely placed in his new home, briefing Ronald on Alice's family tree in case he had to check any archives while Jayne was away, before finally packing all the stuff she needed for her trip and collapsing into her bed.

She had stepped aboard the plane looking forward to a restful time in the air – reading, eating, enjoying the wine – but had promptly fallen asleep, only to wake up when they were somewhere over Bulgaria. The rest of the flight was spent catching up on the last series of Game of Thrones. Unfortunately, the flight landed before she finished the last episodes. They would have to wait until her return to Manchester.

Robert and Vera had been in their element, enjoying all the service for which Singapore Airlines was famous and making friends with the stewardess, ensuring Robert's tea was constantly topped up and Vera snacking like the supplies of chocolate were just about to run out.

Henry Tan had replied to Jayne's email just before she departed.

Dear Jayne,

What a wonderful coincidence that you are coming to Singapore. I can't wait to meet you. Tell me when you arrive and where you are staying, and I will call to arrange a time for us to get together. You will probably be jet-lagged so I'll give you a day or so to relax and sleep.

I don't know much about my family history but what I do know, I will be happy to share.

Looking forward to our meeting,

Henry

She had replied with all the details. He would ring her after she checked into the hotel.

Immigration had been a breeze, and now here she was in Singapore, finally.

Robert and Vera followed her out onto the concourse, pushing a trolley loaded with their bags.

'Phew, it is hot,' said Vera, fanning herself with a brochure.

'Just next to the equator, love, what did you expect?'

'Manchester was seven degrees when we left. It must be over thirty here.'

Transfers to the hotel were part of their stopover package, and soon they were sitting in the back of a large Mercedes taxi on the way to their hotel.

The Chinese driver had the aircon on full and a pleasant, cool breeze took the sting out of the heat.

Jayne looked out of the window as they pulled away from the airport and raced down the modern motorway to the city. In the middle of the road, pink bougainvillea separated the two traffic streams and either side was lined with traveller palms, their large fronds arching like immense open green fans.

To her left she could just see the sea, peeping through the palms and the coconut trees, its flat grey waters dotted here and there with large ships.

'Well, we're here, love,' said Robert.

'I think after we've checked in we should take a rest and then go for a walk to explore.'

'I don't know if I can handle it, love,' said Robert. 'I'm feeling pretty tired after the flight. It's awful hard work eating and drinking for thirteen hours.'

'I'm feeling pretty tired too, Jayne, it must be the jet-lag and the heat doesn't help. Would you mind if we just slept once we get to the hotel? We have plenty of time to go sightseeing and shopping tomorrow.'

'No worries, Vera, I'll probably go out with Henry Tan if he's available. I'm feeling pretty good myself.'

Thirty minutes later and they had checked into their rooms in the Goodwood and Jayne had already had the first of many showers.

The phone rang.

'Jayne Sinclair?'

'Hello, Jayne, and welcome to Singapore. It's Henry Tan.'

'Hello, Henry, wonderful to finally hear your voice.'

'And great to hear yours too. What are your plans? I'd love to show you my country.'

'That would be great. Would it be possible to meet today? My parents are feeling a little jet-lagged after the flight and want to rest. I seem to be full of beans, though.'

'I'm sure you'll hit the wall this evening. I can come over whenever you want, my office is nearby. Is there anything you'd like to see?'

'Well, you know I've been researching the Fall of Singapore. I promised Alice I would go to the Commonwealth War Graves Cemetery out at Kranji and lay a wreath on her father's grave. Plus I'd love to talk to you. There are a couple of anomalies with the DNA results I don't understand.'

'Kranji is in the north of the island, close to the Causeway. I'd be happy to drive you there. I'm a bit of a historian myself and there are a few sites relevant to the Fall of Singapore we can visit. Shall I come over in thirty minutes or so?'

'Perfect.'

'See you later.'

Jayne put down the phone. Henry hadn't really answered her question about the DNA anomalies. Why was that? Was there something he was hiding from her?

She would find out the truth very quickly when he picked her up.

CHAPTER FIFTY-FIVE

February 15, 1942
Singapore

Arthur didn't know how he made it out of the ditch and onto the road. Part of the time he seemed to be hallucinating as they stumbled on towards the city. He vaguely remembered being accosted by a British patrol.

'Where are you going?' asked the lieutenant in charge.

'Back to the city,' Mei answered.

'What's wrong with the captain?' He gestured at Arthur.

'He's been wounded. We came from Alexandra Hospital.'

'Are the Japs there?'

Mei nodded.

'Look after yourself, sir.' The lieutenant saluted him before hurrying away with his patrol.

They continued to stumble forward for what seemed like hours through the darkness, each step becoming more and more difficult.

For a long while they rested in an overgrown graveyard, leaning against a semi-circular monument to some long-lost Chinese merchant. Around them, half-clothed bodies lay like mourners at their own funeral, unmoving and very dead.

'We need to keep going.' Mei touched his shoulder. 'I think the Japanese will attack again soon.'

Gradually, as they moved closer to the city, the road became more built up with a mixture of shop-houses and godowns on either side.

Here, there were more signs of life and of death. A Sikh soldier draped lazily over a hedge, his stomach dripping towards the ground. The soles of his boots were brand new, the maker's mark still visible and sharp.

Further on, an Austin was abandoned beside the road, its back seats filled with opened and rifled suitcases. Next to it, the front door of a shop-house tilted drunkenly on its hinges; inside, voices amidst the wreckage.

All he really remembered were the smells; smoke and fire and burning, all tinged with the pungent aroma of oil, like a forest of car tyres had been set alight in a rubbish dump.

It seemed like they had been walking for years. Past bombed-out buildings, past groups of dazed soldiers, past more abandoned cars, more wrecked shops, more looted suitcases, more corpses lying in the street.

An officer on horseback with red tabs on his collar rode up to them.

'Captain, have you seen the Loyals?'

He couldn't find the words to answer him.

'I think they are over near the coast.' Mei said, pointing to her right.

'What's wrong with him, nurse?'

'He's been shot. I'm taking him to a doctor.'

'You could try the cathedral, that's where they are taking the wounded.'

'I don't know if he can walk that far.'

Ignoring her answer, he saluted Arthur, dug his heels into the side of the horse and galloped up the road the way they had come.

Mei took his arm. 'This way, Arthur, not far.'

They stumbled up the gentle slope of the hill and reached a road on the other side going down toward the city. He could see smoke rising ahead but there were no soldiers. On either side, old black and white houses flanked the road, like some beautiful dream of a peaceful English village.

Then he collapsed.

He could walk no more. He didn't care if the Japs came. Nothing mattered any more

CHAPTER FIFTY-SIX

Monday, December 16, 2019
Goodwood Hotel, Singapore

In the lobby of the Goodwood Hotel, a tall Chinese man approached Jayne.

'Ms Sinclair, I presume?' The accent was very English, almost too English.

'Henry Tan?'

'The one and only. You look exactly like your picture on the website.'

So he had checked her out before the meeting. He was wearing a white open-necked cotton shirt and khaki pants. Perfect for the weather.

'Are your parents resting?'

'I think so, the jet-lag hit them as soon as we landed.'

'But you're okay?'

'Raring to go.'

'You said you wanted to go to Kranji. It's a bit of a drive but we can chat on the way. Let me carry those for you.'

Jayne had visited the hotel's flower shop while she was waiting for Henry and purchased a small wreath of flowers.

'My car is out front. Shall we go?'

They went out through the front door.

'This hotel used to be the German Club until the Second World War, and then it became the Japanese HQ. It was only afterwards that it was turned into a hotel. You should try the Chinese restaurant, the food is fabulous.'

A valet handed them the keys to a black late-series Mercedes. Henry opened the door for her and she slid into the soft leather seats.

'I'm afraid the car comes with the job. I'm a solicitor and we must maintain the appearance of decorum. My own taste in cars is more sporty, but this is far more practical in this heat.'

They started off, going down Orchard Road and then turning left onto a motorway. Around Jayne, new modern skyscrapers soared, almost shutting out the sky.

Henry noticed her looking out at the buildings. 'Have you been here before?'

Jayne shook her head. 'No, never. It's all a bit overwhelming – the modernity, I mean.'

'Singapore has changed a lot in the last twenty years, sometimes not for the best. We have lost a lot of the old ambience that made the city so charming. We have a joke that it will be a lovely place to live… when it's finished.'

'We say the same about Manchester. It has undergone the same change in the last twenty years too. The old Victorian warehouses converted into bijou apartments and trendy cafés for the terminally hip.'

'If you have time, I'll show you some of the older areas that have survived.'

'That would be wonderful, thank you.'

'We're just passing the famous Newton Circus now. Sadly its glory days are long gone, but still worth a visit for the chilli stingray.'

Jayne thought it was about time to broach the subject of their meeting. 'About Alice…'

'My relative.'

'I haven't been able to find any link to a Stephens in her family tree. My colleague had researched her relatives as far back as 1841 by the time I left and he could find no connection either.'

'You are a professional genealogist, aren't you, Ms Sinclair?'

'I am, but please call me Jayne.'

'As far as I understand it, Jayne, given the amount of our shared DNA, Alice must be quite a close relation of mine.'

'You're right, Henry, but until we find the common link in both your families we won't know the exact relationship. Alice was an only child and her father, Arthur Horton, died during the Fall of Singapore on February fifteenth, 1942. He's buried at Kranji. I have the grave registration number.'

'Good, we should be able to find it fairly easily, the graves are well kept and marked.'

'You wrote that your grandfather, David Stephens, married in 1946 after he was demobbed from the army?'

'My mother was born in 1948. We never talked much about him before she died. As far as I know, he set up his own import and export firm just after the war for medical appliances, mainly from Japan. She said he never talked about the war or what happened. In fact, he actively avoided it. She did mention watching Bridge Over the River Kwai with him once. Or at least, watching about half of it before he walked out of the room, mumbling that it was all rubbish. She could never get him to tell her why.'

'I think a lot of servicemen felt the same way after the war. Even those who weren't prisoners of the Japanese, but it must have been far worse for them.'

He pointed off to the left. 'Through the trees you can just about see the old Ford factory, or what's left of it. It was here the surrender of Singapore was signed. There's a famous photograph of Lieutenant-General Percival walking to meet the Japanese, on one side a white flag and on the other a Union Jack.'

Jayne leant forward to see it better. A small, grey non-descript building was hidden on a slight rise.

'I think the British soldiers fought bravely but they were out-generaled and out-thought by a Japanese army that had been fighting in China for five years,' Henry continued.

'Arthur Horton died in Alexandra Hospital. Where is that?'

'It's back on the west coast. It's where there was a massacre in 1942. The Japanese killed many of the medical staff and the patients. My grandmother was working there as a VAD, a nurse, at the time but she escaped.'

'Really? In Alexandra Hospital? I wonder if she met Alice's father, Arthur Horton?'

'She never talked about that period in her life. And now her memory comes and goes. She's old…'

'She was very lucky to escape. From what I've read, many of the doctors, patients and nurses were killed.'

'I'll take you there after we visit Kranji. It hasn't changed much since the war, the old buildings still exist.'

'I'd like to see the hospital to tell Alice what it was like.'

There was a long silence between them, before Henry finally spoke. 'If you have time, we could also go and see my grandmother.'

'Is she the woman who married David Stephens?'

'She's still going strong but her memory isn't as good as it used to be. She's ninety-four years old, after all. But sometimes the old days for her are far clearer than what she did five minutes ago.'

Jayne thought of Robert, who suffered from early-onset Alzheimer's. 'My stepfather has the same issues. It's why he went into a sheltered facility after my mum died.

One day, he put a pan of water on to boil and just forgot all about it. Could have burnt the house down.'

'Age, the one incurable disease.'

'You talk like a doctor.'

'The whole family works in medicine except me. I couldn't stand the sight of blood, still can't.'

Jayne smiled. 'A fear of blood, not the character trait one expects in a doctor.'

'So I became a solicitor instead, swapping the stethoscope for the pink ribbon.'

Jayne stared out of the windscreen. A long straight road was ahead, flanked on either side by trees and the remnants of a forest.

'We're not far away now. The war cemetery is just up ahead on the right. Next to it you'll see the racecourse, which was only built in the last twenty years. Unfortunately land is too valuable to waste in Singapore. Luckily, there are no races today.'

The car swung right, crossing over the main road and onto a narrow avenue. Up ahead, Jayne could see a monument silhouetted against the sky on a slight rise. It looked like a giant upright wing about to take off.

Henry drove on for about 100 yards before stopping in a small, empty car park. 'Not many people come here any more. If you want me to stay in the car, I will do.'

'Please come with me, Henry. I feel you are a part of this search as much as myself or Alice.'

The heat hit her as soon as she stepped out of the car. Jayne stared up at the giant wing at the top of the hill surrounded by long lines of white gravestones, each representing a life lost long ago.

Clutching the wreath she had bought that morning, she began to walk towards the graves.

CHAPTER FIFTY-SEVEN

February 19, 1942
Mount Echo, Singapore

When Arthur woke, he didn't immediately realise where he was. The bed was soft and his shoulder no longer hurt as much.

'It's good to see you've finally rejoined us.'

'Where am I? What happened?'

'You're in my father's house.' Mei looked over her shoulder and Arthur saw an older Chinese man rolling up his sleeves.

'You've had a fever for the last four days, but it looks like it's finally broken. I've given you a light dose of opium for the pain.'

'I dreamt I was sitting in a graveyard.'

Mei looked at her father. 'That wasn't a dream. We had to take a shortcut to avoid artillery shells from the Japanese through Leng See Sua.'

'What?' Her father was angry. He quickly made the sign of the cross. 'You walked through there?'

'We're Catholic, Father, the old Chinese cemeteries shouldn't scare us.'

'I don't care what religion we are, you are not to go there.'

'How did I get here?' Arthur asked.

'I helped you walk for as long as I could, then I ran back here to get my father and my brother. My father re-bandaged your shoulder and we put you to bed four days ago. You've been asleep ever since.'

Arthur nodded for a moment, listening for the sound of shelling or guns, but he heard nothing.

The father seemed to know what he was thinking. 'The British surrendered on February fifteenth. The fighting is all over. The Japanese are in charge now, God save our souls.'

'What's the date?'

'February nineteenth.'

'I need to rejoin my regiment.' He attempted to get up from his bed but a wave of tiredness hit him and he sank back into the soft embrace of the pillows.

The father walked over to the bedside and took his pulse, timing the beats against his watch. 'You're getting stronger, but I think your wound needs cleaning properly. I have done the best I could here.'

Arthur noticed a square blue ink stamp on the back of the man's hand as he took his pulse.

'What's that?'

'Yesterday I had to go to Chinatown with my son for registration.' The man's face darkened. 'They lined us up and examined our hands and bodies. A man with a hood on his head walked down the line, touching some people on the shoulder.' A long pause. 'My son was one of the people he touched. They stamped him with a triangle and took him away in the back of a lorry.'

'We'll find out where he's been taken, Father. He'll be released soon.'

The man closed his eyes. 'I've been praying for him.'

Mei stood up. 'Arthur is tired now, we should leave him to rest.'

They went out, closing the door quietly behind them.

Left alone in the room, a wave of tiredness swept over Arthur and he drifted off to sleep.

He didn't know how long he had been dozing when he heard raised voices from the floor below. He raised himself up from the bed, and gingerly placed his feet on the floor.

He suddenly wanted to be violently sick. He swallowed quickly, forcing himself to remain upright. The nausea passed and he stood up, leaning his weight against the bedside table for support.

Remaining there for more than a minute, he summoned his strength and staggered to the door, reaching it out of breath.

The voices were louder from downstairs now, and clearer.

'He can't stay here. If the Japanese find him, we'll all be murdered.'

'What do you think we should do then, Mother? Throw him out into the street so the Japanese can bayonet him to death?'

He recognised Mei's voice.

'Please keep your voices down, you'll wake him. Mei, your mother is right. The longer your soldier stays here, the more trouble he'll cause for us.'

'What happened to your Hippocratic oath, Father, caring for the sick and infirm?'

'We've been caring for him but we also have to care for ourselves. What good will we be to him if the Japanese find him here?' A woman's voice, louder and higher.

'I can't believe what I'm hearing.'

'Your mother is right, Mei. When your soldier is stronger, he should return to his unit. The Japanese are not killing British soldiers. They've all been sent to prison camps across the island.'

'We don't know that, Father. And you said yourself, he needs his wound to be cleaned properly. Do you think the Japanese are going to do that?'

'Mei, I've decided. As soon as he is strong enough, he must leave.'

Arthur didn't want to hear any more.

He struggled back to his bed and lay on it, staring up at the ceiling.

He couldn't put these people in danger any more. He would leave tomorrow as soon as he could.

CHAPTER FIFTY-EIGHT

Monday, December 16, 2019
Kranji Cemetery, Singapore

Each step seemed to take an age as the heat and humidity sapped every last bit of strength from Jayne's body.

Up above, the concrete memorial dominating the cemetery had become closer and grown bigger.

She stopped. 'There's no rush. Take your time. They'll wait. They've always waited,' she said, to nobody but herself.

She listened to the odd mixture of sounds that surrounded her. To the left, the banging and hammering of construction. On the wind, she heard the shouts of some strange language. Fragments of sound, fragments of words blown away from mouths and ears carried past her, barely heard.

To the right, a valley ran gently down to the road. A few grey birds noisily squabbling, the pungent smell of newly cut grass, the low drone of traffic going nowhere.

She walked upwards, with every step getting nearer to the past. The sun beat down as it had always beaten down. The wind gave a few feeble puffs from the hearth of the earth. The sparse trees barely threw a shadow across her path.

And then she saw them clearly. Long white rows of teeth sticking out of the ground. Each one represented a man who had lived once, and laughed and loved.

They lay in neat rows, aligned as if by the hand of God to cover the broad summit of the hill. Above them towered the giant wing, its columns carved with name upon name of men who had once lived and, perhaps, still lived on in someone's memory, somewhere.

She looked up in the sky.

For a moment, she was transported back into the past. The whine of plane engines as they dived to machine-gun men on the ground. She heard the loud crash and bang of the artillery shells. She felt the earth shake with every explosion. She smelt the cordite, the oil, the burning and death in the air.

It had been so long ago back in 1942, but at that moment in time, every sight, sound and smell was as clear as if they were happening right there and then.

'Are you okay, Jayne?' Henry asked.

She nodded, smiled wanly and continued walking upwards.

After a short search, they found the grave they had been looking for in the middle of a long line of memorials beneath the shadow of the concrete wing.

It was marked clearly with the fleur-de-lys in a roundel at the top. The plain words were chiselled into the white headstone.

3524357 Private
Arthur Horton
The Manchester Regiment
15th February 1942

At the bottom a simple cross finished the memorial.

'Is this Alice's father?' asked Henry.

Jayne just nodded, laying the wreath at the foot of the headstone and stepping back. She stood there for a moment, her hands crossed in front of her, and her head bowed in prayer.

Then she noticed the earth at the side of the grave, where the Commission had planted some local flowers. It was red, as if the blood of thousands of men had seeped into the ground, soaking it for the rest of time.

It had been a journey to discover this man and his life.

Then she raised her head. She knew what had happened to him long ago, and why his descendent stood behind her. It was the only possible answer.

CHAPTER FIFTY-NINE

February 20, 1942
Mount Echo, Singapore

The following morning Arthur woke early, just as the sun began to rise. He listened for movement downstairs and heard nothing.

Next to his bed, a glass of water and a small, vegetable-wrapped rice cake were placed beside a notepad.

For the first time, Arthur realised how hungry he was. He wolfed down the rice cake and drank the water, instantly feeling more energetic.

He felt his shoulder.

It was still painful but not as bad as before. For a moment, his decision to leave this family deserted him. It would be much easier to stay here, build up his strength, wait until the Japanese eventually found him.

But Mei's mother was right, he couldn't put them at risk any longer.

He sat up slowly and began to slip his legs into the army shorts Mei had given him in the hospital. They had been cleaned and ironed since he had last worn them.

At the bottom of the bed, a shirt was neatly folded. It was probably one of her brother's. He put it on. The arms were a little short but other than that, it fitted perfectly. The last to go on was the officer's jacket Mei had given him in Alexandra Hospital. He would remain an officer for a few more hours, at least until the Japanese put him back with his regiment.

Finally, he slipped his feet into the pumps Mei had taken from the orderly. They were clean now, no traces of the blood from the floor of the hospital.

He checked himself out in the mirror. His face was gaunt and there was a thick week-old stubble along his chin, but he actually looked like an officer. All he needed was a proper cap and a swagger stick to pull off the transformation.

He felt much better now – still weak, but at least he could move without too much pain from his shoulder. He picked up the pencil, writing a quick note to Mei.

Dear Mei and family,

Thank you for all you have done for me. I couldn't have got through it all without you. I can't put your family in danger any longer so I have decided to give myself up to the Japanese.

Please do not worry about me. The fighting has finished now and I will be treated as a prisoner of war.

When this war is over, I will return to thank you. Without your help and care I would not be alive. I can never repay you enough for what you have done for me.

Yours faithfully,

Arthur Horton

He placed the note beneath the empty glass of water and took one look around the bedroom. He would have liked to thank them properly but leaving like this was the best way, the easiest way.

It was time to go. He listened once more at the door but heard nothing in the house. Cautiously opening it, he peered out.

Nobody.

He crept down the stairs and out into the day. As he stepped out into the sunlight, he had to shield his eyes. The palls of smoke still hung over Singapore but at least the stench of cordite was no longer in the air.

Taking one last look at the house that had sheltered him, he walked down to the main road where he thought the Japanese would be.

Tears suddenly clouded his eyes. He had lost everything in this war, even himself.

CHAPTER SIXTY

Monday, December 16, 2019
Singapore

They returned to the car and Jayne announced, 'If it's alright with you, I'd like to talk with your grandmother.'

'She's old, Jayne, sometimes her mind isn't there.'

'It suddenly came to me when I was standing next to Mr Horton's grave. She's the only one who knows what might have happened at Alexandra Hospital. She was there after all.'

'She can hardly remember her own name sometimes, Jayne. We have a carer who looks after her full-time.'

'But the science doesn't lie, Henry. Somehow, you are related to Alice Taylor. We can't find any documentary connection, so we have to ask the one person who was living at that time if they know anything. It's the only way we are ever going to solve this puzzle.'

'She might not know anything at all , or she probably won't remember. I saw her just yesterday and she was talking as if it were still 1970 and my grandfather was still alive.'

Jayne glanced back to the cemetery. 'Is it possible to talk with her? I think it's our last chance.'

Henry thought for a long time before finally nodding. 'But on one condition. If she becomes upset in any way I will immediately halt the proceedings and you will leave. Understand?'

'I understand. I was a police officer before. One of my roles was as a family liaison officer dealing with people who had often suffered the loss of loved ones in accidents or in crimes.'

'Nonetheless, if she reacts negatively in any way, the interview will be suspended.'

'Agreed.' For the first time, Jayne saw the toughness in Henry as a solicitor. He would be a formidable negotiator in any deal.

They drove back along the highway to the east coast, Jayne thinking of the questions she would ask the old woman.

'My grandmother lives in an old house on Amber Road. We've been asking her to move into somewhere more comfortable for years but she refuses to leave it. Too many memories, she says.'

He parked outside the small bungalow. At the entrance, a name carved into stone proclaimed the house as 'Seaview'.

Henry laughed, pointing at the sign. 'Once this was beside the sea, but we've been reclaiming land for years now. I think if you look through the trees, cross the expressway and walk about a hundred yards, you might find the water. According to my grandmother, it used to come up to the door once.'

He pushed open the gate and a corgi came rushing out to greet him, wagging his stubby tail. 'This is Rufus, one of a long line of corgis that have been in my family for as long as I remember. For some reason, we have an affinity to them.'

They walked up the raised steps to the front of the bungalow. 'I think we'll take some tea out here. Grandma loves the heat, says it warms her old bones. Is that okay with you?'

'Whatever makes your grandmother comfortable.'

'Take a seat and I'll bring her out in a moment.'

Jayne sat in the comfortable armchair on the balcony. A small lawn, immaculately manicured, lay at her feet. Separating the garden from the road, three of the ubiquitous traveller palms spread their umbrella of leaves. At one side, an old tree was laden with yellow fruit. They looked like the mangoes she bought in the supermarket at home. Here, they could be harvested whenever you wanted.

The whole atmosphere was one of peace and quiet.

'Grandma, this is the lady I've been telling you about, Jayne Sinclair. She's a family history researcher from Britain. Apparently, we have relatives back in England. This is my grandmother, Chen Siu Ping.'

Jayne stood up and held out her hand.

A small grey-haired woman sat in a wheelchair being pushed by a Filipino maid. Her face was lined and wrinkled with age but there was still a sparkle in her eyes as she looked up at Jayne.

'You can call me Ah Mei, it's been my nickname since I was a child.' A moment passed as she stared at Jayne before she finally spoke in a strong, unwavering voice. 'I've been waiting for you to come for such a long time.

CHAPTER SIXTY-ONE

Monday, December 16, 2019
Amber Road, Singapore

The old lady took a moment to compose herself. 'How are you related to my grandson?'

'I'm not related to Henry. I'm a genealogical investigator, working for Alice Taylor, the woman whose DNA was a close match with your grandson.' A long pause before Jayne added. 'She is Arthur's daughter.'

The old woman's forehead creased into a frown. 'Daughter? I thought his daughter died in the bombing of Manchester?'

'We compared DNA, Grandma. Alice Taylor is closely related to me.'

A wry smile spread across the old woman's lips. 'We didn't have DNA when I practised medicine. How the world has changed. If Alice Taylor is Arthur's daughter then she is your half-aunt, Henry – your mother's half-sister.'

Henry looked across at Jayne, his mouth open. 'What?' he finally said.

His grandmother carried on speaking, ignoring him, staring off to one side as if talking to someone unseen. 'Did you hear that, David? Your daughter didn't die after all.'

She cocked her head as if to hear an answer and then nodded. 'It's time to tell them what happened, David, we've kept it secret for so long.'

She then turned back towards Jayne, and spoke in a direct, matter-of-fact voice. 'I first met David, or Arthur as he was known then, in the weeks before the war. He was wandering around near Boat Quay all on his own. He looked so lost and vulnerable – I learned later that his wife and child had been killed in the bombing of Manchester. We started to talk and became good friends.'

'We met a couple of times after that, just to walk around Singapore and chat. He loved to see the temples and the festivals, his favourite was Thaipusam. Of course, my mother and father didn't know. They would have been terribly shocked to see their very proper Chinese daughter walking with a British soldier, a mere private.'

A long pause again.

'My brother knew. He met us once when we were walking along River Valley Road. He didn't mind, though. I think he knew war was coming and the whole world was going to be turned upside down.'

Jayne leant forward. 'You said his name was Arthur…?'

The old woman smiled again. 'My husband's real name was Arthur Horton, Private Arthur Horton of the Manchester Regiment.'

Jayne sat back, finally understanding everything. She glanced at Henry, who was staring at her. That was the connection to Alice Taylor. Her father hadn't died in the war at all.

The old woman carried on speaking. It was as if the memories were real to her now, and she was back in the days of the war, reliving every second. 'We met again by accident on February thirteenth. I was working as a VAD at Alexandra Hospital in the triage section at reception. Arthur, or David as I know him, was brought in. He'd been shot through the shoulder. The surgeon operated on him almost immediately and he was placed in a ward on the first floor.'

Another long pause.

'As you know, the Japanese came in and began massacring the medical staff and patients.' She closed her eyes, reliving the time. 'The screams were awful, bodies lay strewn in the corridors and the wards. David and I hid in a small linen room. He took the jacket of a captain in the next bed. He always thought that it was being an officer that saved his life when he was put against a wall to be shot.'

'Later than night, we crept out and somehow made it back through the lines to my father's house even though

David could barely walk. I think it was the longest night of my life. My father tended to his injuries and he stayed in our house for a few days. I wanted him to stay longer but my mother thought it was too dangerous. He told me later that he heard us arguing one night and decided to leave.'

She opened her eyes again, staring at Jayne.

'I watched him leave that morning from an upstairs window. I suppose I could have gone to run after him, but I knew what he was doing was right. Mother, as ever, was correct. If they found him with us, they would have killed everybody, him included.'

A sharp intake of breath came from the old woman's mouth, as if she had held back the words for so long they now wanted to escape in a rush.

'I didn't know if I would ever see him again. It seemed like a lifetime later when he walked back up the same road, thinner, gaunter, but wearing a fresh captain's uniform. And this time he was carrying flowers.'

'When was that, Grandma?' asked Henry in a gentle voice.

'It was October the twenty-fourth, 1945. I remember the day exactly. The war years had been tough on my family. There was never enough to eat and conditions were harsh. Nobody could pay Father for his work but he kept on treating people anyway. We never saw my brother again. He was one of those who vanished during Sook Ching. So many men were murdered then, so many just disappeared. Father died in 1944, we just couldn't get the drugs to save him. Mother wasn't well then either. She would die in 1951.'

A long pause. Her aged eyes seemed to glass over as she stared back into the past.

'David told me later what had happened to him after he left our house. He had been walking for less than five minutes when he encountered a Kempeitai patrol led by a sergeant. He couldn't understand what they said, but they stole his watch and emptied his wallet onto the ground. He was lined up against the wall of a shop-house. Their rifles were pointed straight at him and he closed his eyes, expecting to die, when he heard a harsh command.'

A maid came bustling in with a tray loaded with tea, cups and saucers. She placed them on the small table in front of them and poured.

'This is Darjeeling, it was always David's favourite. Try the Kueh Lapis too, they still make them the old-fashioned way in Katong.'

The old woman took the tea cup with two shaking hands, drinking the hot liquid through her wrinkled lips. She put the cup down and began speaking again.

'Where was I? That was it, what David told me. He heard an officer's voice saying in perfect English, "I'm awfully sorry. My men are very tired and have been working round the clock. You are a British officer?"

'David didn't answer. The Japanese officer reached into the top pocket of David's jacket and took out his army paybook. "Captain David Stephens, Royal Engineers. Where have you been hiding?"

'David mumbled a few words. "An empty house back there."'

'The officer reached down and picked up the photo that had fallen out of David's wallet. "Your wife and child?" He handed the photograph back and undid David's shirt, seeing the bandage across his chest. "You've been injured, Captain Stephens, this is your lucky day." And he barked an order to the Japanese sergeant.

'David expected to be taken to a POW camp. Instead, the sergeant drove him back to Alexandra Hospital where he was looked after and treated for the next two weeks. The hospital had been cleaned up by then and all the bodies removed and buried. I think the Japanese wanted to remove all traces of the massacre.'

'What happened to him after he was released from hospital?' asked Jayne.

'He was sent to work at the docks, clearing away the debris from the bombing and unloading the ships. He told me he was put to work with some Australian soldiers and they looked after him. Funnily enough, he was billeted at Great World. He always said it was strange to walk back every evening to a place where he had spent so many happy times but which was now a prison camp. Though, by then, the cabarets had closed and the only dancing was when the POWs rushed to roll call.'

Another loud slurp of the tea. 'You haven't eaten any of the cake, Ms Sinclair, you should really try it.'

'I will, thank you, Mrs Stephens. What happened to David next?'

'As he told me, after six months of working with the Australians, he was taken back to Changi to rejoin the British Army. Of course, they didn't know what to do with him.'

Jayne frowned. 'Why?'

The old lady smiled. 'Because he was a private soldier pretending to be a captain. They couldn't send him back to his old regiment and they couldn't denounce him to the Japanese, he would have been shot. So they did what the British always do at those times: they got rid of the problem by sending him on the first troop train to Thailand. He always said this was probably what saved his life, because he ended up working at the hospital in Chungkai camp rather than being sent to the labour camps deep in the jungle. It was in these that most of the men passed away from typhoid or cholera, beriberi or tropical ulcers. Or they just died from overwork and starvation.'

Henry's grandmother stopped for a moment and asked the maid to bring her a case she had stowed under the bed.

'David survived though, just. He came home to me and we married in 1946. My mother still didn't approve but the war had changed everything and I no longer cared about being proper or saving face. I just knew I loved David.'

The maid returned with a small, battered, brown leather doctor's bag.

'He only told me once what had happened to him during the war. It was just before we were married and he made me swear to him that I would never tell anybody about it. I never have, not until today.'

She opened the case with trembling hands, bringing out an old family album. 'This is David and I on our wedding day.'

Jayne leant over to look at a picture of a man dressed in uniform standing in an old-fashioned photography studio. Instantly, she flashed back to the photo Alice had shown her of Arthur Horton and Margaret Elliot on their wedding day. It was the same man, except in the Singapore photo he looked every inch the officer.

'We couldn't afford a proper wedding dress so I scraped this one together from bits of material we had hidden during the war. It's still in my closet. And that is David. I'll never forget how handsome he looked.'

She went to the back of the album and her old, brown-spotted hands searched in a flap, bringing out an old exercise book and a small sepia photo.

'This is David's first wife and the child. He thought they died in the bombing, but from what you have told me Ms Sinclair, it seems the baby survived.'

She passed across the photograph to Jayne. It was just three inches square, creased slightly and well-thumbed. A young woman sat in a studio with a rosy-cheeked child on her lap. Both were smiling at the camera.

'David kept this photograph all through his time in the camps in Thailand and the mines in Japan. I think it was one of the things that kept him alive when all about him were dying.'

She then opened the stained and mouldy exercise book. 'These are the names of all the men he buried when he was at Chungkai, their regiments and the date they died.'

She handed it to Jayne. Inside were long lists of names in faded blue ink or pencil, written on the yellowing paper.

'At Chungkai, David was the clerk, writing the names of the dead. Every day, adding new names to his record. I think he wanted to keep their memory alive, you see. It was his way of keeping them alive.'

The old woman's head bowed down and her eyes closed.

She spoke to her maid. 'I'm feeling tired now, Carrie, can you take me back to the bedroom? And Henry, make sure Ms Sinclair eats some cake.'

'Yes, Grandma.'

CHAPTER SIXTY-TWO

Thursday, December 19, 2019
Changi Airport, Singapore

Jayne relaxed back in her airline seat enjoying a glass of champagne. Beneath the plane, the sea glistened in the morning light with ships dotted amongst the blue waves. The island of Singapore had been left far behind and they had already crossed over Sumatra and were now headed directly for Perth with an ETA in just over three hours.

In front of her, the stewardess was serving Robert and Vera lunch and she could hear her step-father asking for no dressing on his salad because the mustard made him repeat.

You can take the man out of Manchester but not Manchester out of the man.

Their remaining days in Singapore had been hectic. They had done all the usual touristy stuff: the zoo, the night safari, gone on the Eye, visited the Gardens by the Bay and even taken a grumbling Robert shopping along Orchard Road, finally dropping him in a bookstore and going back an hour later to pick him up.

Henry had taken Jayne to see Alexandra Hospital and pointed out the areas where his grandmother had worked and Arthur Horton had probably stayed. Later he had taken all three of them to enjoy Chilli Crab and steamed prawns at an open-air restaurant on the East Coast.

'You know, the Manchester Regiment were based near here during the war, Jayne,' Henry pointed out. 'They were defending this coast as the Japanese crossed on the other side near the Causeway.'

'And now we're eating here, listening to the waves crash on the shore and the wind rustle through the tops of the coconut trees.'

'Are you going to eat that prawn, love?'

Robert reached over and took the last steamed prawn, his fingers covered in sauce from the Chilli Crab.

'You're enjoying the food, Dad.'

'I am. Beats a plate of fish and chips any day of the week.'

Jayne had spent some time explaining what had happened to Alice. How her father thought she had died in the bombing of the Salford hospital and that's why he had not returned from the war, but stayed in Singapore for the rest of his life, marrying Ah Mei.

'But he kept your picture with him always. It must have been sent to Singapore by your mother.'

Jayne had scanned the picture and sent Alice a copy, wishing she could have been there when she saw it. But Alice seemed to handle it well.

'I'm so happy he remembered us. I can understand why he never came back home. He must have felt there was no home to come to.'

Henry had also spoken to her and the two had immediately become friends, with the young man calling Alice 'auntie' and agreeing to pay a visit to Manchester on his next business trip.

Alice had ended the call with the words. 'It's always good to discover new relatives you never knew you had. Now I have a family on the other side of the world and that makes me so happy.'

Henry had taken them to the airport, and both Robert and Vera had decided they were going to have another stopover in Singapore on their way back. 'We haven't been to Raffles yet,' Vera explained, 'I'd love to try a Singapore Sling next time.'

Now here they were just a short flight away from Australia. The stewardess placed her starter on the linen tablecloth in front of Jayne.

'Would you like some more champagne?'

Jayne emptied her glass. 'Why not?'

It was time to celebrate another successful investigation. She had found out what had happened to the missing father. And Alice had discovered relatives she never knew existed. Everybody seemed pleased with the outcome.

For a moment, she wondered whether she should be congratulating herself. Alice, Arthur, Margaret and thousands of other people had their lives irreparable changed after the Fall of Singapore. Some would eventually recover and rebuild their lives, but many others did not. The horrors of Sook Ching and the death railways of Thailand staying with them until their dying days.

But even though Jayne spent her life looking into the past, she knew now was the time to look towards the future. She didn't know what Australia would hold for her.

The stewardess filled her glass from a fresh bottle of Champagne.

Jayne picked it up. 'To life,' she whispered, 'you just have to keep going and enjoy it as much as you can.'

HISTORICAL NOTE

Winston Churchill described the Fall of Singapore in 1942 as 'the worst disaster and largest capitulation in British history'.

This is a work of fiction but, as ever with Jayne Sinclair novels, it has a foundation of fact. It uses parts of magazine articles and a now unpublished book I wrote in 1998, during a year's sabbatical from my job. At the time, I was living in Singapore and discovered almost by accident that the 1st Battalion of the Manchester Regiment had been based in the city from 1938 to 1942. They had been assigned the task of guarding the beaches on the southern shore of the island, looking out to sea. As has been documented extensively, the Japanese actually invaded through Malaysia, eventually attacking the under-defended and unfortified northern border of the supposedly 'impregnable fortress'.

Of the approximately 830 men of the Manchester Regiment stationed in Singapore at that time, fewer than thirty died in the actual fighting, with almost 450 dying later in the camps whilst building the death railway in Thailand. Or were torpedoed and drowned on boats in the South China Sea. Or died from overwork and malnutrition in the mines of Taiwan and Japan.

The death rate amongst the Manchester Prisoners of War was roughly 56%.

It's a shocking statistic.

Many of the men incarcerated in the camps retained a visceral hatred for the Japanese long after the war had ended. To read the books by the late Arthur Lane, a former Manchester Regiment bugler, POW and founder of the National Ex-Serviceman's Association (NESA) is to understand where that hatred came from.

Life in Singapore before the war was that of a classic outpost of the Empire. The Manchester Regiment, a regular battalion, were garrison troops. Placed there to show the flag, perform trooping of the colours and guard the various government departments. The eccentricities of the British Army remained though. For some reason, the Manchester Regiment always spelt Serjeant with a 'j' not a 'g', a spelling I have followed in this book.

Even after World War Two started in 1939, little changed in Singapore. Rationing and the Blitz devastated parts of the United Kingdom, but Singapore continued on as normal; dancing, sport, good food, plentiful alcohol and a friendly population all created an almost halcyon environment for the troops stationed there.

On the horizon, though, was the threat of Japanese expansion south to create the 'Co-Prosperity Sphere'. This expansion, firstly into China, started after World War One and grew in pace following the Marco Polo Bridge incident in 1937. My uncle, a Catholic priest, ran a hospital for refugees escaping from the fighting, in Western Hunan Province.

In Japan itself the militarist faction gained control and in face of increasing American pressure on oil and other commodities, decided to go to war. On December 7, 1941, simultaneous attacks were launched on Pearl Harbour, Hong Kong, the Philippines and Singapore. In fact, the British already knew the attack was in place when the convoys carrying the troops were spotted by reconnaissance planes on December 5th. (They may also have cracked the Japanese diplomatic codes, but this information remains hidden in the National Archives, not to be revealed until 2042, if ever.)

Dithering by both the local commanders and the government in London meant the initiative was lost and at 4.30 a.m. on December 8th, Singapore was woken by the noise of bombing in the centre of the city.

Two months later after a long retreat down the Malayan peninsula, characterised by amazing bravery and shocking errors of military judgement, Singapore Island was invested on January 31 as engineers blew up the

Causeway. The Japanese attacked on February 8 and exactly one week later, on February 15th, the city surrendered and the brutal imprisonment of its defenders and population began.

The incidents described in the book – the massacre at Alexandra Hospital – took place on the day before the surrender, February 14th. The best book on the massacre, the recently published A Bleeding Slaughterhouse by Stuart Lloyd, is a magisterial account, incorporating original research and interviews with the survivors. Well worth reading if you would like to find out more.

Less well documented is the Sook Ching massacre of Singapore civilians, which began on February 18th. Nobody knows the exact number of men who were executed – figures vary from 50–75,000 – but for the next month or so, the bodies of the dead washed up on the beaches around Changi Beach and along the coast: the very area the Manchester Regiment had been guarding during the war.

One last myth to dispel is the commonly repeated misconception that Singapore's famous naval guns were ineffective against the Japanese because they were designed to face south to defend the harbour against naval attacks and could not be turned around to face north.

In fact, most of the guns could be turned, and were indeed fired at the invaders. However the guns were armed with armour-piercing shells and not high explosive shells. The former are used against ships and are not effective against land-based troops.

It is not this book's role to describe the many horrors suffered by the men on the Death Railways. There are many memoirs from men who went through it and barely managed to survive. A good starting point if anybody would like to find out more is the Far East Prisoners of War website (FEPOW).

There are very few soldiers left who suffered the trauma of imprisonment. For years afterwards, as in the case of Arthur Horton, many simply refused to talk about it, trying to forget about the pain and suffering they endured.

These men received no compensation for their suffering until recently. Indeed, the British government, as is its wont, brushed the events under the carpet and forgot about it completely. As ever, the politics of the post-war Cold War triumphed over basic humanity.

The investigation into the background of Alice Taylor has its base in a story from one of my Singapore friends, whose ancestor was a British soldier during this period. They were trying to find their family in the UK but, in the days preceding DNA, this was well-nigh impossible.

However, this is a story and I have created the connections and the family tree Jayne discovers during her investigation. The techniques used and documentation are all available at the commercial websites. The advances in DNA have made such sites as GEDmatch more and more relevant to family history researchers, particularly when documentation doesn't exist or a brick wall needs to be broken. As increasing numbers of people upload their DNA test results to these sites, more missing connections will be made.

Finally, I must thank the librarians and archivists of Ashton-under-Lyne local studies and archives. I spent many a happy day in the Manchester Regiment archives when I was doing my research. There are other oral history accounts available at the IWM North and on its website which offer rewarding, if disturbing, listening.

It has been argued – successfully, in my opinion – that modern Singapore was actually born on February 15, 1942. The day the British surrendered and the day when many of the colonised realised that the Empire which had ruled over them since 1819 had lost its legitimacy to govern.

That is not to discount the hard work of all those Singaporeans to build their country in the last eighty years.

Rather, in the words of the founding father of Singapore, Lee Kuan Yew, 'The dark ages had descended on us. It was brutal, cruel. In looking back, I think it was the biggest single political education of my life because, for three and a half years, I saw the meaning of power and how power and politics and government went together.'

Out of the ashes of the Fall of Singapore, something new was hatched.

It's a shame so many people had to die in order for it to be born.

The final words belong to Mr Arthur Lane of the Manchester Regiment in conversation with a Japanese woman, Kinue Tokudome, founder of www.us-japandialogueonpows.org.

'The past is the past but it is also a reminder to never go along the same road again.'

An epitaph for all those who died during and after the Fall of Singapore.

Lest we forget.

If you enjoyed reading this Jayne Sinclair Genealogical Mystery, please consider leaving a short review on Amazon. It will help other readers know how much you enjoyed the book.

If you would like to get in touch, I can be reached at www.writermjlee.com. I look forward to hearing from you.

Other books in the Jayne Sinclair Series:

The Irish Inheritance

When an adopted American businessman who is dying of cancer asks her to investigate his background, it opens up a world of intrigue and forgotten secrets for Jayne Sinclair, genealogical investigator.
She only has two clues: a book and an old photograph. Can she find out the truth before her client dies?

The Somme Legacy

Who is the real heir to the Lappiter millions? This is the problem facing genealogical investigator Jayne Sinclair.
Her quest leads to a secret that has been buried in the trenches of World War One for over a hundred years — and a race against time to

discover the truth of the Somme Legacy.

The American Candidate

Jayne Sinclair, genealogical investigator, is tasked to research the family history of a potential candidate for the Presidency of the United States of America. A man whose grandfather had emigrated to the country seventy years before.
When the politician who commissioned the genealogical research is shot dead in front of her, Jayne is forced to flee for her life. Why was he killed? And who is trying to stop the details of the American Candidate's family past from being revealed?

The Vanished Child

What would you do if you discovered you had a brother you never knew existed?
On her deathbed, Freda Duckworth confesses to giving birth to an

illegitimate child in 1944 and placing him in a children's home. Seven years later she returned for him, but he had vanished. What happened to the child? Why did he disappear? Where did he go?
Jayne Sinclair, genealogical investigator, is faced with lies, secrets and one of the most shameful episodes in recent history as she attempts to uncover the truth. Can she find the Vanished Child?

The Silent Christmas

In a time of war, they discovered peace.
When David Wright finds a label, a silver button and a lump of old leather in a chest in the attic, it opens up a window on to the true joy of Christmas.
Jayne Sinclair, genealogical investigator, has just a few days to unravel the mystery and discover the truth of what happened on December 25, 1914.
Why did her client's great-grandfather keep these objects hidden for so long? What did they mean to

him? And will they help bring the joy of Christmas to a young boy stuck in hospital?

The Sinclair Betrayal

In the middle of a war, the first casualty is truth.
Jayne Sinclair is back and this time she's investigating her own family history.
For years, Jayne has avoided researching the past of her own family. There are just too many secrets she would prefer to stay hidden. Then she is forced to face up to the biggest secret of all; her father is still alive. Even worse, he is in prison for the cold-blooded killing of an old civil servant. A killing supposedly motivated by the betrayal and death of his mother decades before.
Was he guilty or innocent?
Was her grandmother really a spy? And who betrayed her to the Germans?
Jayne uses all her genealogical and police skills to investigate the world of the SOE and of se-

crets hidden in the dark days of World War Two.
A world that leads her into a battle with herself, her conscience and her own family.

The Merchant's Daughter

After a DNA test, Rachel Marlowe, an actress from an aristocratic family, learns she has an African ancestor.

She has always been told her family had been in England since 1066, the time of William the Conqueror, and they have a family tree showing an unbroken line of male descendants.

Unable to discover the truth herself, she turns to Jayne Sinclair to research her past.

Which one of her forbears is Rachel's African ancestor? And, who is desperate to stop

Jayne Sinclair uncovering the truth?

Jayne digs deep into the secrets of the family, buried in the slave trade and the great sugar estates of the Caribbean.

Can she discover the truth hidden in time?

The Christmas Carol

When an antique dealer asks Jayne Sinclair, genealogical investigator, to discover the provenance of a first edition of Charles Dickens', A Christmas Carol, she is faced with one of the most difficult challenges of her career. How does she find the family of the mysterious man in the handwritten dedication, when all she has is a name, a place, Victorian Manchester, and a date, December 19, 1843?
She has just three days to uncover the truth before the auction.
Even worse, she faces spending her own Christmas alone; her family

having decided to visit relatives in Scotland.

Jayne is in a race against time to find the family of the man and the reason why Dickens wrote the dedication. Even more, she has to dig deep within herself to find the true joy of Christmas. A secret discovered by Charles Dickens many years ago.

Can she find the truth behind a Christmas past to deliver a Christmas present?

Printed in Great Britain
by Amazon